Other Books by Warren Adler

NOVELS
Mourning Glory
(August 2001)

The War of the Roses
Random Hearts
Trans-Siberian Express
The Casanova Embrace
Blood Ties
Natural Enemies
Banquet Before Dawn
The Housewife Blues
Madeline's Miracles
We Are Holding the President Hostage
Private Lies
Twilight Child
The Henderson Equation
Undertow

SHORT STORIES
The Sunset Gang
Never Too Late For Love
Jackson Hole, Uneasy Eden

MYSTERIES
American Quartet
American Sextet
Senator Love
Immaculate Deception
The Witch of Watergate
The Ties That Bind

Books are available in all formats.
Visit www.WarrenAdler.com.

Undertow

by Warren Adler

ISBN: 1-931304-48-3

Inquiries: www.WarrenAdler.com

STONEHOUSE PRESS

To Sunny
Who Shines Always

Author's Note

This is a work of fiction. All the characters are imaginary. Admittedly, there are similarities between the situations in this book and those in our real and complicated contemporary world. It would be unfair to graft onto these situations the flesh of real people—unfair to the author and unfair to the real people who might have been involved in vaguely similar real situations.

On the other hand, art mirrors life; and people who exist in the imagination are just as real as people who exist in the flesh.

I

From where I sat within the screened-in porch, I could see them emerging in the distance through the heavy amber mist. They walked beside an angry sea, a churning mass of whitecaps gliding toward the beaches with ends like frazzled lace. They were two barely discernible human shapes, man and woman, floating in my frame of vision as a subtle detail in an impressionistic painting.

Rehoboth, off-season, in early April, shrouded in a cocoon of early spring haze, offered rare delights. Like now. Sitting on the screened-in porch, soothed by the muffled repetition of the pounding sea, hemmed in visually by a spectacular canvas of changing lights and tingling salted air, I was tranquilized.

Of course, Christine's champagne and orange juice, the bubbling eggs in the electric frying pan, the smell and sizzle of bacon, added infinite embellishments. Behind me, Christine was clinking glasses on the tabletop, rolling bright yellow napkins into tapering wine glasses, placing the centerpiece, a wicker basket of hyacinths.

I watched the figures define themselves as they moved closer, the impressionism defeated by photographic reality. Don, taper-waisted, the belt on his faded denims square and centered, the tucked-in black pullover tight, as if it were painted on, the hair, peppered lightly, parted on the left in a perfect line—one might think it was all contrived, practiced. Never! Don was born that way, a fetus carved in marble. And Marlena, similarly carved out of Swiss chocolate, that long-necked gazelle look, high, smooth cheekbones, polished to a perfect shine, the clipped African hair, the question-mark stance, the dancer's movements. The couple merged together as they turned in toward the house, sprinkling sand as their insteps dug into white mini-dunes. I refilled my glass from the pitcher, holding it up to the light, now sparkling orange.

"You do beautiful things, Christine."

"Only when it seems to be worth the effort."

She smiled and bent over to straighten an errant salt shaker, her breast mounds swinging beautifully free under her long jersey pullover.

"You're worth it," she corrected. "You didn't drink too much. You made love beautifully. You cuddled me all night long, and I didn't hear a single telephone call."

"Just the sound of passion."

"From them, mostly." She pointed toward the couple coming closer.

"They do carry on," I said. "Do you suppose it's true what they say about black girls?"

"Oh, come on, Lou. We're all sisters under the skin."

I opened the screen door for them.

"The good senator arrives from his morning constitutional," I said, bowing cavalierly, with the exaggerated fawning of a Cyrano.

"We must have hiked two miles," Don said. "Like walking out of an airplane into a cloud layer. Talk about being alone." He sat down at the table and looked at the pretty setting with the yellow flashes of color. "That Christine is quite a secretary. What do you think, Marlena?"

"First class. Oh, Christine, you should have let me help. You should have waited."

"You can help with the dishes. Besides, it was fun."

They sat down. Don poured the champagne while Christine dished out the bacon and eggs.

"I would like to make a toast," I said. My voice had a mellow sound. Inside me the champagne was warming, loosening my tongue. "To my friends, Marlena and Christine, all of us, the very beautiful people."

"And to the lovely man who lent us this weekend heaven," Marlena said, raising her glass.

"And to champagne and orange juice," Don said.

I watched him sip his champagne and then put the glass down noiselessly on the tabletop. These little details made the study of Donald James endlessly fascinating. Observing him had been an obsession since our college days. The boy had changed into the man, but nothing seemed to have changed at all. Don always put down his glass without a sound; his movements were fluid, like heavy oil moving down a polished surface. No motion ever seemed extraneous. One could see it even in the way he wore his clothes. He always wore a tie dead center, when he wore one, lined up with his Adam's apple and the slight cleft in his chin, cutting upward in a line through his slightly flared nostrils, equidistant between the eyes, and downward like a plumb line through the perfect center of his balls. Don was the perfectly symmetrical man. All his camera angles were identical, as if, when he had the malleable flesh of a baby, his mother had turned him in his crib, like a roast on a spit, so that every side would be identically done.

Perhaps the real fascination was in the contrast between him and me. I was always askew, all imperfect angles and loose ends, with a soft body, a fat mind, always "his" roommate, always tagging along, an endless example for purposes of comparison.

Senator Donald Benjamin James, senior senator, Democrat, state of California, the unbeatable, unstoppable, sure to be president of the United States. Good old DBJ.

Sitting now, watching him eating his eggs, sipping his champagne and orange juice like an ordinary mortal, with the angry seas as a backdrop and the fine haze, it all seemed like a motion picture frame, fifty times larger than life. How the hell did he do it? How does anyone get to be fifty times bigger than life? I suppose I should know. But lately it seemed that Don's career had picked up a momentum not fueled by the usual man-made sources. Perhaps it was some mystical wind or a hurricane from somewhere beyond the points of the compass. Whatever it was, it was carrying him like a splinter of balsa wood along its mysterious eddies. An old sideman like me only played his end of the music, parading through the political jungle, hoping all the time that he kept in step and played his notes right.

"How can I eat my eggs if you keep staring at me, Lou?" He turned to Marlena. "For twenty-five years this son-of-a-bitch has been staring at me."

"And what does he see?" Marlena asked.

"He thinks he sees me. He thinks he knows me."

"And does he?" Christine piped, daintily, buttering an end of toast.

"Do you, Lou?"

"I'm learning."

"Beats the shit out of me."

"You know it's true. I do stare at him. It's a ridiculous habit, but that's what it is—habit."

We finished the last of the orange juice and champagne and Don slouched into the rattan divan and lay back on Marlena's lap. Her long, bony fingers played with his forehead.

Christine began to clear the dishes. I followed her into the kitchen and picked a dish wiper off its white perch over the sink.

"I'll be magnanimous. We'll let the kid enjoy her moment."

"He really likes her, Lou."

"Yes, he does. But, then again, she's a rather exotic type. Black. Beautiful. Liberated. It's kind of far afield, even for him. Never saw him turned on by a black chick."

Christine kept her head down as she washed away the vestiges of breakfast. She was probably thinking of her time, perhaps ten years ago. How old was Christine then—twenty-three, twenty-four— fresh from a year in New York, trim, sophisticated, knowing, with big puddles of dark eyes. He picked her right off his own tree, as if she was a mature apple ready to fall anyway. It went on for perhaps a year, maybe more, then phased out, sputtered to an end like a steam train that runs out of water—the heat dissipates and the metal grows cold.

I knew the scar was still there, but the festering was gone, die pain dormant.

"What are you smiling at, Lou?" Christine asked, looking up.

"At us, Christine, at all of us."

"We are a pretty strange foursome."

We finished the dishes and went back on the porch. Don was stirring now. He opened his eyes, stretched, and squinted into the haze.

"Anyone check the office?" he said.

"Not yet."

Christine went back to make the call, to plug the brain and nervous system of the octopus into its many arms. Don had turned his switch back on.

"I really miss the papers," Don said. He had sat up and rubbed his eyes.

"Forget about the damned papers, baby," Marlena said. "The world's not goin' to change much today."

"Come on, Lou, go out and get the papers."

"Screw the papers."

"It's mutiny," Don said. He stood up and picked up a beach ball from a corner of the porch.

"Catch?"

Christine returned with a pad on which she had taken some notes. She had put her glasses on, and, despite the long jersey, pullover and suggestive figure beneath, she was the efficient secretary.

"Patterson has finished the speech on the Florida thing. Grogan's called from L.A., and Barnstable has set up the Monday meeting with Fulbright. That's it. All of it."

That was a reflex. Christine screened out all the unnecessary items.

"Come on, Christine, let's play catch," Don said. Christine smiled.

"Man in motion. He's got a hyperactive thyroid," I said. "I'm just going to sit on my tender, active ass and soak up some booze." I reached for the Scotch and poured myself a tumbler. "Marlena?"

"Thanks, no." She displayed the beginnings of a pout on her tight lips. We watched as Don and Christine ran down to the water's edge and started to throw the ball back and forth.

"Doesn't she ever refuse that man anything?" Marlena asked. I could see her tightening, drawing inward like a coiled spring.

"Nope."

Marlena got up quickly, her graceful legs moving, each like a swan's neck, across the room. She poured a drink of bourbon into a shotglass and swallowed it in one gulp. The booze must have burned going down so quickly. She grimaced and shook her head.

Marlena Jackson. Berkeley, 1970. Major in political science. Vanguard of that breed of independent black women who slice their hair down to man's size and wear big "natural" wigs. Bright, sensitive, antagonistic, belligerent. I hired her immediately and put her on the research staff of the committee. It didn't take Don long to find her. She was striking in her grace, and her racial ferocity electrified the air around her. The interview was an experience.

"What does your father do?"

"He delivers white man's trash. He's a mailman."

"Don't blacks write letters?"

"Badly. There are better ways to send a message."

"Are you a radical?"

"I'm a black woman."

"What does that mean?"

"The black woman is America's conscience."

"Well then, if America has a conscience, she can't be that bad."

" 'Bad' is not the question. 'Guilt' is the question.".

"Do you feel guilty?"

"Hell, honky, I'm the victim."

"Why do you want to work for Senator James?"

"He can move the mountain. He has the ability to manipulate the media."

"Where do you want the mountain moved?"

"To the left, man, to the left."

"Are you a Communist?"

"Blacks make lousy Communists."

"Then what do you want?"

"I want more than equal."

"That's greedy."

"I want a hundred years of back dues, baby. Don't throw me no bones. I want all the flesh, too."

"How will working for Senator James help you get it?"

"He's going to need us. He's going to have to turn us on, and then he's going to pay our freight."

"You sound quite certain."

"That's politics, and you know it."

"You may be overrating black power."

"That's why I'm here."

"Why?"

"I want to be near power, and Senator James spells power."

I had never quite seen that raw intensity in any human being. Marlena wore it embedded in her forehead like some tribal jewel. Placing her on the committee was like dropping a bottle of TNT from the top of Mount Everest—a long burst of quiet, and then an explosion as she made her presence felt. In a way, I felt a little sad for her. She was turning out to be a goddamned star-fucker like all the rest of them. Besides, how long can a pure blue flame burn, anyway? Black power! Bullshit power! The power of fuck.

She paced the length of the screened porch like a trapped tigress. "I guess maybe I should thank the guy," she said after a while, her smile pearly, the tension subsiding. "He's made me more tolerant of the power structure."

"Good for you."

"No, bad for me." She laughed.

"Oh, take it in stride, Marlena. Enjoy the moment. It's truce time."

I hoped I was displaying just the right amount of flippancy. If Marlena felt she was more than just a passing fancy to Don, she was acting out a cruel fantasy. Black pussy was exotic, different, a turn on. Soon Don's letch would ebb. After all, hadn't I been doing this sort of thing for so many years for Don? I had even developed a style. It was a combination of casualness and confidence. "Don't take it too seriously, baby" balanced off with "Nothing, but nothing, stops the big show."

How in the name of hell did I ever get into this bag? We were two of the most unlikely characters imaginable, thrown together as roommates strictly by chance. We were like those two guys in *Carnal Knowledge;* I was the Garfunkel kid and he was the tall, good-looking one. That moment when "Mr. Great" arrived at the dormitory door with his footlocker—glistening, of course, everything shiny and perfect—a shadow fell over my image. I became something over which I had no control. I must have liked it. Like the guy who eats too many eclairs, it may not be good for him, but it sure as hell tastes good. Besides, I'm not a winner. Everything I ever did was mediocre—maybe less than mediocre—everything, that is, except fastening myself, like a leather-braided umbilical cord, to Donald James. I guess if I weren't really mediocre, I couldn't walk in his tracks, always picking my way over the fresh droppings. Here again, it's not so bad getting sloppy seconds on the first-class stuff. Better than getting a first crack at the tenth-raters.

I lived with the illusion that Don needed me as much as I needed him. Who but me would tell him the truth? Who could withstand his intimidation?

History is full of such relationships. But, after using them to rationalize my own position, I long ago discarded any ideas about delving into them too deeply. Maybe, under the surface, there's something sexual about it. Hadn't Karen tried for years to shoehorn between us?

Long-stemmed, blonde, blue-eyed, of course, Karen Whitford. To me she was the absolute zenith of the dream girl of my generation. With those beautiful, bronzed legs in tennis sneakers, that tight, small-assed jiggle, and those bras that made her tits pointy under the tight sweaters—the seduction uniforms of yesteryear. She was a sophomore when we were seniors—the perfect complement to what we called a BMOC, "Big Man On Campus," in those days.

I spent many nights bumming around downtown Berkeley waiting for Don and Karen to finish their action in our room, which might have a little to do with present antagonisms. Those were the years of "everything but," and nice, sweet, bronzed, long-legged daughters of rich right-wing doctors just didn't give away their virginity so fast, preferring instead to invoke the time-honored hypocrisy of the intact hymen. Many a man was trapped by this flanking strategy of sexual encirclement in those days. There was that gloriously sweet, clean, juicy pussy winking up at you day after day, enjoying the embellishments of tongue or fingers, while your stiff prick got second-bested by her hand; and still your manhood yearned—cried—from some bone-petrifying tarpit for fulfillment.

For me, the five-dollar hooker stilled the raging ego; but Don, shivering like a eunuch on the day before castration, began to toy with the idea of marriage. Whether it was love, or pussy fever, or peer pressure, they were all doing it. Don succumbed, and we had one of those big brassy bashes at the country club after the sanitary nuptials at the local Episcopal church of which Dr. Whitford was a pillar.

All marriages seemed like clichés in those days. Maybe that's why I never married or maybe no sweet, bronzed-legged, rich, blonde, blue-eyed girl ever tantalized me with that gorgeous goddamned velvet pussy with the invisible bar across the inner labia.

But whatever the mysteries disgorged through the now broken hymen, they apparently weren't as hypnotic as their speculation on the old iron beds of the Berkeley dorm, because Don was using my apartment in Haight-Ashbury less than six months after his marriage. Not that Karen and Don didn't have what was, at least on the surface, a happy marriage. She reveled in the political life and passed from stamp licking, to hand shaking, to speech making with only minor dislocations. They made great press together—"a charming duo," "the delightful Jameses," "the sophisticated," "athletic," "smart," "chic," "with it" Jameses.

There are always competing moths around a bright flame. In politics, a wife can be one big pain in the ass, especially if she doggedly insists on inclusion. Unfortunately for Karen, inclusion did not fit into our plans. You can't spend weekends at the beach if you practice inclusion. So Don made me the heavy, and Karen reacted as if it were a case of "undue influence" on my part, which it wasn't. Besides, Karen's influence, in a purely political sense, began to wane as the stakes became higher, the money freer, and the professionals more numerous. Don became a kind of chairman of the board of a political juggernaut that had a single goal, to make him President of the United States; and on the board of directors, Karen had only one vote, although she was certainly an important, but programmed, performer in the "game to attain."

She knew her bedroom influence had ebbed and if she suspected, or knew, that Don was receiving solace with strange and younger women, she kept it under control, perhaps remembering instinctively the powerful entrapment of premarital days.

I started to reach for the Scotch again, and then checked myself. I was getting a little too boozy.

"In a way, Lou," Marlena said, "I think I'm resigned to the fact that there can be no permanent future with Don." She said it pensively, fishing, perhaps, for a ray of hope in my response.

"That's intelligent," I said.

I looked beyond the rise of her cheekbones into the dark fire in her eyes.

"I mean it. I really mean it. And yet it's scary." She smiled. "It's scary to watch you and Christine and the rest. You're all planets around his special sun."

"But even planets have a life of their own," I said without conviction. How I hated to articulate this subject.

"Not if the sun does not shine. He is the life-giving power for you, for everyone around him. Now even for me."

"I don't think that's sad, Marlena," I said. "What's so damned important about being an island unto yourself?" I've used that bastardized line by John Donne to rationalize my role many times before. That was the trouble with this Marlena. She was always starting these philosophical psychodramas. I was in no mood for one this time.

"Why don't you go down there and play some ball?"

"I guess it's more fun to sit up here and throw harmless little bitchy darts." She smiled, stood over me, and planted a cool kiss on my cheek.

When Don had exhausted his interest in the game of catch, he and Christine came running up to the porch again, slightly reddened with exertion and the rays of the sun which had penetrated the mists. Don grabbed Marlena and embraced her with both hands around her tight buttocks. He kissed her full on the mouth. Then, arm in arm, they proceeded into the bedroom.

Christine and I played gin rummy.

II

Later in the afternoon, Don and Marlena scooped a hole in the sand about twenty feet from the house and built a coal and wood fire. Christine brought out a jug of wine and a box of marshmallows. I found some long thin branches to spear the marshmallows. Don lit the fire and we sat cross-legged around it, warming ourselves against the chill of the late afternoon, as Marlena rolled some joints.

Pot was not a new experience for us. We had attended countless private bull sessions on college campuses and invariably there was grass.

It really turned on the kids to see Don puff deeply on the battered joints, his pinky stiff, as he had seen the kids do it. He really wasn't much for pot, though. As always, he confined his public actions to what was politically important.

Marlena passed the joint around. We watched how she did it, cupping her hands around the stick, breathing deeply, holding the smoke in, then slowly exhaling, following up with a little pull on the community wine jug. Christine coughed a little on the first puff.

We passed the joint around again and again, sipping the wine, toasting the marshmallows. The haze, as the sun angled closer to the western horizon, deepened almost to a rust, darkening our faces. In this light, Marlena's face and hands looked like well-polished onyx.

"You know," Don said, "This is good. This gets us out of our skin. God, how I hate my skin sometimes."

"Why?" Marlena asked.

Perhaps it was the reference to skin that made her speak.

"Yes, skin," Don said. "Skin is the right word. For skin is the façade. Ever notice how the holes in our skin, I mean the orifices, tell our story? The eyes, for example. You learn a lot by reading eyes. When I speak before an audience, I read eyes. They tell me how I'm relating. Stage actors will tell you that. Real stage actors. People that can't act before a camera. They see eyes through peripheral vision on stage, and they can trace the emotional impact they are making through the eyes of certain people in the audience."

"I like that about eyes," Christine said. "I hope my eyes speak. My mother always used to say, 'I see it in your eyes.' I became very conscious of my eyes. That's why I hate to wear my glasses."

"The mouth, too," Don was saying. "What goes into it and what comes out of it. You can, for example, tell an awful lot about a man by the way he eats, the way he chews, the way he smiles."

"And words," Marlena said.

"Words will never tell you much. Words are a voluntary act. That's the politician talking, Freud notwithstanding. Words can be practiced. They can be sounded in the mind before they reach the voice mechanism. Words are a manipulative tool. Words are media."

Don, like most successful men in public life, was obsessed with the idea of the media, especially as to how it had constructed him. Only a politician with a sixth sense of how to confront the media could possibly make it in the big leagues of the American political rat race. And this sense was a gift. Don had this gift. He could reach out deep into the television tube, sending the fruits of that gift outward into the electronically charged air, and it would redefine itself again, almost as he had willed it, charging electronically into the home of the most casual viewer. There was a mystique about it. Most politicians worked at it, and the more they worked, the more they stumbled and diverted the energy that was supposed to pass between the people on camera and the people at home.

"Then what the hell is real?" Marlena said suddenly, the smoke billowing from her nostrils.

"Real?" asked Don. "I'm real. Here, feel me." He reached out and put a hand on her breasts.

"So you are," Marlena said.

"But how real are you on the boob tube?" I asked. The combination of alcohol and pot had made me giddy.

"I am as real," Don giggled, "as they want to make me."

"But how real are you to yourself?" Marlena asked.

"That doesn't matter," Don said. "It's how they vote that counts."

"Now we get to the heart of the matter," Christine said.

"I want your vote," Don said, standing up, staggering slightly, pointing a finger at Marlena, as if he were Uncle Sam in the World War I recruiting poster.

"You got it, baby. You got my vote." She caught his hand and pulled him into the sand.

"I can't screw everybody," Don laughed.

"Why not?" Marlena said.

There was silence while we each took another drag on the joint.

"I just wanted to say one thing more," Marlena said. She paused. "I think you are the biggest bastards I know in the whole world."

"You're getting sentimental, Marlena," I said.

"I say," she said, "if you're going to do it—go fuck an elephant."

"You said it," Don agreed.

"And if you're a politician, it's best to be unreal," Marlena said.

"Invent yourself," Don laughed. "I invented myself. I fucked myself. I conceived myself. I gave birth to myself. Who am I?"

"I give up," I said.

"I am the African Ouji bird," Don said.

"The one that flies in ever-decreasing concentric circles and loses itself up its own asshole?" I asked.

"Something like that."

"I think you're beautiful not to exist," Marlena said.

Don laughed.

"She's a real smart ass, this one is, a real smart ass." He reached over and buried his mouth on hers. He could see her hand reach for his prick, as if to confirm to him that he was alive, after all, a man, real. This is real, I imagined she would say as she brought the live hard-on into the depths of her being. This is the real thing, big baby.

It was obvious that they were turned on and that they were oblivious to the eyes around them, mine and Christine's. I sensed Christine's discomfort and took her by the arms and pulled her out of the sand.

"Let's walk along the beach."

She looked out into the roaring ocean and shivered. I put my arms around her. "Shall I get you another sweater?"

"No, this is better."

We started toward the water's edge. Looking over my shoulder, I could see Marlena's long dark fingers gripped around a bare buttock cheek as they merged into the private secret that suddenly they alone shared. I envied them, feeling, as always, in the presence of his conquest, inadequate and frightened.

III

Christine and I walked along the beach. The sea seemed to grow in agitation as the sun lowered itself in the west, deepening the tones of rust, reddening the beach, bloodying the water. High dunes formed by generations of wind eddies prevented our seeing any signs of life. We were alone, it seemed, in a peopleless void; and the very idea of it was miraculous. We walked as if in a seasonless, endless, beautiful desert. When we grew tired, we rested against a high dune and looked out to sea.

"You know, Marlena is probably right."

"About what?"

"About us. We are in fact, just planets in his solar system."

"Is that what she said?"

"She was right."

"Of course she was right. Now she's part of the same bag."

"Maybe. But the options of the very young are much different."

"Your middle age is showing."

"Yes, it is."

"When I hit thirty," Christine said, "I thought it was the end of the world. Most of my friends were married. Some had kids. When you see other people's kids, you feel so—so barren."

"I know what you mean."

"We're feeling sorry for ourselves, aren't we, Lou?"

"No, I think we're feeling nothing, Christine. I think we've lost our ability to feel anything."

"That's not entirely true. I do feel warmth for you, Lou. Not excitement, but lots of warmth. 'Comfortable' would be a better word. And you do meet some basic physical requirements. No, on balance, I think we have a very intelligent relationship."

I picked up a stick and threw it into the sea. It got carried away in a moment, lost among the foaming crosscurrents. "Our whole lives are wrapped around him, and you know it. And that's what bugs me. Because I like my life to be wrapped around him. I like the whole political rat race, the whole lifestyle. And I've enjoyed the climb right up to now."

"So have I."

"Two stereotypes."

"We're like his appendages."

"Inseparables."

"We're his family."

"We're more than his family."

"Do you think he can make it, Lou?" Christine asked, after a long pause. We always avoided such a reference, as if by speaking it we would put a damper on his chances.

"We've got 14 months to the convention. Can you think of anyone in our party who can touch him? Better yet, can you think of anyone with a better organization?"

"That's only the nomination. Can he beat the president?"

"By the time we get finished with that man in the White House, the world—the world, I said—will see him as a fascist pig—which is what he is."

"Won't it be great—" Christine checked herself.

"To be in the White House. All that power. My God, it scares me."

"It doesn't scare Don."

"That scares me, too."

Christine shivered. "Isn't it amazing how politics dominates our lives."

"It's a full-time game."

"You're telling me. It's my husband."

"And my wife."

We sat for a while watching the sun, like a big red pumpkin, drop further into the horizon.

"You know, you're a very attractive person, Christine," I said suddenly, putting my arms around her waist.

"I guess you might say there's a certain cool attractiveness about me. That comes of an Italian mother and father."

"What was it like to be his mistress?"

"How do you answer a damn question like that?"

"Were you in love with him?"

"First, flattered. Later, I loved him."

"You know something? I was always around during the whole time. I saw nothing. I questioned nothing. Even when we traveled together. I never really thought of your reactions to anything. You were simply a new piece."

"That was ten years ago—ten long years ago. There's been lots of girls since then."

"But they've disappeared, lost somewhere along the way. You've stayed on."

"I'm part of the family. Even Karen thinks of me as a kind of fixture, the loyal retainer. I haven't told her a truthful word in ten years. As a matter of fact, she trusts me implicitly. She's right, too. I don't think of Don as a sex thing anymore. I've always been suspicious that Karen knew about us, but she's never let on. I think she thinks that you and I have something going."

"She's right."

"We're the world's two most unlikely lovers. We sleep together because it's convenient. We don't have to go through the whole mating game."

"I do you and you do me."

"Somebody has got to do us."

We were both silent for a long time. Christine closed her eyes.

"Did Don ever lay you on the beach in broad daylight like that?"

"I was just thinking in the same terms." She laughed. "Don was and is the most spontaneous lover I've ever been with, not that I'm the most experienced girl in the world, but that must be part of his thing. He wants what he wants when he wants it. It's like a form of greed."

"That's my most vivid recollection at college, always walking in on one of his episodes."

"It kind of turned me on at the time. He used to straddle me on his desk, on the floor, on his chair, in the wardrobe. I enjoyed every minute of it, I must confess. I used to go to the office without panties, ready for instant action. Sometimes he would talk on the phone while we did it. Once he even laid me in his own home talking to Karen in the next room."

"Were you frightened?"

"No."

"Why do you suppose he does it?"

"Why not? He enjoys it. It's only once around the track."

"Aren't you bitter?"

"Not at all. My time was over for him. I understood it. I like my life as it is. I'd never be very important on my own."

"Nor would I."

"That must be the reason we're here. Don is important. And then, by proximity, we're important. Would you believe that my wonderful Italian mother thinks of me as a walloping success?"

"So did mine, before she died."

"He makes us important. We're important because of him."

"Do you feel important?"

"Yes, I do."

"So do I."

"That's the answer then. Egoism. All those people along the way that put us down. We're getting back at them. We're somebody. They're nobody. We get our names in the papers. We're a kind of celebrity. We're identified as his people."

"I like being his people."

"Can you imagine—if he makes 1600?"

"I'd love it."

"All that power. Think of all those people who would lick my ass. Hell, I'd be the keeper of the keys. What a fantasy I'm having. Do you think it will corrupt us?"

"Totally."

"Good. I'd like to wallow in it."

"And Don?"

"He'll wallow more than any of us."

"But will he be a great president?"

"Sure. He'll charm the whole damned world."

"Is that enough?"

"Sure."

"God, we'd be on top of the world. It reminds me of an old song."

"Which?"

"You're too young. We've hitched our wagon to a star. I can't remember the tune, but the image is there."

"I can hum it." Christine hummed a few bars. "To tell the truth, Lou, the real scouts' honor truth. I don't care about saving the world, or even helping other people. I don't relate emotionally to the whole idea of doing things, of getting the country moving in this or that direction."

"Does that trouble you?"

"A little. I'm just here for the ride. I really don't care where the wagon goes, as long as it goes."

"I guess I feel the same way."

"No identity crisis?"

"None."

"Think he has?"

"None at all."

"I'd like him to be a great, a loved president."

"He probably will be."

"Do you love him, Lou?"

"Yes, I love him, and I know you do. About the only person who never loved him was his father."

"How do you know that? I never ever heard him speak of it."

"College incident. I met his father only once—a violent man, a carpenter by trade, a drunk by avocation. He showed up drunk one day at school. Had some kind of loud argument with Don. I could hear them through the door of our room. Then the old man walked out, red in the face, unshaven, spittle hanging at the ends of his beard. Don was crying. The old man had punched him pretty good. Last I heard, the old man died soon after. Don didn't even go to the funeral."

"Are you chilly?"

"Yes."

IV

We started back toward the house. Miraculously, the mist had cleared at last, and while the sun still hung at the end of the earth, we could see the clear beginnings of the moon. As we got closer to the house, we could make out two figures running towards us along the water's edge. It was Don and Marlena. From where we stood, with the rays of the diminishing sun slanting over the water, they looked like the pas de deux of a ballet. They were playing some kind of tag, splashing along the water's edge, apparently ignoring the iciness of the water. Don was in light blue jockey shorts and sweatshirt, while Marlena wore a glistening white bikini bottom and black sweater. They splashed along the edge of the angry foam. Occasionally, Marlena was caught and pulled toward the dry sand where she was firmly held, and then she escaped again to the water's edge.

"There he goes again—Mr. Energy," Christine said.

Now it was Don who was being chased. He ran toward the ocean, slowed up as the water reached his knees, and then, like a broken field running halfback, headed straight for the charging Marlena, sidestepped when he reached her, slapped her hard on the butt, and ran off again. We could hear their laughter as we got closer.

"I'll be damned if he's going to get me going on that one," Christine said, slowing down. "I would put nothing past him when he gets overenergized. He'll think nothing of throwing us both into the water."

"Not this boy. Maybe they'll get tired if we walk slowly."

We were still about an eighth of a mile from where they cavorted; and as we approached slowly we could see her lunge for him and miss, fall, then rise again like a track runner to the count of go, and

23

run off after him in a relentless ritual. When she seemed to falter, he
would stop, head for her again, stand within her reach as she waited, knees together, catlike, coiling to pounce. Then, energy gathered, she sprang forward, reached out and missed, then ran after him
gathering speed with her long graceful strides, slower than his, but
covering distance always a short way from him. He led her again
straight into the sea, further than before, up to his thighs. She followed, kicking outward and sideways for balance. Then she was
nearly upon him, lunging to catch him around the neck, but he
ducked, shifted stride, and headed back toward the beach again.

Her lunge had harvested only pure air, and she fell, slipping like a
brown stick into the churning surf. He turned when he reached the
white part of the beach, pointed, laughed, and sat down. She got up,
fell, got up, and fell again. Then she began to drift outward on the
tide, caught in a cross fire of breakers. It was too close to shore to gen-
erate panic, until one realized that there was an enormous hump in
the near-shore carved by the pounding. But the realization was
inescapable. Marlena was in trouble. Don seemed rooted to the
ground; then suddenly he was jumping into the surf, diving in head-
forward, and in a burst of adrenalin-charged energy, I was running,
then following him blindly into the surf. He was by far the better
swimmer. He would jump, come up angled like a porpoise, look
about him to that spot where he had last seen Marlena's head, then
jump again. I followed his movements, trying to stay afloat and close
enough, peering into the thumping sea for some signs of Marlena, listening for a sound. We were well over our heads, although close
enough to see Christine, petrified with fear, standing on her toes
along the water's edge, holding her body from jumping in behind us.

The sun had disappeared, it seemed, almost instantly, and the
darkness came swifter than it had ever come before, as a kind of ret-
ribution, as if lights were going out in a blackout all over the shore.
Then I couldn't see Don anymore. I thrashed about, desperately trying to keep my body buoyant, hitting each wave and crosscurrent as

if my fist would have the strength to stop its onslaught. I dived, saw nothing but the dark sea, surfaced, dived again. My lungs felt as if they were bursting. It must have been panic or pure instinctive self-preservation, but suddenly I felt myself fighting to reach the shore. My mind was only on my own survival. Then, as I struggled flaying the mad waters with my arms, something struck my thigh. I put my hands down and felt human hair. I grabbed it, lifted the head and looked into Don's tortured face, the eyes open, the lips distorted. I held on and struggled toward Christine, who had waded in up to her thighs, following our life and death struggle as the waters carried us sideways with the tide.

She was crying something unintelligible. I tried to hear. I was beyond my strength, lost in a nightmare of salt and foam and enveloping darkness. I told myself to be calm. I told myself to live. The waters swirled around me. I swallowed mouthfuls, choked, vomited, but held on to Don. The scalp must be a tough part of the human anatomy. I wrapped my fingers round his hair and pulled inward as I fought to reach firm ground. Suddenly, I found a rhythm to my movements, a kind of step in time with the tide, and I was moving inward, finding the push of the tide. Then, not knowing how long the struggle continued, conscious only of the night and Christine's outstretched arm, we reached the hump of the water's edge and fought our way to the top. At that point, there must have been a loss of consciousness. There was no telling how long it lasted, but when my lungs functioned again, I was under a blanket, still clutching Don's body, my chest freezing against the wet beach, and Christine's body astride us both, giving us whatever warmth was available. I felt her breath on my neck. I turned around.

"Marlena?"

I saw Christine's eyes. She could not speak. Then I was crawling up toward the beach house. I made the front porch and pulled myself up by the doorposts. My knees sank. I tried again. Without quite making it, I stumbled toward the whiskey table and found a bottle of Jack

Daniels. Opening the top, I sucked out a swallow, then vomited it up, did it again, held it, felt the warmth hit my stomach, recoiled, swallowed again, and then, somehow, made it back to where Don lay. He was faintly conscious, and Christine was applying mouth-to-mouth resuscitation with almost instinctive efficiency. Don coughed. She released his mouth and massaged his body with her hands. We didn't say a word to him as I joined her in the massage, then dragged his body along the sand to the drier beach. She brought out more blankets. I buried him in them as we rubbed him.

He was chilled, but conscious now. I put the nozzle of the Jack Daniels in his mouth and he gulped, coughed, held it down, and sat up. He put his head between his knees and held it there, reaching for the bottle again, drinking and coughing, but regaining his strength.

"Marlena?"

I stood up and started back to the nightmare of the sea, perhaps angrier at us now that we had partially defeated her. Conscious of my nudity, my clothes apparently ripped off by the ocean's wrath, I stood at the water's edge and looked up and down the ends of the beach, now becoming moonlit.

"Marlena," I shouted, summoning every bit of my strength for that one shout. I walked first one way down the beach then the other.

"Marlena," I shouted again, but even the sound of my voice could not be heard over the ocean.

Soon Don was beside me; we pulled Christine's blankets around our bodies.

"Maybe she was carried sideways and is washed up not far from here." We clung to the hope. I ran down one end of the beach; he tried the other. We all shouted Marlena's name, like some weird chorus counterpointing the ocean's mad melody.

There was no sense of time. Only the physical act of searching and the panic of what was swiftly emerging as reality. Soon we fell exhausted on the beach again. Don was crying and pounding his fist into the soft surface. He was screaming and flaying the sand until it appeared that he would soon start swallowing it. Christine and I, still not speaking, reached him and held him down. Soon he was quiet but still on the edge of hysteria.

"This is a dream and soon we're all going to wake up from it. Isn't that right, Lou? Christine? This is a dream. We're having a bad dream, a nightmare, and Marlena is in the house."

"Sure, Don. That's what it is," Christine said. Her face had gone chalky white and her hair lay matted and sand-soaked on her head. She appeared to find some solace in looking at her fingers.

In our whole lives, I don't think any of us had ever experienced such terror. We were worldly, wise, sophisticated. Now we were benumbed, actionless, wishing that it were us beneath the sea. The confrontation of the present reality was unbearable.

"Now what?" Don said suddenly, and we knew his mind had begun to function again.

"I don't know," I said.

"Let's just sit here and wait," Christine said.

"Wait for what?"

"I don't know."

"Maybe that's a good idea," Don said. "I don't know what to do. I can't believe that any of this has happened."

I shivered. "We'll freeze out here."

We huddled together, our arms around each other for warmth and—perhaps, more so—for security.

"We should do something," Don said.

"What?"

"Call for help?"

"Help?" Don shrugged. "Who can help?"

V

We sat silently for a long time, without the sense of time-passage, frozen into inactivity, peering into the sea. For Don, there was more than the shock of death. There had passed between him and the dead girl something beyond what we could experience. There was a sense of loss.

For us, there was only the sense of tragedy, certainly less of a feeling of loss—pity, rather. Here was a beautiful, pulsating woman, full of vigor, one moment alive, then gone to some horrible Valkyrie, punished for some nameless sins.

By degrees, the event, the death, the near drowning, became a secondary consideration.

"What happens now?" Don had said it, certainly out of his own concern for what had always been the look ahead. Don was not one for nostalgia. What was past was past. He had always looked ahead, relentlessly. I had the feeling that if our positions were reversed, he would have known how to advise me.

"That person," Don said suddenly. "I keep thinking of that lovely person. The thing is simply too big for me to understand."

He put his head in his hands and sobbed. I had only seen him cry once in the twenty-five years of our friendship, that time after the visit from his father. But then, looking back, his life had been touched with a minimum of tragedy. All the people he had ever cared about were still alive. His mother. Friends. Children. Even old loves. He had never been in combat. He had rarely confronted death. He had never even attended his father's funeral. Death was a foreign visitor.

Soon we found the strength to move and made our way back to the house. The night was clear and cold, even for late spring. The sky was a canopy of stars, and the moon gave off enough light for us to pick our way back to the house. Christine put a kettle of water on the range and brought out a change for Don, who toweled himself listlessly and dressed in the living room. His hands were shaking and it was impossible for him to button his shirt, which he left opened and tucked in.

I poured out two heavy tumblers of Jack Daniels and we drank it down like water. It burned deeply. Christine showered and emerged shortly, wearing slacks and a sweater.

"Well, what happens next?" Don said. It was the third time he had asked the question.

"Well," I said, "I think maybe we should discuss the options."

"Options?"

"There are options, you know, Don."

"In the face of this horror, there are no options."

"Life goes on," Christine said, voicing the eternal platitude.

"Not for Marlena."

"But for you."

"You know something? I don't give a shit. I don't give one shit."

"Well, there are lots who do."

"We should have called for help. Why didn't we call for help?" Don stood up and paced the narrow room. "Why didn't we call for help?"

"Don't throw that monkey on my back," I raised my voice. "You had that option, too."

Don softened.

"I'm sorry, Lou, I really am sorry."

I knew, though, that for the rest of his life, the idea would bother him. Facing reality, I would say that Marlena was beyond help, lost in the deep somewhere. I looked at the little cuckoo clock in the corner. It was ten o'clock. It took only a few minutes for a person to drown. What good would help have done? Forever, now, we must assume that help could not have taken back Marlena from the sea. You might say, surely there was some chance. No. There was no chance. This fact is incontrovertible.

"I still ask," Don said. "What happens now?"

"We go over the options."

"Options, again."

"All right," I said. "Let's not go over any options. Pick up the damn phone and call the police. You tell the police that you, Senator Donald James, were up here for the weekend, shacking up with this black chick, and while high on pot you ran into the water. The temperature of the water was about forty degrees. She tripped and fell and drowned. There's the telephone. That's the simplest way. Go on and do it."

"Leave him alone, will you, Lou?" Christine said.

"How can I leave him alone? We've got to come up with an idea, and he's got to be a part of it."

"Lou, can't you see he's in no fit condition to make any sensible decisions?" Christine was right about that. Don was shaking uncontrollably. I poured him another tumbler of bourbon. His hand could barely retain the glass. I wasn't too steady myself. But of one thing I was certain—Don needed me now. He needed his old buddy badly.

"Okay, I won't go over options, just possibilities," I said, "Don, please listen." His eyes were filled with tears, his shoulders shaking with sobs.

My mind was functioning now. It was a strange kind of lucidity. "Christine, we must make him understand."

Christine went to him and put her arms around him gently, as a mother might confort a troubled son. He let her caress his damp hair.

"You've got to listen, Don," she said.

"I know this must sound like it's reverberating in your head from a great distance, Don, but there are other considerations—political considerations." At last, I had spit it out. It was the unspoken, the all-pervasive, the reason for everything. "Unless you're ready to quit," I said.

"I'm finished, Lou," Don said, pushing Christine aside, his voice returning to its strength, the reality of his position at last infiltrating his consciousness. "Maybe I deserve to be finished."

"Maybe," I said, "and if you accept that, then I would advise picking up the phone and calling the police."

He seemed quieter now. He got up and moved toward the screened porch. I followed him. He walked out onto the beach and looked toward the ocean. The moon in its three-quarters phase gave enough light to pick up the swirls of the sea.

"Do you suppose—" he said, turning an anguished face toward me.

"Not a chance," I answered. "How could there be?"

"Was it my fault, Lou?" he said.

"No."

"She had a right to life. She would have been alive if I hadn't brought her out here."

I did not answer him. He was working things out for himself. He had to.

"It was an accident," I said. "A freak! A one-in-a-million accident."

"Did we do all we could to save her?"

"All we could? We nearly died in the process."

"Did we nearly die?"

"Yes, Don."

"Why do you suppose we were saved?"

"Pure chance," I said.

"Lou—" He turned to me. His face was black. The light of the moon did not reveal his features. "How can I face anybody? How can I face Karen, the kids, the public? I just don't think I can face anybody. On top of it all, through all this misery and grief, I'm ashamed." An involuntary sob escaped from somewhere deep down in his being.

"Now I want you to listen to me, Don," I said. "I'm going to try to be pragmatic. Do you understand what I mean? I'm going to try to face the facts of this situation. Will you listen to me? Can you listen?"

He shrugged his shoulders indifferently. The shock had obviously taken its toll. He seemed barely able to comprehend. He seemed beyond the ability to understand.

VI

"Come on into the house," I said, leading him back to the living room of the beach house.

"I called the Rehoboth Hospital," Christine whispered, "on the off chance that someone had discovered her, washed up along the beach. I was anonymous and discreet—told them I was looking for my sister—nothing."

"I didn't call the police," she said, anticipating the question. I put another glass of Jack Daniels in Don's hand, encouraging him to gulp it down. I hoped the liquor would shock his nervous system into some sense of coherence. There were things that had to be done. We needed his mind, and we needed it reasonably clear.

"Did anyone know she was coming out here?" I asked Christine.

"Yes. They knew she was going to the beach with me. Everyone in the office knew. I wouldn't be surprised if they knew that Don was going with us. You know these things have a way of being open secrets. She was also very close to her father. They exchanged letters. He's a mailman in Philadelphia. No. There's no way to escape from that one. She very definitely came here with me. You remember we came in the same car. And people knew it."

"Suppose no body is ever discovered. Suppose she never gets washed up on the shore. Can we explain her disappearance? Call it suicide or something?"

"How do we get Don off the hook?"

"We get Don out of here. Hole him up in a hotel somewhere. Then we establish a threesome. All three of us went out here together for a quiet weekend."

"It's believable—I guess."

33

"Just as soon as we get him out of here, we'll call the police and pronounce her missing. But we've got to find a way to get him out of here." I pondered the possibility for a moment. No. It would be a tough story to establish. Where was the senator last night? That was the problem. A good detective could punch holes in the story quickly. Besides, Washington was a network of gossip, all kinds of gossip. Someone would know that Don and Marlena were having an affair. Someone had to know.

"It won't work," I said.

"No, it won't work."

"And, even if it did, I don't think we could all live with it."

Don was sitting on the couch curled up in the fetal position. His eyes were open; his expression, blank.

"Look at him, Christine. What are we supposed to do? It's one helluva responsibility. I don't want to make the wrong move. I'm getting frightened now. I wish I weren't so meldramatic, but I simply don't want to tell the world about this. I'm caught in limbo. If only we had more time."

"I'd say we were running out of time. In a few hours, it will be Monday morning. The calls will start to come. The whole organization will be thrashing about. There are appointments to be filled. Marlena, too, had things to do on Monday."

I went over to Don and shook him by the shoulders. He looked up at me and nodded.

"Don," I said gently. "You've got to help us think this out. There's no sense waiting for something to happen. We've got to do something. We've got to make something happen."

He sat up. Then he put his head in his hands. "Let me walk along the beach for a bit," he said. "Let me just be alone."

"Don—" Christine was about to say something, then checked herself.

I guess moments like these must come to every man, moments of mental paralysis. It was not simply a question of not knowing what move to make. Rather, it was a wish, a compulsion to make no move.

Don's whole life was built on weighing alternatives, options, shoulds and should nots. He always squarely faced two, three, four sides of a question. That was his greatest strength, that uncanny ability to sift the right move out of a hash of alternatives.

"I want to walk on the beach," he said. I blocked his way. He pushed me gently aside.

"I'm going with you."

"I've got to be alone."

He walked out onto the beach, a sad, hunched figure. There was no point in following him.

VII

When he had gone, Christine and I looked at each other. Near where she stood, in a neat little pile, were the beautiful yellow napkins that had so happily punctuated the morning. What a beautiful morning it was! A century ago, it seemed.

"I feel so damned helpless," I said.

"So do I."

"Do you think we're too close to the situation to make a rational evaluation?"

"I hope not."

"Do you think he'll do something stupid?"

"Oh, my God."

We walked out to the beach. At a distance, we could make out his figure walking slowly beside the water.

"Should we follow him?" Christine asked.

"I'm afraid we'll just have to take our chances. The ball is in his court."

We went back into the house and sat silently in the living room for a long time. I was disgusted with myself, with my helplessness, my inability to work up a plan. I felt, somehow, without courage, unbrave. It is a terrible frustration to be ineffective in a crisis.

And this was a crisis. It was, indeed, much more than that. It was an incident that would have reverberations around the world. There was one thing that being with Don all those years had taught me—to respect the sense of history, to follow destiny. Senator Donald Benjamin James was the most important political star in the American galaxy. In that context, he was hardly a man. He was an organization. He was DBJ, a point of view, a catalytic force, a symbol, carefully constructed, painstakingly assembled, ready to be launched into an arena where the big prize is the ultimate power trip. In fourteen months, the Democratic convention would begin. Soon a decision would have to be made on the primaries. But now was the crucial time, the fund-raising time, the jockeying for position time; the galvanization, the careful work of years was all coming together. The presidency! It seemed like some shimmery blue lagoon in an arid landscape, visible to the eye, the path through the parched desert barely discernible, but beginning to throw off bolder and bolder outlines.

But even Don, with all his attractiveness and organization, knew he stood on ever-shifting sands. Those winds were tricky. Things happened. Nothing stayed quite the same. Especially now.

A politician was not simply a man. Like Don, he was only pieces of different men, scraps of imagery and imaginings, a media creation. From state senator, direct to the Senate of the United States for two terms, a campaign of uncounted nights, meetings, speeches, strategies, echelons of advisers, cadres of people, strung out and lined up throughout the length of the country, waiting for the signal to go forth and capture the holy grail. To recognize that Don was, after all, only a man, a man who defecated and fornicated and felt pain or anger or sadness, was admitting a lapse of faith in the political system. Even Don would never allow himself such a delusion.

Did Don's trail end on some lonely beach, the soul revealed, an empty shell of a man baying at the moon? It would seem so. The facts—notice, I did not say the truth of it—were perfectly suited to both creating the man and, therefore, killing the image of the man at the same time.

Put it in these terms. He is the beautiful, symmetrical man who shows up well from every angle on television. His voice is distinctive, individual, warm, reassuring, the words he speaks are well tuned, and the ideas carefully created, served up like a delicate soufflé. His style is envious, active, athletic, vital. His family is a perfect complement to the man of action. But he is not all putty and geegaws. Hasn't he

stood sweating under the TV lights and allowed the skilled newspaper boys to play darts with him as target? His is the body by which
every woman dreams of being entered. A leader? He is a leader
because he attacks the opposition. He is a leader because he instills
hope in empty hearts, that is his greatest talent. He is the promise,
the resurrection. Issues? He stands with mankind, the poor, the dis-
enfranchised, the blacks, the Chicanos. You see them, lined up, like
scraggly bums before a soup kitchen, banging on their bowls. But
that only shows compassion, for he is not for the kind of change that
will change. That kind of change will undermine the middle, and it
is in the middle that the treasure is buried. Nor is he a fraud. He cannot be a fraud, because he is not real. The technology of politics
makes it impossible for him to be real, and he knows it.

Now take this figure, precariously perched on the limb of history,
ready to build his nest in the highest branch-pit of the tree, and
reveal him as vulnerable, a miserable man, an adulterer, a smoker of
pot, a cheater, perhaps a murderer, and you have the ingredients of
political suicide at your door.

That was only one side of the coin. That was the wherefore of it.
Where was the why? Why did Donald Benjamin James want to wield
the ultimate power of the state? That was the dark side. I had watched
Don's ambition grow, not like some rotten malignancy taking posses-
sion of a life; rather, it was like a flower springing up from some stray
seed, perennially in bloom, with blooms creating buds, then more
blooms, until the thing was growing beyond anyone's wildest imagination, enveloping all, soaking up earth and moisture, bloom upon
bloom. He could have been a very successful lawyer. He could have
been anything. He could have made barrels of money, could have fitted well in the modern Babbittry of country clubs and charity balls
and "Kultur," a "credit" to his community. Instead, he chose this
power thing, and I had come to learn that this was the headiest thing
of all. Power! Even the word had its own sinews and suppleness.
Power! The quintessence of being, the rarest prize of them all. Who

had planted the seeds of this thirsty flower? What did it matter? It was there. Let explanations lie. Let it suffice that I understand its force and temptation, as do all men who hover around a power source.

And I couldn't tell, really, whether I mourned for Don or for myself. Certainly, it was not for Marlena. What was Marlena to me? Who cared about Marlena? That must sound callous. But it is honest. What was she to me?

Now, in practical terms, here is what could be expected. The police would be notified. Don's involvement would be revealed, and the informers to the world would descend upon Rehoboth like a community of ants attracted to a melted caramel.

And the fornicators of the world would head for the hills while the hypocrites rubbed their hands together in anticipation of the dismemberment of the political corpse of Donald Benjamin James, DBJ. Headlines would be composed with cleverness and zeal by curmudgeon copy editors for ten-dollar prizes. "DBJ Takes Pot Luck. Comes up with Black Corpse." And the TV boys, all eyes and cameras doing a recap of the weekend. "And here they had breakfast. And here is where they lit the fire and smoked the pot." It would be the most delicious scandal of the century, the kind that years from now becomes the big movie of the season. Then the interpreters would follow, all compassion and kindness, all superior in their knowledge, all knowing, all omnipotent, all humble. Eric Severeid—rosy cheeked, grey perfection, nobility of articulation— would intone wisdom, like oil from an eyedropper. And then the conclusion: "There but for the grace of God go I."

Americans might excuse the philandering, but the death would be hard to swallow. Sex made great media grist. Combined with death, it was sure fire. The challenge to Don's credibility was mammoth.

Had Don yet to comprehend all this? And having done it, would he throw himself into the sea, not after Marlena now, but in denial of his own fate? That thought made me run out to the beach again. He had stopped going away and was now coming back.

His face was white, almost transparent, even in the yellow bulb light. He shook his head. "I've really bought it this time," he said. It was then that I knew he was beginning to reach inside himself for some lever of control.

"What were you saying about options, Lou?" he asked.

VIII

It was nearly midnight. We moved into the kitchen and seated ourselves around the table of an old-fashioned dinette set with a plastic top and thick, round aluminum legs. Christine poured us each a cup of steaming coffee. We sipped deeply, ignoring the burning against our lips and tongues, perhaps welcoming the pain. Christine had moved a brush through her hair and lightly painted her lips with her special brand of shiny orange. Don was sitting erect in the chair, as if the act of keeping straight was holding him together and any movement or slouch would cause his joints to collapse.

Christine brought out a dictation book and pen, crossed her legs, and perched her large-framed glasses on her nose. We were what we were, and while the terrible events of the past few hours had broken the rhythm of our lives, it did not change who we were and what we had to do. A stranger peering through the window might have taken it for an ordinary business meeting, perhaps two writers working on a play with their secretary.

"Do you believe in miracles?" Don said suddenly, breaking the silence, and, appropriately, opening the strange meeting. And yet, this was always our method—Don, Christine and I. This was always the way we attacked a problem—sitting around a table, boiling down the options, recording the results.

"No," I said. "I don't believe in miracles."

"Neither do I."

"Let's start with a fact, then," Don said. He was recovering the strength of his mind, although his physical appearance belied the fact. Deep black pockets had suddenly embedded themselves under his eyes, and the firm mouth seemed slack at either end. "Marlena is dead. That is an incontrovertible assumption. Marlena has drowned.

Marlena could not have been saved. Marlena is dead." His voice broke for a moment and then firmed. "No sense asking why. Only how. The ocean wanted her, trapped her, smothered her."

"Accepted," I said.

"Now what is the likelihood of the body being washed ashore?" Don asked.

"I have no idea."

"If there is no body, there can be no autopsy," Don said.

"And if there is no autopsy, there would be nothing to indicate sexual encounters or pot. That's an important consideration, Don. Call it option one, Christine. If there is no body, then there can be no autopsy. If there is a body, there could be an autopsy, although I think you need the permission of next of kin. In any event, if there is no body, then we have the option to eliminate certain details of the events, like the question of sex and pot."

"You're probably right. Make a note of this, Christine. Whether they find Marlena's body or not, they must first establish cause of death. In this case, drowning. Then once they've determined that there was no foul play, the question of autopsy becomes moot."

"Unless the next of kin asks for it?"

"Which could happen."

"That means we've got to speak personally to the next of kin, to Marlena's father."

"I don't know how the hell I can face him. If it weren't for me, his daughter would still be alive."

"And that's another thought you've got to put out of your head. Marlena's death was an accident. It was in fact an accident. In the eyes of the law, it was an accident. Don, you've got to look at this rationally and solely from your own point of view. You've already established your humanity to your public, to the American people. That's not your problem. You've now got to prove that you're not an adulterer, that you don't cohabitate with women other than your wife, much less black girls, that you don't carouse, that you're hap-

pily married and that one of your staff simply got herself drowned
by accident while you were working in this house, lent to you by an
old friend, for the weekend. People can believe that you worked all
weekend. Hell, you had your secretary with you and the most trusted member of your staff. If you keep your cool, you could be home
free. Do you understand?"

"You make it sound so simple. The smart money will know
I'm lying—"

"You mean, suspect. Knowing is something else."

"The self-righteous will want to believe it."

"And they will."

"The blacks will think I've exploited one of their women."

"And secretly admire you."

"The kids will know I'm full of shit."

"And love you for shoving it up the ass of the American people."

"The question then is, Is there more currency in telling the truth
straight out or fudging the whole scenario?"

"Can a politician really show his weaknesses? A king descends
from the gods."

"Frankly, Lou, a full confession, the whole truth, is the course I'd
really like to take. Call it expiation. I'd feel a hell of a lot better."

"So what?"

"You think there is no forgiveness in the electorate."

"Oh, come on, Don—you sound like a ten-year-old in a 1935
civics class. Forgiving, perhaps, Remembering, definitely. Do you
want their forgiveness or their votes?"

"I would still like to tell it like it is."

"It won't come out like that, because like it is to you is not like it
is to others. You'd have to be almost omniscient. Almost, hell—
you'd have to be totally omniscient, and a brilliant performer, to pull
it off. You may be the latter, but not the former. Now, Don, I think
you're good. You're great. But bringing off the pristine truth—there
are too many possibilities of failure."

"Put it down as an option, anyhow. Let's not strike it out completely." Suddenly Don stood up. "I think this is ghoulish. I just
can't believe that this is happening and Marlena is lying out there
somewhere in that black, lonely sea. It makes no sense at all."

I could see his point. Hell, I'm not inhuman.

"We're just outlining the situation," I said.

He turned angrily and beat his fist on the table. "Hell, don't you
think I wouldn't like to find an easy way out of this mess? Don't
you think I'd like to spare my family the humiliation? Not to mention the party and the organization out there that thinks Senator
Donald Benjamin James's shit doesn't stink. Well, they're about to
find out that it does, just like everybody else's. How gullible do you
think they are out there? How much of a massage do you think we
can give them?"

"A big one," I said.

"Not big enough."

"We're exploring options."

"Options—horseshit. I haven't got many options."

"If you'd calm down, we'll go over them."

"No, I'll read them out to you. Option one: Tell the simple truth.
Report the drowning. Let the chips fall where they may. Option two:
Report the drowning. Tell lies. Hope that time will make the story
believable. You remember Goebbels and the big lie? Repetition of a
lie equals truth. Option three: Just resign. Walk away. Fuck it all.
Option four—"

"You're oversimplifying," I interrupted. "That's the whole point. We
can't make it simple. You've got to come out of this thing with the benefit of the doubt. That's all we can ask for—the benefit of the doubt."

"Do you suppose I'll get that from Karen?"

"Privately, no. Publicly, undoubtedly."

"God, that will make me sick. Karen in the role of the gallant
wife, long-suffering and noble. She'll love playing that role."

"She's always played it."

"And pretty well, at that."

"But, Don," I said. "She could balk. She can really hurt. She can murder you with a word."

"She's not going to be overjoyed when she gets this message."

"Would you be?"

"Ecstatic."

"You see," Don said, "the deeper we go, the murkier it gets. And, how do you think Barnstable will react? Hell, he's given me twenty-five years. He's primed our pumps. Raised millions. And, Max Schwartz, old Max—not to mention my mother, my kids. These people will be mortified."

Christine poured him another cup of coffee. He put his hand around the cup, ignoring the handle, perhaps greedy for as much warmth as he could get. He looked a pitiable figure. It annoyed me to think in those terms. He had never been an object of pity. That would be the last reaction people would have had. He gulped at the coffee and shook himself, like an old dog after a nap.

"I think one option has very definitely emerged," I said. "And that is dependent on two basic factors. Either the body is found or it isn't. If it is found, we must prevent an autopsy. If we can do that, then you'll have the benefit of the doubt in that at least you didn't have sex with her, and that would eliminate the dope problem as well. People will say, Who is he kidding? But at least none would know for certain, and we could construct a plausible story that would eliminate any hard facts which could point conclusively to a—a scandal."

"If we take that route, then I'm forced to lie outright. I told you, Lou, I don't think I can do it. It's not like a simple, ordinary political lie. This is a blatant head-on fourteen-karat lie. It's too vulnerable."

"That's the gamble you may have to take."

"That's an interesting observation."

"Maybe we should get you a great lawyer. There are many legal ways to insulate the public from the facts."

"I disagree." He was absorbed in his own thoughts, fighting to find some concentration, working to survive.

"About a lawyer—"

"If we hire a good lawyer—perhaps Ed Williams—think of what we've planted in people's minds."

"But everyone is entitled to good legal counsel."

"My problem is not a legal one. Hire a lawyer of that stature and there is an implication of—foul play. Murder. People will want to grasp at that straw first. People are conditioned to think in those terms. After all, haven't we got all the ingredients of a murder mystery here, and isn't murder a national passion? People will construct all sorts of scenarios. Like this one, for example: Marlena was his mistress; she would expose him unless she extracted something from him."

"Like what?"

"Like some radical goal, some trade-off on a political goal. Not money. If I refused, she would expose me to the world as a fraud. There. That's a motive. I found a way to kill her."

"I think you're exaggerating."

There was no question now that he was gathering his forces. It was good to see him coming back. A red flush had begun to creep around his cheekbones.

"But it all hinges on the elimination of an autopsy," I said. "Suppose an autopsy is insisted upon. Suppose Marlena's family insists upon it. Suppose nothing we say can persuade her father not to proceed with an autopsy. We are, after all, whites; and you know how she felt about that. Worse yet, her father might use the occasion for a vendetta, a vendetta against the whole white community. After all, we can expect him to occupy center stage before the media if he so chooses."

"If he insists on taking that tack, we'll be creating some new options."

"I have another wild thought," I said. "But please, Don, don't go into a tailspin."

He shook his head. He seemed so fragile, sitting there slumped like a wavering image on a trick mirror.

"Suppose the body is washed ashore. Near here. Let's assume that, simply for the sake of my impending suggestion. Suppose we got out within the next few hours and found her body along the beach."
He looked up at me, fires of anger in his eyes. "I don't want to hear it," he said, standing up. "I don't want to hear it."
"I know you don't want to hear it. But we might as well throw it on the table. It has got to cross our minds sooner or later."
"As an option," he said sarcastically.
"As an option."
He doubled over, slammed a fist into his mouth and gagged. It was a dry heave. I held his head down over his knees until he signaled with his hand that he was all right. He straightened up and pushed me away.
"I know there are limits, Don, but—"
"I'm walking on the edge, Lou. Don't make it any tougher."
"You know what I'm saying, though, don't you, Don?"
"Yes, I know what you're saying."
"I'm lost," Christine interjected. "Somewhere along the line, I've lost you."
"He wants to eliminate Marlena's body."
"Oh, my God."
"It's an option," I said stubbornly. "It's only an option."
"It's disgusting," Christine said.
"Is it?"
It was too late to go back. It was impossible to retrieve the thought, return it to the inchoate darkness of the mind, frozen beyond inarticulation. Too late. We had crossed the Rubicon. Their thoughts had to be no less different than mine. It was, very decidedly, a clear-cut option.
"Shall I continue?"
Don grunted. It was a kind of a involuntary sob.
"The whole story is in the body," I said. "We could simply find a way to get rid of the body. We could bury it, for example. After all, what is it?"

"I can't believe that this is you talking, Lou," Don said. "Do you really think I can live with such a monstrous thing?"

"I don't know, Don. But you must remember. We didn't murder this girl. We are dealing with an accident on the one hand, and a career that plays for pretty high stakes on the other. I truly believe we can rationalize the act."

"I don't think I have it in me."

"Well, it was an option. It had to be said."

"Fuck that option. I couldn't live with it."

"All right, let's forget it," I said, but I knew we could not forget it, that it would come swirling back, like a candy wrapper caught in the crosswind of a courtyard. After all, what was the human body after death? Just so much garbage. Dust to dust.

"Well, we've solved nothing," Don said, somewhat regaining his composure.

"We seemed to have agreed," Christine said, reading over her notes, "that at all costs, we must prevent an autopsy."

"Everything, the whole credibility of our approach, depends upon the elimination of all hard facts. We volunteer no information other than what is beyond question. A girl drowned. It was an accident."

"And why did we come to Rehoboth?"

"A working weekend—the only logical explanation."

I was quite serious about this point. At last a reasonable exit was becoming visible. I was sure, Don, too, had begun to see a slight ray of hope for his position.

"It does have some logic. Let me see if I'm able to understand it. We report a drowning, whether the body is found or not, preferably before it is found. We offer as little explanation as possible—an accident—a working weekend. We pick our way across the public record as if it were a mine field. Our goal, the ultimate option, is to keep everything shrouded in mystery—everything vague, no facts, nothing definite with which to achieve a firm conclusion. We keep all comment from reporters in person."

"And we control, as much as possible, the outflow of information."
"We issue bland short statements, filled with sentimental asides, like 'regrets,' 'shock,' 'tragedy.' " Don had the reflexes of the consummate politician and the feel for public persuasion with its style and idiom. "All right," he said. "We've explored some options. Now, let's list priorities."

He was becoming extraordinarily businesslike about the whole episode. I couldn't tell whether he was on the verge of hysterics or simply cool and confident. It was that thought that had begun to gnaw at me. Was all this really happening? Was he putting me on? Was this really a test of my mettle? Had he staged all this just to test his power over us? His voice seemed sharper, his lips tighter, as if he were spitting out the words, forcing them out one after the other.

"Priority one," he said. "I've got to appear at the local police station and report the drowning. I've got to make a statement. I should probably appear with you, Lou. I play out my role, cool but contrite. Let's face it, she is a member of my staff. I do not answer any questions. Perhaps I can cleverly intimidate the local gendarme who is suddenly confronted with the celebrated Donald Benjamin James. Can you just see the look on his face? He's just bursting to tell the wife and the local representative of the Rehoboth Bugle. I tell him I'll be here when he needs me. I assure him of my availability. I betray no guilt, no remorse. Only pity. Only sadness. He sits by his broken down manual typewriter and types out my statement. I sign it, once again assure him of my availability, and take off back to the house to steel myself against total destruction of my whole world. I stand here like Sampson among the Philistines, pushing the whole hall down on my head. Would you call that priority one, Lou? That's priority one, right Christine? I got it down pretty pat, don't you think?"

I had never questioned his ability to grasp his situation, only the need for him to recover his senses and act. But would he act? Was this only a kind of verbal hysteria that had seized him and was quickly exhausting him?

"Priority two. I'll bet you don't know what priority two is, Lou."
"You seem to have most of the answers."
He stood up. His face was in a deep flush. He looked feverish.
"Priority two will be Karen. We've got to convince her to keep
her public cool. I really feel sorry for her. What a humiliation. The
beautiful Karen James, with her fantastic charm, all her youthful
good looks, couldn't keep her boy on the string. Karen must be carefully fit into the charade. You know something, Lou, I hope she
refuses. I hope she blows the whole lid off the whole thing. I hope
she speaks the unspeakable. 'This crummy bastard was two-timing
me and I don't care what happens to him!' But she won't. Not
Karen. She's too damned smart. She'll hold me up for ransom."
"She's had to be a dummy not to have suspected that you were
cheating on her all these years."
"That's the most insufferable part of her character. She wouldn't
even raise the point. She never raised the point."
"Maybe it's because she didn't want to know the truth,"
Christine said.
"The truth—don't talk to me about the truth," Don said. "I
don't even want to hear the word. There is something repulsive
about the word."
He walked across the room, poured himself another tumbler of
Jack Daniels, and drank it in a gulp.
"How am I doing on my priorities, Lou? Are my priorities okay?
I've snowed the authorities. I've snowed Karen. Now comes the hard
part. Priority three. I've got somehow to get to old Mr. What's-his-
name. What was her last name? Jackson. Yeah, Jackson. I've got to
go through with that confrontation. I've got to tell him about the
death of his beautiful dream. How he must have sweated for that kid
to get an education. How he must have worked to make something
of his pride and joy. And I, the hotshot politician from the West,
busted up his dream. I've got to lay my heart out in front of this
black man and ask his forgiveness and his silence. I must say to him,

'Black man, don't trouble the waters; let sleeping dogs lie. Don't rock the boat.' Words he has swallowed before—words that stick in his craw every day of his life."

He started for the Jack Daniels again. This time I got there first. "Don't be a damn fool, Don. You're going to need all your wits. The worst thing that can happen is your appearing drunk."

"I appear as I appear," he said menacingly. I thought he was going to wrestle me for the bottle. Instead, he threw the glass against the wall with all his strength. It splattered over the tile floor. Then, spent, he sat down again.

"I suppose you're right," he said after a long silence. "Well, we beter get on with it."

There was no question about the course of action that lay ahead. We had only to decide upon the details of execution and hope that somehow Don would be able to sustain himself through the ordeal. Obviously, Karen was our first problem. She had to be called. She had to come out here. Don's two sons were both away at school. And Barnstable, as staff director, had to be filled in. And Don's mother. Who else? My God—the world, the whole damned world.

IX

Of one thing, though, I had become certain. Donald James was not bugging out. He probably didn't realize it yet, but he had made the decision to stand and fight. Without voicing our thoughts, we had calculated the odds. What did we have to lose? In the gloom of the early morning hours, tired, our energies spent, panic and confusion lapping at our guts, we seemed to have reached the bottom rung of despair. There was nowhere to go but up.

Don stepped into one of the bedrooms to make the call to Karen, not the room he had shared with Marlena, but the one in which Christine and I had spent the night. We could hear the low drone of his voice through the closed door. It was strange, this sense of urgent privacy that he felt the need for now, as if in the act of shutting out "strangers" he was somehow making it up to Karen.

Karen's reaction to Don's dilemma was moderately predictable. Would she go along? How could she do otherwise? Marriages to politicians are cemented by ambition. After years of conditioning, of licking envelopes, of shaking endless lines of hands, and of the fixed, frozen smile of the banquet circuit, surely she was conditioned to understand her role. But then, Karen could be difficult. And humiliation is an eccentric emotion.

After fifteen minutes, he opened the door of the bedroom and returned to us. He looked stronger, more confident.

"She's on her way. I told her to call Jack. They'll drive out together. I'm sure Jack will call here as soon as she gets to him. Poor Jack."

Jack Barnstable was staff director on the one assignment that had absorbed his life from the very beginning of Don's career, the presidential campaign of Senator Donald Benjamin James. He was a pro, a man of gargantuan size, appetite and mind. Jack Barnstable was indispensable to our future strategy.

"What was her reaction?" I asked.

"Well, I was pretty vague. I gave her just enough details for her to get the message."

"Evasion again?"

The telephone ring blasted its way into our consciousness, frightening us with its sudden intensity. Christine picked it up and handed it to Don.

"Yes, Jack." He listened patiently. "That's about the size of it, Jack." We could hear a muffled voice at the other end and could visually observe the impact of the words on Don. He looked at his watch.

"Well, I guess I owe you that much, Jack. Briefly, this is the story. . . ."

He outlined the bare details. He did not hide the fact of his having an affair with Marlena. One did not hold these things back from Jack Barnstable.

"I'm sorry, Jack," Don said, after he had given him the story. "Yes, we do have some ideas. We, we've considered that. No, don't bring any lawyers, not yet."

He hung up and looked at his watch again.

"We should go now. We should report to the police," Don said. He stretched out his arms in front of him. His hands shook. "I need time," he said. "I'll blow my cool. I need time."

"Let's wait for Jack," I suggested.

"Three more hours." He thought for a moment. "I have got to have more time."

"Maybe you should try and get some sleep," I said.

"Who the hell can sleep?"

"You're going to need all your wits, Don."

But instead of answering, he walked out into the night again. I followed. The beach seemed a wasteland of deadness. The waters had calmed. Heavy clouds obscured the moonlight. It seemed as if the world had simply stopped. He looked in either direction, his eyes making an effort to penetrate the inky darkness. Then he shrugged and came in again.

X

I watched Christine typing on the blue portable that was always an essential part of her baggage. Businesslike and alert, her glasses slipping halfway down her nose, she was typing a memo to Jack Barnstable. It was a reflex of her way of life. Perhaps a painter would paint in her situation. A writer would write. A carpenter would chisel wood.

Don had gone into the bedroom, Christine's and mine, and was, hopefully, asleep. I looked in and didn't see a stir. I couldn't sleep. My mind was busy with details on how we were going to cope with the next twenty-four hours. The crucial twenty-four hours—the onslaught of the news media, the pressures of political allies and enemies, the reaction from friends and foes from abroad. Barnstable would have the toughest assignment. He would have to keep the whole organization in line, not only the sixty-odd staff people on the campaign payroll, but the bankrollers, who would be quick to panic, and the amateurs, who, in the absence of any payment, would be the toughest to hold, especially the women. It was not simply the case of an indiscretion by, perhaps, the head of a corporation. Hell, he could be replaced. But how could you replace the man who was the organization? That was the whole point of the game. He was not a man. He was an entity, an organization. He presided over a closed world of bright young men and women with burning eyes who wrote long memos and filled pages of printed loose-leaf books: the "DBJ Advance Man's Manual"; the "DBJ Index of Past Policy Guide"; the "DBJ Audio-Visual Policy Line"; including the authorized pictures, the authorized poses, the authorized words, the authorized method of endorsement; the "DBJ Foreign Policy Index"; the "DBJ Past Poll Index"; the "DBJ Supplementary Staff Guide" (the campaign staff as opposed to the senatorial staff); the "Green Book of Contributors"—three copies, Jack's, mine and Max's.

It was an endless mountain of paper, like lava coming down from Mount Olympus, covering everything. Like the library of position papers, computerized, a staff of fifteen was required just to keep the input catalogue. How does DBJ stand on Pakistan, the Middle East, devaluation—it was an endless potpourri of issues, all carefully boiled down into options, simple enough to evaluate during the time it takes to produce a good shit. All these geegaws are fucking necessities if you want to get elected president. The days of bulling your way through are over. You can't stand up in front of the media and leave the audience with gaps. You've got to know the bare rudiments of everything and have enough style to embroider the facts. Hell, you're not expected to have any deep knowledge. We've got an army of professor types writing position papers. This makes them feel like they're making a contribution and gives us the aura of expert knowledge. Who the hell has time to read all that shit? We've got all those smart-ass young people reading and writing and talking, but the name of the game is to boil down and squeeze out the essence—just enough essence to give DBJ a good whiff, enough to go on. Throw old Don a cue and he's beautiful. Who the hell is watching that old boob tube anyway? If they were so damned smart, they'd be reading books.

The whole operation had begun to develop a life of its own under the sure hand of Barnstable. Jack Barnstable was indefatigable. The best compliment you could give him was to call him a pro—even better, a real pro.

It was an organization that fed on itself. We all knew that when you called Jack Barnstable in, and it was absolutely essential, you were bringing in the whole root of the iceberg. If there were enough time, which there wasn't, Jack would have the whole pattern of options on a computer readout.

Unfortunately, there just wasn't enough time. The revelation would be a savage blow to the organization. The big question was,

What was the recovery potential? Even the language of this business was peculiar unto itself, as if it were some new semantic technology that had gotten encrusted onto our language. Don literally had to check himself to prevent his speech from reflecting these new words. Input, for instance. Don and I talked a lot about these things. How, with this mass of information and knowledge, could our country's leaders make such dumb decisions? Like the Viet Nam war. Incredible. Which brings us to another subject—the "DBJ Manual of Attack Positions." This was literally an arsenal of words, or paragraphs, neatly arranged to provide DBJ with an attack on every conceivable position that could embarrass an opponent, particularly the incumbent; for while the researchers were putting together DBJ's positions, a parallel team was putting together his anti-positions.

So here we were with all the heady benefits of this efficient organization. And now the whole menagerie was trapped, out on a limb because of a simple human need—to love (that may be too strong in this case), and a simple human experience—death. I must admit that I was satisfied that we had come up with the right decision, that we had picked the right options. It is always good to be secure in the decisions you make. If you psych yourself up to believe you made the right decision you have more strength.

None of us could have lived with the idea of hiding the body. That was a ghoulish thought. I'm even ashamed of having made the suggestion.

Christine finished her memo and gave me a copy. It was two pages long, and under the text was written: Destroy after reading.

XI

Karen and Barnstable made the trip in three hours flat. I automatically looked at my watch as I heard their car crackle over the pebbles in the driveway and come to a halt. They must have been going at a pretty fast clip. Don was up in a moment, bounding toward the door, opening it, gathering Karen in his arms. She just stood there, rooted to the floor, like a statue, not moving, not returning his caress. Who could blame her? She was wearing a turtleneck sweater and slacks, and her soft blonde hair was tied back with a long kerchief over it. She wore, appropriately, dark glasses, although I couldn't help thinking that it was an affectation. She barely looked at me or Christine.

Don led her into the bedroom—ours, again. He couldn't bear a confrontation with us looking on. I led Jack, looking as if he had slept in his clothes, to the other end of the house, in an effort to shut out the sounds of Don's and Karen's voices, although I had this tremendous urge to listen. Jack saw the bottles lined up outside the screen porch. He went out, poured himself a Scotch, and sat down heavily at the kitchen table. He looked lost and defeated. Finally he looked up at me.

"You stupid bastards," he said. "You stupid bastards."

"It was a freak," I said. "A one-in-a-million chance."

"I was driving along and thinking. Karen wouldn't open her mouth. How stupid can you be? Then I began to feel sorry for myself. Hell, I gave that son-of-a-bitch all those years, nearly twenty fucking years, and because he can't keep his cock in his pants, we've all got to suffer."

I didn't answer him. It would have been futile. What did he expect? Christine looked particularly disturbed. He went on for ten minutes in that vein, getting it all out, letting the words tumble over, his big

63

frame shaking with anger as he poured out more drinks for himself and gulped them down. Finally I had no choice but to stop him.

"Okay, Jack. We've listened. Now it's time to stop and get back on the tracks. We went through all this earlier. We've got a plan. Christine's got a memo."

"A memo? Jesus K. Christ—" She handed him the memo. He put on his horn-rimmed glasses, which he had laid carelessly on the kitchen table, and read the memo. When he was finished, he shook his head. "I can't believe you put this in writing. Are you crazy?"

"We had to put it down," Christine said. "We had to."

Jack took a match out of his pocket, stood over the sink, lit the end of the papers and watched them burn. Then, as if they were diseased, he flushed the bits of ashes down the drain. He turned to us. "He's probably right. There doesn't seem to be any options left on this baby. Besides, I think he's got enough guts to pull it off. Has anyone been contacted besides Karen and me?"

"No one," I said.

"Good."

He went to the phone and called the number he had written down on a piece of paper.

"Check in at the Rehoboth Motel. Take three rooms. Just stay there until I call. Don't ask me any questions."

"What was that all about?"

"I'm staffing up."

"Do you think that's wise?"

"We're going to need statements. Media people are going to crash down around our heads like hailstones. We're going to need bodies."

"Has Max been called?"

"Not yet."

"We need Don."

"Leave them alone, Jack. Give them a little more time."

"I'm not so sure we have any left. In a little while, the sun will be rising. If that body is going to pop up, it will ride in on the early tide."

"How the hell do you know?" I asked.

"I grew up in San Diego," he said. "I'm an old beach bum."

Jack rose, went to the bedroom door and knocked.

"Let's go, Don. We've got to move."

There wasn't a sound behind the door. Then Don opened it. His eyes were red. Karen was behind him, her face like flint. She followed Don out to the living room and sat down on a stiff-backed chair. Don wouldn't sit down.

"The way I look at it," Barnstable said, "there's no room for wasted, counterproductive action. Karen, do you understand?"

"I understand," she said. Her voice was tight. She looked at me. "I understand a lot of things. I'm numb. It's one thing to be simply betrayed, but to be the victim of an intrigue, a conspiracy—that makes me want to puke."

I'm sure everyone in the room felt embarrassed for her, and she knew it. The truth was that she seemed sort of extraneous. Can you believe that? She considered herself the injured party, and yet her injury didn't matter to us at all. She had to be fitted into a specific role, and, beyond that, we could not afford a single drop of compassion for her. About all anyone could be expected to say was "Isn't that a damn shame?" and pass on to the bigger issue.

She simply had to swallow her humiliation. She was gagging on it, as we all knew she would. We sat around silently, avoiding her eyes. Don leaned against the wall, nervously running his fingers through his hair.

"I'm supposed to be 'Miss Good Girl,' 'Miss Keep Your Big Mouth Shut.' I've been in a state of shock since that damned phone call. So you were making a speech in Philadelphia. Some speech."

"Karen, please," Don said. "You promised at least to discuss things calmly—and privately."

"Well, would you believe that," Karen said. She was making a great effort to keep her voice from becoming shrill, holding herself back. "Private. The whole world is going to know about this. What

do you think I'm about to become? Have you given that some
thought in your calculations?"

She looked at me and Jack. "Have the two wizards even considered that one?"

"I," she had said—that damned first person pronoun that comes
shouting at you through the ether. It was that fucking "I." And she
really gave herself a big "I."

"—am about to become an object of pity. Can you imagine that?
Little Karen Whitford, the perennially pursued female, about to
become an object of pity."

"Karen, I beg of you," Don said. "I understand how you feel—"

"Oh, bullshit. How can you understand how I feel? We had a marriage. We're a team. We *were* a team. Haven't I been good about
everything, Don? Haven't I been the faithful wife? The good political wife? My God, haven't I paid for your success with all those lonely nights? All those endless lines of people. All those faces. All those
bright smiles. I've paid my dues."

"Christ, Karen, you've been marvelous. You've been the best."

"Apparently not the best."

"I know how you feel. I know how I would feel. The question is,
Do I stay in this business or get the hell out? Do I make my stand
or kiss it off?"

That thought seemed to sober her.

"Who cares?" she said, hissing the words. I knew she didn't
mean it.

"I have mixed feelings, myself," Don said.

"What did you expect, that you were going to get away with all
this forever?"

I wanted to say to her, "But you knew. You acquiesced." I held
my tongue. Anyone with any semblance of sanity would have done
the same.

She stood up and put her glasses in her pocketbook. Her eyes were
slightly puffy, but for a woman in her early forties, she was quite

handsome. Physically, they were both unusually good-looking people. One would have thought that they could have found sexual satisfaction in each other. Think of all the women in America who simply would not understand why he would cut out on this beautiful wife for a—for a nigger.

"Forgive me, boys," she said. "I've not quite learned how to cope with this as yet. It will take a bit of time. Don't worry, though. I'm a damned good actress. I've had a lot of practice out there in front of those cameras. Don't worry about me. I'll pull it off. But don't expect any more of me." She looked at Don. "At this moment, I can't stand the sight of you. I'm rather an old-fashioned girl. I don't really understand what's going on in the world, you know. Even more than twenty years of marriage hasn't quite made me callous about the old virtues, like being true blue to your mate. I was thinking about all this in the car coming out here. And you know what's begun to bug me? My own identity. All these years, I've submerged myself for the cause, the great cause of Donald Benjamin James. But who the hell am I? Oh, I admit to plenty of vanity. Who wouldn't want to be the First Lady of America? Well, maybe there are lots of people who wouldn't. You know, that's pretty predictable. After all, I've got two sons who worship their father. I guess they'll be the same way when they go out into the world. Maybe all men are hunters like that. Maybe women are expected to let their men run wild. I just never could bring myself to be unfaithful. It's like a commitment that you make with your whole being. Maybe men don't do things like that. I even think that I'll be an object of pity only to my own age group. Because I don't think the young people will think it's wrong. They may even suspect that I, too, was running around. Ha! What a laugh. Look what I'm dwelling on. My own hurt. Perhaps I should be like those big jungle animals who, when injured, crawl into a cave to lick their wounds. That's what you'd all like, I know. I'm afraid all this talk doesn't matter much to any of you. I feel so stupid, running off at the mouth."

Don walked over to her and tried to take her in his arms. I could
see that he was genuinely moved. You don't cut away twenty years as
if you were trimming the fat off a steak. A lot of private, secret things
had passed between them in all that time. In his mind, at that
moment, she was more important to him than his career. I guess you'd
have to have a wife to understand what was going on between them.

Frankly, I was busy looking at my watch. So was Jack.

Karen pushed him away. "Just keep your hands off me, Don,"
she cried. "I don't want you to touch me. Please." She sat down
again, took a mirror out of her pocketbook and inspected her face.
Jack took it as a sign that it was time to act. Outside in the east,
the sky was lightening, although the clouds had continued to
thicken. It looked like the beginning of one of those terribly
gloomy, beach days.

"Don," Jack said. "I'd suggest you get cleaned up. Shave. Comb
your hair. Put on some clean clothes. If there are going to be cameras, let them at least get some shots of you looking good, not like
some stumblebum. Lou, I guess you should go with him. I'd like to
go too, but I'm afraid I would lend an air that was too professional,
too studied."

Jack had that marvelous take-charge way about him. We all
respected his ability. He was especially needed now. Both Don and I
were physically and emotionally drained. We needed time to replen-
ish ourselves, and there wasn't going to be any for the next few hours.

Christine came out of the bedroom. She had cleaned herself up,
trying to look presentable, but the bags under her eyes were beyond
redemption. She motioned me to come into the bedroom.

"I've packed up Marlena's clothes," she said. "As soon as we can,
I want to shift her clothes into our bedroom and you move your
things over here."

"I never even thought about it."

"I'll tell you something else. She had some pot in a cellophane bag
stashed in her valise. I've emptied it down the toilet, but I think

we've got to get rid of this plastic bag." She held up the plastic bag.
I took it from her and burned it in an ash tray. "I also found some
strange pills. They're probably only sleeping pills, but I threw that
down the toilet, too, along with the little label." She held up the
vial. I took it from her. "I also went through her things pretty carefully. Nothing special.
I really feel sorry for that kid. Can you imagine? She'll be the forgotten person in this whole episode. God, I feel sorry for her." Tears
welled in her eyes.

Don came in and went into the bathroom without a word. I
looked out into the kitchen. Karen was sitting alone now on the
screened porch, her coat wrapped around her, looking out to sea, lost
in her own thoughts. I shifted the valise quickly into the other bedroom and began to change my clothes. When I had finished, I
brought my suitcase into the room that Don had shared with
Marlena. The bathroom door was open. He saw me put the suitcase
in the closet and nodded.

XII

The police station was less than a mile from the beach house, on the main street, which at this moment in time was totally deserted. Even the reception room of the police station was deserted, although we could hear an occasional burst of sound from a police radio. A soggy container of cold coffee and an adventure magazine lay opened on the front desk, indicating that someone was around. A young patrolman arrived from somewhere in the rear of the station and greeted us with the familiar deadpan look of the disinterested civil servant annoyed by an uncommon intrusion.

"I'd like to report a drowning," Don said. He had that sixth sense about just the right tone, just the right look.

"A drowning?"

The young policeman looked at us, and then bit his lip. He saw in Don's face something vaguely familiar.

"Yes, an ocean drowning. One of the members of my staff. A woman. Age, twenty-four. Black."

"Black?"

"I really think you should check to see if there have been any bodies washed up along the shore around here."

"Yes, I'm going to do that. There have been no reports so far, but then, who would be out on the beaches at this time of night. Hell, we're off season. Don't I know you from somewhere?" Recognition was slow in coming, but it was coming.

"I'm Senator Donald James."

"Senator James! Holy shit—" The policeman was embarrassed now, the mask of indifference cracking, the boredom now gone. "Now what were you saying about a drowning?"

"One of my staff—a black girl. She's missing. We did see her jump into the surf. Mr. Castle and I. This is Mr. Castle—Louis Castle."

The young policeman held out his hand, brushing it first on his shirt (perhaps a reflex that revealed more of a class complex than cleanliness).

"Officer Benton."

He was in his early twenties, his black hair pasted against the side of his head (an anachronistic hairdo, but somehow not out of place). Without his uniform, he could have been pumping a gas tank or delivering groceries.

It was better than we dreamed. A green kid. We were able to use the subtle intimidation that only a celebrity could carry off on this type of person. Don sensed this. He was calm, deliberate.

"I'll tell you what we do. I'm staying about a mile from here. Why don't I give you a statement. It may be we're unnecessarily alarmed. Maybe the girl is safe, after all. Just you write it down, and I'll get back to My place, and you can have the chief call later in the morning. I think, though, that you should at least get the facts down and start to proceed."

"Yes, sir," Officer Benton said. He pulled an electric typewriter on its stand toward the desk, put a piece of paper in the carriage, and proceeded to take our dictation. Don devised a short, quick statement. Heavy tide. Slipped. Got carried away. Tried to save her. No details of time or place. Vague. All as agreed. It was a lot less painful than we had expected. He signed the statement and made sure the boy gave him a carbon copy.

The young patrolman looked at it, then pulled another piece of paper out of the drawer. "Can I have you autograph?" he said.

Don signed the paper. "I would appreciate your giving me a call if anything turns up. I plan to be at this number all day."

We left the station house and got back into the car. It was all so simple, so casual. One had the feeling the young patrolman even welcomed our quick exit so he could call his wife or mother about this sudden difference in the dull pattern of his days.

"Okay, that's done," Don said. "So far, so good. But the shit is now about to hit the fan. At least I can gather my wits now. Could you imagine if we had some son-of-a-bitch at the desk? He would really have killed us."

"The old James luck."

"Yeah. I'm real lucky, Lou."

"He could have been one of those officious crew-cut types who talk like a book of regulations. I think we've passed this hurdle nicely."

"And I think we took advantage of the kid. He'll pay for it someday."

XIII

Back at the beach house, Jack had literally sprung into action. His glasses were on his forehead as he barked orders into the telephone.

Don was getting retrospective again, slipping deep into himself. This could be disastrous. He looked around for Karen. "Where's Karen?"

"She was here a bit ago," Jack said. "Try outside." He peered through the screen. We could see Karen in the distance, along the water's edge, a huddled figure in the gloom and chill of the early morning. Don started out towards her.

"Hey, Don," Jack called. "We've got things to do." Don ignored him and proceeded to the water's edge.

I showed Jack a carbon of the statement we had signed at the police station. He read it while still on the phone.

". . . and I want that AP and UPI wire watched. Just keep the line open at the motel. One line only. Don't hang it up. All we've got here is one phone. Just dictate it and shuttle it over to us. You're about a half mile from the house."

He hung up.

"The way I figure it, the first bulletin will come over the AP or UPI. I've got someone covering that base. At this point, all publicity is the enemy. We've got to see what the enemy is up to."

Jack Barnstable was one of those people who get turned on by crisis. He was like a lion who spots a kill—all tense, every nerve taut, with calculating intelligence, alert, with all energy and concentration on the prey.

The two sounds were almost simultaneous: the earsplitting siren, as it shattered the early morning stillness, and the unfamiliar, tinny ring of the telephone. The siren stopped outside the door. We heard car doors slam and the march of heavy footsteps outside. Jack looked out the window.

"Here they come. Looks like the chief and two patrolmen. I'll get them. Take the phone."

I answered the phone.

"This is station WSIL. My name is Cleveland. We just got a police bulletin about Senator James—some drowning. Could you give me the information?"

"Where did you say you were from?"

"Station WSIL. I'm the night disc jockey."

Another burst of luck. Another amateur. If only the professional will stay hidden for a while, I thought.

"Okay," I said. "Here it is. Ready? One of Senator James' staff people fell in the ocean and drowned. At least we think she drowned."

I gave him nothing concrete. No names. No race. No age. He would call it in to the wire services and get his $2.00, and that's the way the world will first get it.

Almost as soon as I hung up, the telephone rang again. From the corner of my eye, I could see Christine emerge from a bedroom, and it occurred to me that the typewriter had been clicking since we arrived.

"Yes," I barked into the phone. The police chief had been shown in by Jack and was being taken out to the screened porch, outside my field of vision. The voice on the telephone was that of Henry Davis, one of Barnstable's bright young political P.R. types, apparently staying at the Rehoboth Motel.

"Give this to Barnstable, Lou. We're ready to make our calls to the state coordinators. We need word from you fellows on what the line is. We need some answers if the calls are to be credible." He lowered his voice. "I wish you could be more explicit as to what's going on. We'll sound like dummies when we make those calls."

"You'll know soon enough," I said, hanging up.

I called Christine and took her out of earshot of the police, who were standing in the sun porch watching Don and Karen on the beach.

"Just stand by the phone. If it's the press, no comment. I think we might be lucky on the first break. No need to complicate anything with any additional information."

Jack was waving me toward the screened porch, a sense of urgency on his face. I could hear the police chief's voice.

Chief Bernhard was one of those leathery types, with a face all lined and wrinkled. One might take him for retired navy. Even his voice had that same leathery quality, worn and gravel toned. From his very first words, I got the feeling that he was skeptical, not only of our own story, but of all human aspirations. Perhaps it was the nature of his job. But distrust was written all over him. I introduced myself to him and made an attempt at small talk; then, seeing that I was getting no reaction either out of him or the two stony-faced types beside him, I gave up. There is no more frustrating experience than being up against a nonreaction person, a blank.

"I'd like you to point out to me where she went in," Chief Bernhard said. I obeyed, showing him just where she had begun to slip. Then I showed him that point where we both went in after her and where we lost her.

"Has her body been found?" I asked.

"Too early. We figure she'll come up at Buzzards Point in about an hour or so. I've got men out there, waiting. Tides at this time of year point to that area."

Frankly, the information relieved me. It, once and for all, blotted out the possibility of getting rid of Marlena's body.

XIV

Don and Karen started back from the water's edge, their faces tight and grey in the morning light. We all watched them silently as they approached. I introduced them to Chief Bernhard and the patrolmen, who had their names engraved on little black plates across their right-hand vest pockets: Officer Barker and Officer Sims. Both Don and Karen flashed their best political smiles, that casual, relaxed lip smile, showing lots of teeth, the mouth opened slightly, the head back a bit, as if they were on the verge of unparalleled joy. Force of habit. They picked out the most incongruous weapon from their arsenal. Chief Bernhard showed no reaction. The effort was wasted on him.

He did, however, shake hands—a kind of limp, suspicious, and perfunctory movement. Both patrolmen had their pads and pencils ready, and, as if on signal, both began to jot down some notes.

"Would you mind if my men went through her effects?" Chief Bernhard asked. Don looked at me and shrugged.

"I suppose," I said. "If you think you ought to."

He nodded to his men who went off into the interior of the house.

I had half expected him to say something like "just routine," but he disappointed me. He very definitely was not a cliché of a police chief.

"Now, will you tell me exactly how she got into the water, Senator?"

Don explained, as carefully as he could, the technical aspects of the drowning, beginning at the point when Marlena got caught in the swirl of the tide. It was as if the entire episode had begun at that point in time. Don, as always, was quite articulate as he explained the sequence of events, both during and after we had lost her. The details were merely that—pure details, facts, bare of observation, stripped clean of any emotion. Chief Bernhard listened intently, watching Don's lips move, as if he were deaf, reading his lips. It was a peculiar trait, watching a person's lips, especially in a man who could hear. I hadn't noticed it until he began to listen to Don. It was extremely annoying. Perhaps it was just a device to make the speaker uncomfortable. I wondered if Don noticed it. If so, he didn't reveal himself but just went on with his description, almost as a small child tells a story in perfect chronology. "And then I did this. Then this. Then this." Don's voice was strong and confident. Karen sat beside him on the rattan couch, where yesterday Don and Marlena had slept and felt closeness. The brief image of that scene chilled me. I involuntarily shook my head, as if I had swallowed something too sour.

"I appreciate your thoroughness, Senator," Chief Bernhard said. "But what I would like to know is how she got into that water in the first place."

"We were sort of jogging along the beach."

"Jogging?"

"More like tag. You know. One person chases another. We were all taking a little exercise."

"And she simply ran, or was chased, into forty-degree water?"

"More or less."

"Was there any drinking?"

"We had just had lunch. Some wine."

We both knew that he was skirting around the edges, that he was narrowing his base until he had worked himself into the eye of the target.

"Do you always come out here, Senator?"

Don looked at me. For a moment, I could detect some helplessness, some brief indecision. It was like reading sign language. In that split second, he had made up his mind. He knew what he was going to say.

"Only occasionally, Chief. One of my Washington neighbors, Harley Donovan, owns this place. We've come here for years with the family. Occasionally we use it for working weekends, like this one. I brought my staff people this weekend. Lou Castle here, my administrative assistant, my secretary, Christine Donato, over there by the phone, and, of course, Marlena Jackson, one of my staff assistants on the education sub-committee of the senate, of which I am chairman. She was working on the problems of minority education, which you know have been absorbing the country. Bright girl. A damned shame. She had a great future."

It was difficult to read anything in the chief's face. Don had hardly answered the question, although to an untrained ear it might have sounded like it. I knew by his next statement that the Chief was not buying the explanation.

"Oh, a working weekend—is that what you'd call it?" It was half statement, half question. Since it was not clearly defined as a question, Don remained silent.

"Was your wife here, too?" Chief Bernhard asked, looking at Karen. She smiled, a little too toothily again.

"No. I was back in Washington. Came in early this morning. Don called me. He was so upset. It is upsetting, you know."

"Yes, I can well understand," Chief Bernhard said.

"What time did you say it all happened?"

"Well, I'm not exactly sure. Lou?"

"About sundown," I said, feeling a tightening in my throat. "It suddenly had gotten dark."

What the hell. It had to be said. It was in the air now. No way to avoid this turn of the road. This was the point that required real finesse.

"Why did you wait so long?" Chief Bernhard asked. "Nearly eleven hours." I thought he would go on with some admonishment. Instead, he clipped the sentence short—cleverly, I thought—letting the thought hang there like an accusing finger.

"I really can't offer you an explanation of that, Chief," Don was playing a strong game with a weak hand and knew it.

"Eleven hours, Senator."

"Yes, eleven hours."

"You don't think that's strange?"

"Strange?"

"Yes, strange. Eleven hours. Did it ever occur to you that fast action might have saved her?"

"Nothing, in my opinion, could have saved her. We tried. We searched. It was hopeless. We searched for hours. It exhausted us."

"Why didn't you call for help?"

"We were so damn busy trying to find her. It probably never occurred to us."

"Never occurred to you," Chief Bernhard said.

"It's hard to keep your wits about you in such circumstances."

"You say you searched for that girl for eleven straight hours."

"Most of it."

"How do you search a single stretch of beach for eleven straight hours?"

"We felt it was worth the time."

"I doubt it."

"Well, that's what we did."

"I just don't understand it," Chief Bernhard said, still stoic, neither smiling nor frowning. "In any event, we haven't got a body yet."

"That's right."

"The body will tell us something."

The implications were impressively clear. We had agreed not to be baited by inferences, and, I must say, Don was masterful. He held himself in check. The chief was trying to break our cool. Hell, we couldn't blame him. That was his job, and he was doing it well, in the face of great intimidation.

"I think the implications of that remark are insulting," Don said.

"You don't think I have the right to make it?"

"You're questioning my integrity?"

"I am."

"I am a United States senator."

"Yes," Chief Bernhard paused, "and a senator in deep trouble, I'd guess."

"That's obvious."

"I'm not a fool, Senator. There's a young woman involved here, a weekend at the beach. You've got to admit there are ingredients here that are suspect."

"Yes, I have to admit that."

"So let's not be thin-skinned about implications."

"I know. You're only doing your job, I suppose."

"Yes. And I promise I won't make hasty judgments."

"That's all I can ask."

"I believe the body will tell us something."

"Yes, I suppose it will."

"Like cause of death, for example."

"Cause of death? I told you the girl probably drowned."

"We shall see."

"You sound ominous."

"It's the business I'm in."

"I think you're subjecting me to a suspicion that I don't deserve." Don paused, but I could see his hands begin to tremble. "Even an inadvertent hint of such a suspicion can have a fatal effect on my career."

"Suspicion of what?"

Don backed off. He restrained further comment. "Come on, Chief. You know what I mean."

"I'd be less than honest if the possibility were dismissed."

"I suppose."

"The sea is a potent weapon. In this area, it cannot be discounted."

"Of course. I was unnecessarily indignant." Don's tone was apologetic.

"There is always a thin line here. Accident, suicide—murder."

"Yes, I understand," Don said hastily. "I guess I can only hope you believe me."

"About the accident?"

"Yes, the accident."

"Senator, I must impress upon you. It's too early for conclusions."

"I understand."

"Thank you."

Chief Bernhard stood up. He did not shake hands. Without a word, he walked out to the beach in the direction of the water's edge. We said nothing to each other. The chief stood looking out over the sea.

After a while he returned. The two patrolmen had finished their search.

"Nothing unusual," one of them said, looking over his notes.

"We'll be back, Senator," the Chief said. He left by the front door. From the window, we could see him talking to his men. One patrolman stayed behind. He took up a post in front of the door. Then the chief and the other patrolman got into the car and drove off.

The siren was silent.

XV

When they had gone, Jack Barnstable stood up and stretched his long frame.

"We've got a fox on our backs," he said.

"I hope he's a good investigator," Don said. "That's all I can ask."

I knew what he meant. We all knew.

"There is only one conclusion," I said, hoping that I could believe my own words.

"It was an accident," Don said. "It was an accident."

"It's on the ticker," Christine interrupted. "AP got it first. Just one paragraph."

"Was it carried as a bulletin?"

"Yes."

"Shit."

"It said, 'Senator Donald Benjamin James today reported the drowning of a young woman staff member during a weekend outing in Rehoboth Beach, Delaware. The staff person, whose name was not immediately known, was a twenty-two-year-old black girl. According to police officials in Rehoboth Beach, Senator James and his Administrative Assistant, Lou Castle, reported the drowning at 6:00 A.M. this morning.' "

"I don't like it," Jack said.

"I know what you mean."

"It's the word 'outing.' They could have done it without the word 'outing.' The sons of bitches."

Christine handed the paper to Don. He was slumped in a chair. He let the paper fall. Karen picked it up.

"How wonderful," Don said. He crumpled the paper and threw it on the floor. It had to hurt to see it on paper like that, so blatant. The telephone rang again. Jack and I ran into the living room. Jack reached the phone first.

"More on the ticker," he said. "You sure—they've got Marlena's name in the story? Here, give it to Christine." She took the phone from him and began to get it down into her shorthand book. When she finished, Barnstable grabbed the phone from her.

"Henry. Bring Al Simon and Joe Kessler and come on down to the house." He gave them directions.

"Step on it. Leave Steve at the motel and stand by. No. Call Washington. Put out a staff bulletin. No comment. No one is to comment. Tell the whole staff simply to clam up. Get it?"

XVI

When I got back to the screened porch, Don was still slumped in the chair, sipping a drink. He looked slightly catatonic.

"I'm beginning to worry, Lou," Karen said. It was the first remark she had addressed specifically to me since arriving. "Now, I'm getting scared."

"How the hell do you think I've been feeling?" I said.

"Do you think he can take it?"

"What do you think?"

"That's a question to a question."

"— don't know, Karen," I said.

Her jaw seemed firm, her lips pursed, as if she was gathering her forces for some sudden resolution. There is a mystique about marriage. Something does pass between two people in a marriage that is not articulated, that only a threat of extinction brings to the surface. With Karen and Don, it was down to the nitty gritty now. We both looked at him. He must have caught our expression of despair.

"I'll be okay. I'll be fine," he said, his voice shaky. "Just let me get over the shock of it." He stood up, turned white, seemed about to faint, then sat down again.

"How about lying down for a while, Don?" Karen asked.

She helped him up and took him to one of the bedrooms. He lay down heavily and closed his eyes. He was, quite literally, physically and emotionally exhausted. She covered him with the bedspread and shut the door.

"He might as well get some sleep. Things are going to get a hell of a lot worse." Then she looked at me. "I'm going to call the boys. I'll try to explain. What can I say?"

She went to the other bedroom to make the calls.

By the time Jack's staff assistants arrived, bedlam had broken out in front of the house. The press had begun to descend, and a little knot of mangy men and women stood across the street, just watching. Photographers were shooting pictures of the front of the house. One had even tried to break inside from the rear, but Jack Barnstable had thrown him out. Soon we heard sirens again, and two carloads of state police arrived. They took up posts at all sides of the house. We were besieged. The price of fame!

As if by instinct, the staff men pulled up chairs and sat around the kitchen table. Jack sat at the head of the table. I was beside him, and Christine, pad ready, sat next to me. There was Henry Davis, greying early at thirty-two, a kind of public relations theorist, intense and humorless; Al Simon, research and polling expert, twenty-nine, Ph.D., Harvard, balding; and Al Kessler, AA to Barnstable, the next link in the chain.

"All right. Here it is," Jack said. He looked over his shoulder into the other room. "Where's Karen?"

"On the phone," I answered.

"You all know what has happened. Marlena Jackson was drowned. I'm not going to bore you with the facts. There will be hundreds of interpretations and opinions. None of them will matter. We've got to construct a rebuttal—one that holds water, one that gives us a chance to recover. Frankly, I don't expect miracles. It may take years to gain the same momentum we had before yesterday. We have one job, and one job only, to prevent the political assassination of Senator Donald Benjamin James."

I assumed that it was my turn then. I outlined the strategy that Don and I had agreed on last night. I stressed the importance of being vague and the need to control, as much as was feasible, the outflow of information. They all agreed that we had picked the most persuasive options.

"All right, Lou," Jack said. "We've been brought to this point. The opening story, unfortunately, had a bad smell to it."

"I think," Davis said, "we're going to have to learn to roll with the punches, at least at this initial stage, and milk enough out of the peripheral details to work out a 'let's wait until all the facts are in before I judge' kind of reaction. Naturally, our opening statement has got to have the seeds of the entire scenario."

"Like what?" Jack asked.

"We've got to give them something to rationalize, an 'out' for the senator. One: we've got to imply that this is a monumental tragedy, not only the loss of a human being, but the potential loss of a brilliant mind. Note the emphasis on the mind. Really gush over this one. And two: express extreme confidence and bullishness over the senator's political future. Any doubts here will plant bad vibes. There will be plenty of commentators who will write us off summarily, just to overdramatize. That point is essential."

"Any comments?" Jack asked.

"I think we've got to stress a moral position," Al Kessler said. "I mean moral, not in the sense of values but in the old-fashioned sense, as opposed to the immoral. Somehow, we've got to get the point across that the senator was acting within the bounds of traditional morals—in a sexual sense."

"By all means," Davis agreed. "We've got to blunt the inference that the senator is an adulterer."

"We are hoping that there won't be any hard facts to go on," I said. They all looked at me, waiting for me to continue. I thought better of it. My silence confused them.

"Hard facts?" Al Kessler asked.

"You mean evidence," Al Simon pointed out.

"Evidence of intercourse. That would mean an examination of the body," Davis said.

"I think we should assume at this stage that such an examination won't take place," I said. "If there is an autopsy, we've got to change the strategy."

"That means there won't be any hard facts—hard facts of adultery," Davis said.

"Unless there's admission," Simon said.

"Admission?"

"On the part of the senator."

"That would be political suicide," Jack Barnstable said. The thought agitated him. "That would be the end. We couldn't recover from that one."

"You're undoubtedly right," Davis said, "but for reasons that are far more complex, in my opinion, than the simple fact of adultery. It is adultery with a black girl. Then there is death connected with it. Drowning—a death by violence. Then consider the other aspect, the lag of time in reporting the incident. That implies two things rather vividly. One: panic. Two? Foul play. We're talking here of the presidency, a presidential election. There is an instability of character that reflects itself in these two points; at all costs, we've got to checkmate that kind of thinking."

"That's laying it on the line," Barnstable said. "You seem to be saying that the challenge is insurmountable."

"I'm saying that we've got our work cut out for us," Davis responded. "Some people, you know, might excuse adultery. Lots of people would feel genuine compassion for the senator; the capacity for forgiveness is enormous in us sentimental Americans. But will there be enough to forgive? How many votes will we lose from those who will not forgive? And how many votes will we lose from people who do forgive? And how many are there in this country who won't forgive the fact that the girl was black? Then there will be those who have lingering suspicions of murder. Yes—murder. We grow up on a diet of murder and conspiracy. There are still voices that won't be stilled on the matter of the Kennedy brothers. Besides, doubt sells. People write books about doubts, and other people buy them and believe the books. Above all, we can't look or smell conspiratorial. And then, suppose we cross all those hurdles and get the kind of ratios we need; what about those who will simply lose confidence in the ability of the senator to act in a stress situation, one that requires quick, decisive action. You see the problem?"

"We've seen the problem from the beginning," I said. "We chose to wait until we had come up with a plan. We deliberated. Deliberation takes time. We didn't shoot from the hip."

"Calculating," Henry Davis said. "Substitute calculation for deliberation. That makes it something sinister."

"What the hell are you getting at, Davis?" Jack said. "Somewhere along the line, we've got to grasp the threads of optimism. I appreciate your being the devil's advocate, but we have committed ourselves to saving the senator's career. We wouldn't be spending this much time on the problem if we had meant to surrender."

"I am completely aware of the problem. That's why I have been the devil's advocate. I've just put into words what we are all feeling. We're not fools, any of us. Neither is the senator. Least of all the senator. Our one hope, as you must already have doped out, as your initial strategy suggests, is to befuddle the public with vagaries, platitudes and bullishness. I'm with you one hundred percent. But, let's not kid ourselves. Let's not pretend among ourselves that the senator didn't have an affair with Marlena Jackson; nor can we deny that he waited until he had worked out a plan before he acted."

"He's still the same person he was before all this happened," I said. "He's got to have collected some brownie points with the American people."

I was conscious of saying something not quite in the league of the men around the table. These were the pros. Who was I kidding? The American people? That was a phrase that one didn't use in this company; that was only for the consumer. Who the hell were the American people? They were the one hundred twenty million who voted, the mixed bag of conflicting demography that lay out there like the animals of Noah's Ark, all greedy for their own particular brand of nourishment. The cows ate grass. The pigs ate corn. The monkeys ate bananas. The giraffes ate leaves. Relate it to ethnic groups, young and old, black and white and yellow, union workers, farmers—menageries.

"Okay," Barnstable said. "Let's convert all this talk to practicalities, to a course of action."

While we were talking, Kessler and Christine were busily taking notes.

"The way I see it," Davis said, "we've got to write a statement, the initial statement—short and sweet, along the lines originally suggested. I'll write that. But that will only be the initial counterattack. It's got to appear in time for tomorrow morning's papers and the six o'clock news. For TV, we've got to have another dimension. The cameras will be coming down here as fast as they can."

He looked out the window.

"They're not here yet. That's because we're a little removed from the big markets. Probably, the Washington guys will get here shortly. We have got to give them some footage of the senator and Mrs. James. That's essential. Hopefully, the body will be found either before the cameras arrive or after the deadline for the six o'clock. The juxtaposition of the body and the senator and his wife would be unfortunate. The footage has got to imply that there was no adultery, that senator and Mrs. James are as one, true to each other beyond a shadow of a reasonable doubt. That's a tough order but it will help."

"That makes a lot of sense, Davis," Barnstable said. "Christine, get that down."

"Do we all agree?"

None of us was certain that this was necessarily the right course of action, but Henry Davis was persuasive and logical.

I tried to put myself in the role of the viewer on the Monday night news. I had just gotten home from work. I was tired. The mortgage was bugging me. My wife was bugging me. The kids were costing me a fortune. Then, looming up at me, momentarily, was the juicy story of America's shining knight, Senator Donald James. What would my reaction be? Well, the son-of-a-bitch finally got caught. How does he pull out of that one? You poor bastard. You poor bastard. You poor, dumb bastard. But I would have some doubts, seeing that pretty wife of his with him, standing by him. Maybe . . . "Naturally," Davis continued. "That wouldn't be the whole story. There'd be sidebars. Interviews with the police chief, possibly with the girl's father, with her friends. Hell, if they catch the father at the moment of his fresh pain, that will make one hell of a visual. And it won't be very good for our team. A good TV editor and the networks are masters of this; they will be able to practically pin a murder rap on the senator. Tht's why I say that our first counterattack can only be the statement and the husband and wife footage. We've got to let the story blast off fast, all the flack out of the way as quickly as possible. Leave 'em with the image of family solidarity and condolences for a member of the staff. That's providing we can maintain control. We have only two factors to worry about; statement and footage. The senator simply says nothing. He looks serious, but not remorseful. With the right breaks, we would muddle through, depending on what else is presently traumatizing the American people."

"Then what?" Barnstable asked. "What happens tomorrow?"

"Tomorrow, hopefully, we make contact with the father. This relationship is crucial. We have got to make contact with the father. He has got to be persuaded that the senator is genuinely bereaved. That is essential. If this doesn't work, we've got problems. The visuals of the relationship have got to be genuine. The senator must establish his humanity and concern for the feelings of the father. People will understand that. And, of course, Mrs. James has got to be present while the cameras work. If we're clever enough, we can get the father in the middle of a group shot, perhaps at graveside. It must remove the cloud of guilt. It must clean up the story as much as possible."

"Suppose the father doesn't cooperate?" Al Simon asked.

"He has got to cooperate."

"There's many a slip between the cup and the lip," Jack Barnstable said.

"This is not an exact science," Davis said.

"But please understand we are dealing with media only, the extension of the mind. We create only what we wish to create. The media will help us expand the dimension of our actions. I'm not saying that this course of action is foolproof. In any event, the impact of the follow-up is also essential."

He paused and looked about the table. He appeared neither confident nor arrogant, always coldly logical, speaking in terms that we all could understand, hammering out a course of action that seemed to lead us through a minefield.

"The follow-up is equally important. By the third day, the story will have begun to run its course. It will have dropped from the number one story of the day to two or three, depending on what is happening in the world. Hope for a declaration of war, an assassination, something cataclysmic. But don't bank on it. Now we've got to get a syndicated columnist to write a sympathetic review that will appear to be inside dope. You know, throw open the human side, explain anguish—a kind of philosophical look into the senator's psyche."

"What columnist?" Al Simon asked.

"Someone with a good sense of justice. Not a liberal. I'd pick a conservative on this one. Someone with a noblesse oblige point of view. Liberals tend to be rather snotty and holier than thou. You know, they don't think their shit stinks."

"You're probably right."

"The big danger, it seems to me, will come from left field."

"Left field?"

"Some obscure, investigative type of reporter determined at all costs to search out the truth. He's probably just a few years out of college and just burning to sock it to the system. The big reporters will never get off their fat asses. They'll spout philosophy and write about the whole affair with broad abstractions. But keep a sharp

lookout for that scrupulous, thick-lensed, eager-beaver who'll sneak
up on you and get the whole chain going."
   I watched Davis's eyes when he talked. They were ice blue under
wire frame glasses, giving him a look of uncommon intensity, like
some overzealous one-track idealogue, a fundamentalist preacher
exhorting the gullible in some dimly-lit tent in Kansas.
   "I suppose we can also expect a flood of magazine copy," I said.
   "Exactly," Davis agreed. "That's why those stills taken during the
next day or so are so important. A bad picture in a magazine could
damage us. There's something about the magazine environment that
has a lot more integrity than a newspaper."
   "Okay," Jack Barnstable said. "Suppose we follow the script and
get all the breaks, how can we expect to come out?"
   "I think that's a fair question. Unfortunately, I can't give you a fair
answer. I don't really know. I'm not clairvoyant."
   "Well, then speculate," I said.
   He was such a smart-ass that I had to hear his prognosis. We all had to.
   "Do I have to?" he asked, smiling, enjoying his expanding role.
   "I think you owe it to us."
   "Well, in the first place, I think he will slip considerably in a pres-
idential preference poll if it were taken within the next seven days."
   "How badly do you think he'll slip?" Barnstable asked.
   "Badly."
   "Permanent damage?"
   "Nothing is permanent in our business. We're in the manufactur-
ing business. If our product loses some demand potential, we'll give
it a new wrapper. Add some exotic ingredient."
   "Like beefed-up toothpaste."
   "I would hate to put it on that level," Davis said. "That makes us
so damned—crass. But, in terms of television, I'm afraid it's true.
Television, as the kids say, is where it's at."
   "I guess it's an unfair question," Barnstable said. "We'll just have
to see how our strategy unfolds, but we can, at least, use the tradi-

tional measuring devices." He turned to Al Simon. "Today's Monday. In one week I'd like a poll taken, on a national level, with a state breakout. I want to know how the senator stands in peoples' minds. Not a presidential preference poll, although I have a feeling Harris and Gallup will do it. I'm looking for some fix on his lowest ebb. I figure that time will bring him up again. And our people, particularly our money people, have got to see recovery—tangible recovery. We'll do it maybe three weeks from now, then three months."

"We'll need some strategy to hold them in line during that period," Kessler pointed out. "In any event, our financial situation is thrown all out of whack. I'll have to check all the accounts and start really watching the buck. I have a feeling that our contributions will dry up for the next few months. We may even have to cut payroll, although to do so would indicate that we were hurting. You've got to look like a winner if you want backing, and Max Schwartz must be persuaded to stick with us."

"And, Davis," Barnstable said. "I really would like a running analysis from you on the efforts of our media strategy, in addition to the poll material. Put two or three of your brightest guys on it and come up with, say, a daily verbal report for the next two weeks. Nothing elaborate. Just the parameters. But nothing, absolutely nothing, in writing."

"Should be no trouble," Davis said.

"Another important point is security," Barnstable said. "Let's not stretch this operation beyond what is manageable security-wise. A leak from any of us, no matter how inadvertent, could be damaging. So, please." He paused. "Do I have to say more?"

The meeting broke up. Henry Davis found the typewriter, rolled up his sleeves, and began pecking away at the statement. Outside, the crowd seemed to be gathering in numbers. Curiosity about other people's misfortunes is a powerful force.

There was something eerie about everything that was happening. Besides, it was happening so damned fast that it was hard to get a fix on it, hard to get your bearings. But the thing that was really annoying me was that the whole episode was losing its human dimension—at least, to me. We talked. We analyzed. We came up with strategies. But everything seemed so remote from—let's call it humanness. It seemed so unmanageable. Maybe I was just pissed-off because we weren't in control. We had been in control for so long, and suddenly we were floating on tides over which only the cosmic force had control. Cosmic force—Christ, is that me talking?

XVII

From somewhere far away, through heavy layers of unconscious fog, Ernie Rowell could hear the flat, even voice emerge talking about the weather being partly cloudy; and then his eyes blinked open into the darkness. He seemed to emerge from one of those deep blackout sleeps, because it took him a long moment to find his bearings, replete with the beginnings of panic, lapping at the edges of his mind.

The warm, silken flesh of Ellen's body restored his confidence. He was at Ellen's. It was five-thirty in the morning, still black as pitch, and he had to get his ass out of this safe cocoon and into the cavernous city room at the *Washington Chronicle*.

"This is cruel and inhuman treatment," he hissed, pressing close to Ellen, cupping her right breast, then teasing the nipple. The nipple hardened. Ellen stirred.

"Something to remember me by," he whispered, then cleared his naked body of the covers, hoping the chill would encourage his awakening.

"Off to fight the windmills," he cried, bounding out of bed.

He dressed in the half-light, poking around on his hands and knees for his undershorts and socks, misplaced in the heat of urges that had washed over them last night. It was good, he remembered, and then sadly recalled that it could have been a great Sunday—a languid morning of sex, coffee, croissants, the *New York Times* and the *Chronicle*, then later bicycling across Memorial Bridge along the Potomac. He found his clothes and dressed.

Peering back at him through the mirror, he saw himself—a roundish face, the beginning of a whiskey bloat, hair curly and falling in sloppy ringlets over the ears, eyes myopic in their gold-rimmed lenses. As always, he was missing his collar stays, and his shirt had the look of long, hard use emphasized by the badly knotted tie, slightly stained. Ellen, in their six months together, had tried to unslop him, but he unfailingly fell apart by the end of his day, which always finished when the bureaucracy's began. When everyone was fresh, he was stale.

He bent over the sleeping figure and blew in her ear. She stirred, lifted a bare arm from under the covers, and stroked his head.

"Be back by three," he said, kissing her earlobe.

"You'll know where to find me."

"Don't bother to dress."

"Ummm." Her hand dropped and she sailed off to sleep again.

From her apartment on New Hampshire Avenue, he began the four block walk to the *Chronicle*. The streets were empty and the lights still on as he quickly walked east, conscious always of the fear that, despite his protestations to himself, danger lurked in these streets. Such exaggerated fear will destroy our cities, his head would say, but somewhere at the base of his spine he was still afraid.

But he did enjoy walking down deserted streets. Even when he lived in New York, walking at odd hours from his apartment at First and Sixtieth to the *New York News*, there was the same feeling of delicious aloneness and, at the same time, omnipotence, as if the city and all that was in it belonged to him, was his to do with what he wished.

And if he really could do what he wished, he would erase the filth and decay, inanimate and human, and make the world one big festival of life, perhaps complete with rock bands and pot and good vibes and love—like Woodstock, where he had been, and which was the high point the absolute high point, of his twenty-six years. His mind stubbornly refused to inhibit the intensity of the memory. It was like an instant playback, complete with smells, sights, feelings, all that mass of humanness, his heart racing in tandem with the sweet electric joy of the scene, an ocean of throbbing life.

Even now, years later, the memory recharged him, with its assurance, and most of all, its hope. We must never again be bullshitted. We are the generation that will unite the world. God, was he proud of his generation. We taught the bastards a little religion. We rammed it to them because of their stinking war. We made them see how pollution was strangling the country—not just smoke or sewage or physical waste, but the other pollution, the pollution of lies, deception, and bullshit. Of course, the bastards had not yet learned their lesson, but the denouement was coming, because he and all that generation were moving in on them, eating, like termites, into the very foundations of the system, like a vast underground army. And he was one termite burrowing into the media. He knew who his comrades were and they knew him. They spoke in signals—symbols—and collected acts of faith like stamps or coins.

Six months at the *Chronicle* had shaken, but not yet wholly obliterated, his faith that the movement's center was holding. But his faith, like Job's, had been sorely tried. He saw venality and deception on a grand scale in the panorama of events that cascaded over the lens of his vision with ever-increasing velocity. And yet through the gushing, trembling white water, he could see, still see, some pure blue sky. Toilers in the movement were still to be found, standing like missed targets in a shooting gallery. They were in the back row to be sure, but there they were, writing speeches, influencing political policy, criticizing, putting the liars down, burrowing in.

Was he measuring up? The question gnawed at him, a constant irritation. There was always that conscience reading terror that he was walking the thin line between copping out and making out. He had come a long way from Williamsport, P.A. where the old ethic had sunk its roots from the courthouse in the square to the very center of the earth's guts, where it had found some magnetic mother lode. For no matter how far he and all the sons and daughters of Williamsport, P.A., had strayed from that place in the square, they could always feel the pulling power of that magnetic force. And it made them feel guilty, because they had left the town to the termites. But even through the guilt, they secretly longed for it, knowing, at the same time, that it was gone.

No matter what events had intervened, the good old American fantasy of returning to the faded main street of Williamsport, P.A. on a great white charger, preceded by the high school band and the good old boys of the American Legion, with all the good citizens of town lining both sides of the street and his mom and dad up there on the reviewing stand along with the mayor and Aunt Charlotte and Uncle Jim and the rest of them, still had the power to crowd out all the new dreams. When he was weakest—like the time his first by-line popped up on the *Chronicle*—he felt, he truly felt, that he would do almost anything to get more and more recognition, and hang the movement, for that one glorious moment on the White Charger down Main Street in Williamsport, P.A.

Even his knowing that the fantasy was a mendacious myth could not cool its ardor. It was like some lustful temptation that would never, could never, be consummated. And if what was happening, was really happening, then Main Street, and all the Main Streets of America would be, or had become, little more than a stagnant, open sewer with all the dead dreams of the national pride scumming the top.

He truly believed that it was his generation above all, who had first seen the stagnation take hold; had seen it in the obscenity of the men who ruled their lives, bullshitting them with their artful little tricks, pandering to the prejudices that had been put inside them by their fathers.

Tell us the truth, by God, his generation had shouted. He could still hear the sound of it through the din of the shooting gallery. And hearing it so clearly made him sure again that he was still among the standing targets. He prayed that he had the strength to remain standing, for he could now see the casualties of his sweet generation flopped over beside him, falling daily. Someone, he was sure, would emerge to lead them, to galvanize them into a force that would strike back, a spearhead right into the barrels of their guns.

Those we lose, we lose. Fuck 'em! Natural genetic selection. He hoped he would find the strength to stay angry. Sometimes he had to dig far, far back to find that pure anger again—maybe even as far as the funeral of Hank Petrucci, who came back from Vietnam in a telegram. They all went to the service at the Catholic church, which smelled of wet stones. The sound of Mrs. Petrucci's wailing drowning out the priest's intonations seemed to heighten the frustration and futility of the service, since there was no flag-draped coffin at the time and a piece of the grief was handed around to each of them like communion wafers. It was not the memory of old Hank, pumping gas, fixing cars, greasing up his crew cut, strutting around town in his leather jacket with all those shiny buttons, dumb and cocky but alive, that sustained the anger. Only later, after the service had locked itself in the memory bank, when people talked about it and wrote about it in the papers and put flags at half mast and added another gold star to the memorial plaque in the town square that it began to sink in that none of them really knew why Hank Petrucci had hung up his oil streaked jeans and had his ass blown to bits.

Mr. Petrucci's gas station had become a shrine to Hank with a gold star hanging in the office window and pictures of Hank in uniform and other memorabilia on the dirty walls—a track medal from Junior High, a copy of the telegram of death, even a picture of himself and Hank when they were kids, before divergent aspirations intervened. He even understood when Mr. Petrucci treated him like crap when he came by the station during a Penn State recess with his long hair and wire-rimmed glasses, "Hank would've kicked you dumb hippies right ina labonz," he had mumbled.

"Hey, Mr. Petrucci, it's me, Ernie."

"Hey Ern, whyn't you cutcha hair. Don't be like dem bums. Goddam commie shits."

It was being a pariah in those early days that pushed them in among their own kind, the kids about his age, to whom Vietnam was a sword of Damocles and, above all, definitely not worth dying for. What the fear of this foreign death had done was to open their eyes and shake them loose and make them promise themselves that the big boys would never again move them around like chess pieces. "Don't trust the bastards" became the slogan.

Sometimes, he had all he could do to hear it again through the earsplitting roar of later considerations—earning a living, thinking of the future, knowing that the thirties were coming up fast and seeing his contemporaries flop over into the stagnant pool of the middle class with its view of America as a clipped front lawn and two squirts of an aerosol deodorant.

In the city room, the night city editor clacked away at his typewriter, doing the assignment sheet for later in the morning when the bulk of the staff would arrive. Ernie Rowell went to his desk at the far end of the room, lit a cigarette, and uncovered the hot, black coffee that he had bought at the vending machine near the elevators. He picked up the phone and dialed the night city editor.

"What's on?"

"I got some routine rewrite jobs. Get off your ass and walk over here."

He put the phone down and laughed. That Brady was one mean son-of-a-bitch, a relic of the old school although he was not yet fifty. But he was taught the old ways by the Hecht and MacArthur types and looked on the crowd of newly arrived long-haired men and women with their funny glasses as putrid dung.

"Snotty, wet-behind-the-ear crud," he would say, tempting them to bite at the bait. As Ernie walked over to him, container in hand, cigarette dangling from his lips, he could hear the hoarse bell of the wire service bulletin.

"Rip that," Brady yelled at a copy boy who was busy slitting through a mountain of handouts. The boy, eager to please, rushed to the wire room, tore off the copy, and brought it to the city desk, reading it as he came.

"Shit," he said. "Senator James got a problem."

Brady read the copy and whistled. He handed it to Ernie Rowell.

"How do you read that, hot shot?" he asked.

"I read it as a good story," Ernie said, his stomach tightening. People from the movement were banking on James. Christ! He could be their man.

"So the cocksucker finally got caught," Brady said, his eyes glistening, enjoying the moment. He sat back and put his hands behind his head. Here was one focus of his bitterness, Ernie thought. Scratch Brady and you'd find a bigot, a hater. The whole world was too dumb for a heavy failure like Brady. Perhaps that was why he never made it at the *Chronicle*. After all, Chuck Chalmers, the executive editor, was James's friend and politically the *Chronicle* and James were right in line.

"I think you're jumping to conclusions," Ernie said.

"Outing—see the word outing?" Brady said. "What do you think that means?"

"I still say it's not conclusive." You cynical bastard, Ernie thought. Brady smiled and dialed the phone.

"Chuckie baby will have to call the shots on this one."

Brady played it straight with Chalmers. He read him the copy, then looked up at Ernie Rowell.

"Ernie Rowell's here. He could get up there in two and a half, maybe three hours by car. I'm sure we could pick up wire photos. Okay, we'll send our own photographer. Here, Rowell, talk to Mr. Chalmers."

It had all happened so fast. Ernie felt his voice waver.

"I want you to call me personally just as soon as you get the lay of the land. We'll probably put a few reporters on it once we see how the story is rolling. I know you can handle it, Ernie," said Chalmers.

"I'm sure I can."

"But keep in close touch with me."

"Yes, sir."

"One question."

"Shoot."

"How do you personally feel about the senator?"

"Very good vibes."

"Good." There was a pause. "Boy, that son-of-a-bitch at the White House will enjoy this one with his morning Sanka," Chalmers said. Then he hung up.

"Okay, Rowell, start rolling."

"I'm off," He started to leave.

"And don't get your cock caught in your zipper."

It wasn't until he picked up his car and was heading out toward the Beltway that he began to think of that parting remark of Brady's. He wants me to discover the worst, he thought. Some people are happiest when helping to increase other people's misfortune. But then again, Brady was a professional, and the business had made him a cynic. Or was it simply that Brady hated the paper, hated his failure, hated himself, like all the pigs in this country, all the rest of the unfeeling bastards that run the system?

He checked himself. It wasn't professional. His job was to write the truth and let the chips fall where they may. No matter how it hurt. And so what if the Senator was shacking up with a broad over the weekend. What's wrong with that? Hell, he understood. It took the pressure off. It was healthy. He thought of Ellen, her lush naked body tucked away between the sheets. The movement would understand.

But would the others? There's the rub, he thought. Middle class morality. No, the country wasn't quite ready to have a cocksman at its helm. He enjoyed the pun. Not that we didn't have one before. He shook off the thought. It was corroding his objectivity. He was first and foremost a journalist, a reporter for America's most powerful newspaper. He must take this responsibility seriously. Besides, for a young reporter, this was the opportunity one fantasized about. He flicked on his radio to WAYE and let the rock music soothe him.

"I'm gonna be as objective as hell," he said aloud, pressing hard on the accelerator, "no matter how much it hurts."

XVIII

Don slept for two hours. By the time he had put himself together, the crowd in front of the beach house was enormous. The television boys had arrived. I counted six crews, not to mention the nest of still photographers and a growing cluster of seedy looking reporter types. The area around them was littered with coffee containers and sandwich wrappers, the inevitable trademark of the traveling press. Thankfully, there weren't any vendors of souvenirs. Ordinarily, the crowd of news hawks would have been a welcome sight, but in the cold greyness of this particular morning, they were depressing.

We filled Don in on the results of our meeting. He listened thoughtfully. The brief sleep seemed to have refreshed him. He even managed a thin smile. He had good recovery powers. They say it's all in the genes, and Don must have had good genes. Karen went to work in the kitchen to scrounge up some sandwiches. Barnstable kept the telephone busy, and Christine was at his side taking notes.

There were two details which dominated our minds. One was in the hands of fate; the other had a more human controllability. There was, first, the question of the body. Apparently, it hadn't arrived on the morning tide as expected; at least that was the information we managed to squeeze out of the state trooper lieutenant, who nervously came in and out of the house, probably out of curiosity. Every time he came out, the press would hammer at him, as if by the act of coming inside, he had received some magic piece of earth-shattering communication. The second thing that concerned us deeply was our attempt to get in touch with Marlena's father. Apparently, he had been told of the tragedy, had been given time off from his mail rounds, and had disappeared. He was probably on his way to Rehoboth, a distance of about three hours by car from Philadelphia.

Barnstable had put some of our staff people on the job of tracking him, but it was like looking for a needle in the haystack. Naturally, we wanted to intercept him before anyone else did.

There was surprisingly little communication between our besieged command post and the outside world. Our one link, the single telephone, was in constant use. Don sat slumped in a rattan easy chair, his legs crossed, lost in thought. He was never a man to sit silently for any length of time. We had to make some move shortly. It was simply unthinkable to go through another day and night stuck out here, literally trapped in space and time.

Davis finished the statement and brought it in for us to read. I was surprised at its brevity.

"The loss by drowning of one of our most dedicated staff members comes as a profound shock to me. Marlena Jackson was a woman of towering intelligence, perception, wit and charm. Her contribution to our cause will be sorely missed.

"Her people will, however, suffer the severest loss by her untimely death, for she was destined for leadership, marked for great things in the timeless battle to undo injustice and right wrongs. We do not question the motives of Divine Providence in taking her so soon. We can only mourn her loss and hope that there will be others to take her place.

"On behalf of myself and her fellow staff members, I extend to the bereaved family our heartfelt condolences."

"Don't you think that 'Divine Providence' stuff is a little too purple?" Barnstable asked. "What do you think, Don?"

He looked the statement over thoughtfully.

"Divine Providence," he repeated. "You know, that may be just the right touch. Divine Providence. It may be true, you know."

"I thought it would be bigger," Davis said, "than simply 'God.' 'Divine Providence' takes in the whole psychic universe, so to speak. The words convey an image of tremendous spirituality."

"I think it's corn," Barnstable said. "Pure corn."

"What's wrong with corn?" Davis said.

"No, Jack," Don said. "I rather like the connotation. I also like the wit and charm touch. She had that. She had those qualities and more. You know, seeing this in print is so damned incongruous. And yet, I think I can sincerely say these things. I believe them to be true. Marlena was a most unusual personality."

"Well, I'll buy the 'Divine Providence' bit," Barnstable said. "But this 'contribution to our cause' material leaves something to be desired. Cause? What cause?"

"The implication is the cause of the good as opposed to the bad," Davis argued.

"How about the cause of the presidency?"

"I see what you mean, 'cause' is weak here."

"I think you're right, Jack," Don said. "There is a political implication here that detracts from the integrity of the statement."

"You mean we have no cause?" Davis said. But he was overstepping. Like all stubborn minds, criticism was tough for him to take. Sarcasm was a good defense, but it was only halfhearted and he beat a quick retreat. We, of course, had created our so-called "cause," definable as a better world, more things for people, no disease, no poverty, no pain. That was "our cause." Only, all of us knew better. The "cause" was getting the presidency. That was the long and short of it.

"Let's dump 'cause,' Davis," Barnstable said. "You really don't need the phrase 'to our cause.' Her contribution will be sorely missed." He crossed out the words.

"Do you think we should say 'black people'?" Barnstable asked.

"Here I'll stand my ground," Davis said. "Black is a polarizing word. Why use it? Everybody understands a sense of peoplehood, even the worst bigot. If we say black, I think we'd sound like we're pandering."

"Okay, I'll buy that," Jack said. "Now let's read it over again."

Don read the statement again, over Davis's shoulder.

"You don't think we should say anything like 'accident'? 'Drowning' seems so cold, somehow."

"You mean like 'accidental death'?" I said.

"Yes," Don agreed. "I think 'drowning' leaves something indefinite about the how of it. I'm really concerned about that. So was Chief Bernhard. It's too inconclusive. How did she drown? You know, there are going to be lots of people who will believe in their hearts that I caused her to drown. Let's not have any illusions here. No, I insist upon 'accidental death.' We don't have to mention drowning. Put in 'accidental death.'"

Davis made the change.

"Now how do we get it out mechanically?" Davis asked.

"Christine will type a number of copies, and I'll phone it in to the office for massive distribution," Barnstable said. He looked at his watch and then out the window. "Here come the TV boys. I can't imagine what they'll be expecting."

"I hope there's no sign of a body until later," I said.

"Frankly," Davis said, "I hope they don't find it until after the deadlines. As a matter of fact, I don't care if they never find it."

"I don't agree, Jack," Don said. "There's got to be some finality to this thing. We've got to get this thing behind us."

"We sure do," I said.

We were all silent for a moment. Barnstable broke the silence.

"There's one other thing that bothers me about that statement."

Davis looked up.

"Towering intelligence," Barnstable said. "The word 'towering.' It's too much of a build-up, too big a word."

"She was very, very bright," Don said.

"But towering?"

"People expect superlatives in eulogies," Davis said. "It's part of the ritual."

"Maybe 'towering' is too heavy," Don said.

Davis, obviously piqued, struck 'towering' and handed the statement to Christine.

"Let 'er rip," he said. She called it in to the senate office for reproduction and began to beat out a quick tattoo on the typewriter. The statement was a good one. It left just the right gaps to be filled in by the information consumer out there in the ether.

XIX

There was a sudden burst of activity outside of the house. We heard the last gasp of a siren. Chief Bernhard pushed himself through the crowd of television cameramen and reporters and worked his way to the door. Flashbulbs popped. The television men were shouting for people to get out of the way. Chief Bernhard's face as it approached was a mask of stone, lined and immobile. I opened the door for him to pass, and then quickly shut it. He walked into the living room and made straight for Don. He looked around at the little crowd that had gathered in the living room. We all searched his face for some sign. He simply could not be read. He moved to where Don was sitting, faced him squarely, legs spread slightly, firmly planted.

"We found her," he said flatly.

Don swallowed hard. I could see him fighting for control again. Another hurdle to be jumped.

"She came up where we had expected, only a little late. Brought her to the hospital. The doctor at the hospital made the preliminary report. Death by drowning." He hesitated and took a little book out of his inside jacket pocket.

"She's lying in a ground floor room of the Rehoboth General Hospital, ready to be claimed by the next of kin. A black female, early twenties, she was dressed in white panties and sweatshirt. No marks on the body indicating a struggle, except against the sea. Classic drowning, the doctor said." He paused.

"That it?" I said.

"I don't know," Chief Bernhard said.

"What does that mean?" I asked.

Chief Bernhard looked at me, his watery blue eyes encased, alert and cryptic, in their wrinkled pouches.

"Well, I've got to make a report," he said. "We have to satisfy ourselves and the district attorney that there are no grounds for prosecution."

"Prosecution?" Barnstable shouted, standing up.

"Take it easy, Jack," Don said. He turned to the chief. "I really would like some better explanation."

"Well, when a woman is drowned in mysterious circumstances, you simply would have to have some kind of an investigation. Let's face it, Senator, girls don't just go swimming in their underwear this time of year with the temperature of the water at forty degrees. The circumstances are unusual."

"Don't you buy our explanation?" I asked.

"Would you buy it if you were me?"

I was annoyed at my own hesitation.

"Yes," I said, conscious of my own foolishness. "Considering the source. Yes, I would buy it."

"We can't look at it quite from that angle," he said. He had bested me and he knew it. "Without casting aspersions, there is a certain equality under the law, at least in this jurisdiction. Even the victims have rights." He was needlessly sarcastic.

He was a challenge, this Chief Bernhard. Davis was right. Each new situation required a new set of options. Here was a golden opportunity for an obscure police chief to make himself a national figure. I looked at his lined and sphinxlike face. As usual, it told me nothing. Who knows what dreams such a man might harbor. A giant killer. Here was that once-in-a-millenium opportunity to be a giant killer. Was it time to bring in a lawyer?

"I need," Chief Bernhard said, "an explanation of how or why she got into that water. That's the problem."

"We gave you one," I said.

"Yes, you did."

"And you don't believe us?"

"I wouldn't say that," Chief Bernhard said. "You know, I'm just a country cop—" There it was, the eternal hatred of the rural for the urban, the simple for the complicated, the bumpkin for the slicker. It lay there exposed now, revealed, the perennial little man who suddenly finds himself holding the tiger's tail. He was our most dangerous threat. None of us could have failed to see it.

"—Lots of things don't make sense to me. I don't consider myself any smarter than the next guy. And I'm well into my fifties; so I've lived a while. But it simply is not plausible for a girl to have gotten herself drowned under the alleged circumstances. She was tall and athletic. She had strength—"

"Well, then, Chief," Don said suddenly, his voice strong. "What is your implication?"

"She wasn't in full control."

"What does that mean? Just stop talking in riddles," Don's short fuse was functioning again, a good sign.

"I'm not talking in riddles, Senator. She could have been under an outside influence—drink, drugs, despair. Or—she could have been helped."

"Jesus Christ," Don said. "You're implying that I murdered the girl."

"Look, I'm a cop, gentlemen. I'm not a politician."

There it was again, the hatred of the public servant for the politician. This fellow was dangerous.

Silence, at times, seems far more eloquent than speech. It hung in the air, eloquent as hell. The four of us, Barnstable, Davis, Don and myself, were of one mind, confirmed as we traded looks, locking our eyes briefly with understanding. The one mind fixed itself on the one immediacy. What strategy do we now adopt? Where are our options now? The chief was displaying no more than understandable curiosity. It was hard to see him as a stereotype because he was so expressionless. He could be that wise old fox, Maigret, lurking there behind the marvelously wrinkled skin, soaking in what was coming through the electric air, understanding through his pores. Or that has-been, inarticulate cynic, Lou Archer—world-

ly and sad, all illusions dead or dying. But, whatever he was, he had
a curiosity that was not going to be put down. He wanted to know.
Then, suddenly, Don was speaking, and we all knew what strategy
he had opted for.

"I think you're entitled to have all doubts erased from your mind,
Chief. I'm fully prepared to be interrogated."

He looked toward Barnstable and Davis, who, understanding, got
up and left the room. I stayed. I sensed that Don wanted me to stay.

"Fire away, Chief," Don said. He straightened in his chair,
antenna up, eyes alert. He had fully recovered his faculties. He was
strong again.

Chief Bernhard kept his eyes on Don as the strength, from Lord
knows what hidden inner resource, flowed into him. There was a
barely perceptible bracing of his back, a tightening of his hands
around his notebook, a narrowing of his eyes. It was as if both men
were getting ready for an impending duel—which, indeed, was true.

"Was the Jackson girl your mistress?"

"That's an irrelevant question," Don responded quickly.

"Why?"

"Because it won't explain what you're looking for."

"What am I looking for?"

"Motive."

"That's right."

"You've got to establish motive before you can proceed logically
to the next step, the criminal act."

"Standard police procedure."

"All right, suppose she was my mistress. Mistresses, from what I
have read, can use threat of exposure as a weapon. In my case, that of
a national political figure, it would be a powerful weapon."

"Logical."

"She threatens this exposure. It is obviously a damaging, even a
possibly fatal prospect to both my family and career. I cannot abide
this. I kill her. I drag her screaming to the ocean and push her in."

"Such a possibility crossed my mind."

"Reject it."

"Why?"

"Because it is fantasy. If I did kill her, I would be exactly where I am now. In the uncomfortable eye of suspicion. This would be the least logical method of removal. Hell, the whole world will think she was my mistress, anyway. For a man in my position, drowning, especially under these circumstances, would be the least logical of my moves to eliminate her."

"It could have been a crime of passion."

"There would be evidence of that."

"Probably so. There was no sign of a struggle. Even the doctor didn't suggest the possibility."

"Aha! But there are other possibilities. Like suicide."

"This has always been prospect one. In my business, though, murder is a commonplace, typical situation."

"Not in my business."

"It does strike in the strangest places. At this point, though, I see no evidence to suggest it. We do develop a sixth sense about it. No, I think murder is a long shot."

"Thank you."

"There are other ways of dying."

"Okay, then. Let's work on the suicide. From your point of view, that is."

"You know my point of view then?"

"I am assuming that if you are viewing the suicide possibility with interest, it would have to follow that you believe she was my mistress."

"You're correct, Senator."

"She chooses to take her revenge through suicide, drowning. She is going to expose me to the world as a philanderer, an adulterer. By her death, she attempts to destroy me. Correct?"

"Correct."

"You've got to admit that her drowning has had a profound effect on my career. The whole world is as curious as you."

"I'll admit that."

"In fact, the blow is so severe that I'll be lucky if by morning I find myself a viable political commodity."

"Yes. Yes, to all of that."

"Then you've established motive? She wanted to do me in. She committed suicide. She did me in. Logical?"

"Not as logical as you think, Senator. We policemen do know a little bit about the patterns of suicide. Taking one's life for a cause is serious business. It is normally preceded by some rationale—a note, a recording, a sign of some sort. We found nothing."

"So what you have is only theory, speculation."

"That's right."

"So write off suicide. Is it back to murder then?"

"You're harping on that unduly, Senator."

"I know it. There's a mystique about this whole episode that suggests murder. Murder by manipulation. The athletics was my idea."

"Your thoughts have no legal bearing on the case, Senator."

"Well, then, how do you read it, Chief?"

"You really want to know?"

"Yes. I do. Here we are sparring around like two fighters in the preliminaries. Let's get to the main bout. If I'm under suspicion, I'd like to know. I've never quite been in a situation like this before."

Chief Bernhard suddenly grimaced as if he were in pain. It was the first tremor of expression that I had noted during their discussion.

"You know, Senator, neither have I."

It was just then, watching this inexplicable police chief, that I began to see his dilemma. He was concerned about his own role in this episode. We had, it seemed, all been looking down the wrong alley. He had his own image, his own niche in life to protect. He, too, had been weighing options. There was simply no end to the complications that presented themselves.

"This is no ordinary case, Senator," Chief Bernhard said. "It puts us all on our mettle. No, I don't really think you're guilty of anything but indiscretion. That's my gut reaction. You don't have to respond. I know the fix you're in, and believe me, I don't want to make things worse than they are. But look at it from my point of view. I could make the determination myself. That could be interpreted as a whitewash. On the other hand, I could draw out the investigation and buck it upstairs. That's the easiest way out for me—a typical bureaucratic reaction."

"Why the hell don't you vote your conscience, then?"

"Why don't you?"

"Frankly, I think you're needlessly torturing me."

"I guess I am."

The extent of Don's luck never failed to amaze me. If I believed in God, I might attribute it to—what did we say in the statement?— "Divine Providence." What had been revealed in this crackling discussion was that under his blank exterior, the chief owned a rather highly versatile intelligence. This was no stock character police chief, no one-dimensional "pig," stereotyped in our brains as unthinking, unwise, and above all, sadistic. Chief Bernhard was none of these things. The problem was that he saw through us. Now the question was, did he see through us because our strategy was so transparent, or was his intelligence so keen that he grasped the truth of it by clever and imaginative observation. It gave me a cold shudder to think that our plans were not good enough to get past a single small-town police chief. Of course, now that I had vested him with superior intelligence, I suppose the plan had regained its credibility again.

This man, Bernhard, could murder us. He could raise doubts. He could do a big job with innuendo and half truths. Hell, he could get his face on network television. How many men tucked away in a small town like this dream of miraculously being plucked out of their anonymity? Overnight, Chief Bernhard could be a national, an international figure—fleeting, yes, but there are many who must yearn for such a moment. Bernhard was no fool. He knew the extent of his power.

"I think I'm entitled to know which way you're going to jump," Don said.

"I've been thinking about this all day long, Senator. But only now, only now that I have the body and we have had our talk, has it become obvious to me what I must do. You see, I detest you politicians. As a man who deals strictly in truth and facts, I have no use for the lot of you. This whole episode is a case in point. You'll do anything, pretty nearly anything, to fudge up the facts."

"Your judgment is harsh. You don't understand. Politics is a business. It has its own vocabulary. Its own idiom. Its own way of doing things."

"I know. It makes me want to vomit."

"Well, here's your golden opportunity to have your revenge."

"You've got the wrong boy. I haven't got the stomach for all those lies, and I'm too damn old to be lying myself. There's no reason for me to continue my involvement in this case. The girl drowned. The drowning was an accident."

"That's pretty damned obvious."

"Yes, Senator, it is. But so is your attempt to block out the truth."

"Nothing is that black and white."

"Aside from despising politics, I detest your point of view. Promising all the downtrodden that you're going to make them have a better world—bullshit. You're lucky, in a way, that I feel the way I do. If I didn't detest all that you stood for I might have done it differently."

"Done what?"

"I could have brought the reporters to the beach, had them take pictures of the body. I could have asked the coroner to determine if there were evidence of intercourse. I could have asked for an autopsy to determine whether she was under the influence of anything. I

could have tipped off reporters. Believe me, Senator, I know what I
could have done. But I didn't."

"Thanks."

"You're not out of the woods, by any means."

"You make me feel dirty."

"You are dirty. You know why—because you're a damned liar and
a cheat. We both know that. The worst part is that people might
believe you. God help us all if that happens."

"I am an innocent victim of a strange set of circumstances."

"You're not an innocent anything. Just a petty liar. But just
remember. You don't own the world. You can't always do what
you want."

"Okay. I heard your speech. Now stop preaching."

He stood up; the eyes behind his mask said nothing. He looked at me.

"I'll issue my report—and I'll tell them." He pointed to the reporters.

"What will you tell them?" I said hesitantly.

"The truth."

"And as you see it, what is that?" Don asked.

"That a girl, race black, age about twenty-three or four, drowned
and was washed ashore at Buzzards Point—" He looked at his book.
"—at about 11:15 A.M. I will say that this girl meets the description
of your staff person who was reported missing at 6:00 A.M."

"And what about the big question?"

"You mean the lapse between the time you knew the girl had disappeared and the time she was reported missing."

"Yes."

"Nearly eleven hours."

"My God, you'll finish us," I said.

"The truth is the truth."

"You can't do it," I protested.

Chief Bernhard looked at me and then at Don.

"We have no choice. Everything has an Achilles' heel. That's
mine," Don said, shrugging.

"We could deny it," I said.

Don paused.

"Do what you have to do, Chief."

"I fully intend to."

"He can't—," I began.

"Shut up, Lou—will you please just shut up. We'll figure—" He checked himself.

"I'm sure you will," Chief Bernhard said.

He turned and, without bothering to say goodbye, walked out the front door. The press mobbed him. He talked to them briefly, then made his way to his car.

"Every dog has his day," Don said when he had gone.

"My God. You should be ecstatic. He took you off the hook," I said.

"Off the hook? I've swallowed the damned thing. It's like I'm on a roller coaster straight to hell. He saw me. That son-of-a-bitch saw me. He's worth a hundred of any one of us."

"Come on off it, Don. What did he see? He doesn't understand your orbit. It's a different world from where he sits."

There's nothing more discouraging than being exposed to a politician in the midst of moralizing. To a realist, fantasy is a put on. And Don was putting me on. Believe me, I understood. It was like getting laid, that brief release of pure ecstasy and then the reality of the soft cock again.

"He knew," Don said.

"I think you're damned lucky."

"Yeah, I'm lucky."

"Now you've got to see the girl's father. That's going to be a tough hurdle. He may not buy the chief's report. He may have ideas of his own."

"He might. But the ironic thing is that the chief's report is true," Don said.

"Who knows what's true?" I said.

I mean that. I'll say it again. Who knows what's true?

XX

"We need a performance now," Jack Barnstable said.

It was nearly one by the time Chief Bernhard had left. I briefed everyone on our conversation, with appropriate editing. The conclusion was satisfying to everyone.

"That's a big plus," Don said. "Depending on the way the chief handles it."

"You needn't worry," I said. "He has lots of contempt for politicians and newspapermen."

"I hope you're right," Barnstable said. "Okay, Davis, would you bring the senator up to date?"

We were all in the living room now. Karen had combed her hair and put on makeup. She looked younger, more composed. The resourcefulness of the human spirit never ceases to leave me in awe. You see a lot of it in this business. Where in hell did these people, Don and Karen, get their reservoirs of strength? Maybe that's what set them apart, this wellspring of constant replenishment.

"As we had expected, the stories in both print and the electronic press are catering to everybody's baser instincts," Davis said. "Some of the afternoon papers are writing headlines with question marks, like 'Did He or Didn't He?' TV and radio all put out special bulletins. They're now following up with fill-ins. The coverage is one of unremitting blackness from our point of view. Our statement was given to the press outside here and distributed in Washington and by wire. It's our opening gun, and should give us the edge in the morning coverage and certainly in the early evening news shows. If the chief handles the situation correctly, he should upstage us in the stories, which would be great. Our statement logically should follow the verdict of the police chief. Now comes a little of the hard part.

Senator, you and Mrs. James have got to go out there and face the cameras, and you've got to make it look good. No statements. We want silent stuff."

"What would you suggest?" Don said. "Just walk out there like a dummy and say nothing?"

"I've already arranged for everything. Take a look outside—the beach side."

We followed the direction of Davis' pointing finger. There was a large knot of people standing on one spot along the water's edge. We made out a nest of cameras and a number of ladders on which photographers perched.

"I told them," Davis said, "that I'd let them take you while you walked on the beach. I thought it would be a nice touch. And for Pete's sake, try not to smile. This is strictly for the photo boys. They were happy for the opportunity. There'll be no funny stuff. I told them I'm doing them a favor. They're here to get footage. This will placate them temporarily. I left an opening for later in the day."

"What's that mean?" Barnstable asked.

"It means that I lied to them. I promised them something that I have no intention of delivering."

His arrogance was beginning to grate on me. He was so damned cocky and had this positive way of putting everything as if he were so certain, so sure of his approach. I guess maybe in situations like this a guy like Davis shines. He gives you the impression that he has weighed all the possibilities and come up with the only answer, the only option. Even Don wasn't bucking. He understood exactly what his role would be. He and Karen would walk arm in arm on the beach along a prescribed route in the path of the cameras. They would first walk away from the cameras, then towards them, pausing to look out to sea. This would give lots of pensive sideshots. They had to look regretful. That was most important. They were playing strictly for the cameras, following Henry Davis's script; and, apparently, the cameramen had agreed to take his direction. He

explained the conditions carefully to Don and Karen, pointing to little, unobstrusive markers that he had placed along the beach indicating where to stop, how far to go.

"It's a fifteen-minute deal," Davis said. "I've paced it off exactly.
At the end of the fifteen minutes, head back to the house. The TV
boys will hold their ground—the state troopers will make sure of
that. I told them to stay out of sight. Expect the TV people to shout
questions at you. Don't answer them. Don't acknowledge them.
Have you any questions?"

"Lots," Don said. "But no answers."

"And put some TV makeup on," Davis urged. "The darker kind.
Mrs. James doesn't need it."

"Should I wear my sunglasses?" Karen asked.

"No," Davis said. "That will give you too much of a mysterious,
glamourous look. The audience we're playing to will resent that
look." She took her sunglasses, which were lying on the table beside
her and with a testy shrug, put them in her pocketbook and snapped
it shut.

At one o'clock precisely, Don and Karen emerged from the
screened porch and headed toward the water's edge. They walked
hand in hand. Even from their backs, you caught a clear picture of
what they were trying to convey. Closeness. Sadness. Poetry. The
enigma of the sea. The sanctity of marriage. From the moment they
stepped onto the beach, they became media, both the content and
the media itself. This was the extra measure that gave Don his
uniqueness, that marked him for the power role he was seeking in
the context of present-day politics. He could rise up and accept the
role and play it to the hilt with skill. He had the ability to play all
the instruments in the orchestra, and, consequently, he orchestrated.
He was admirable.

"He's been a good soldier," Barnstable said. "He hasn't let us
down yet. I hope he makes it."

"There's still a hell of a lot of mine fields ahead," I said.

We stood on the screened porch watching the performance. The cameras were grinding. Flashbulbs were popping, and, as if indifferent to all that was happening, two lone figures picked their way along the ocean's edge. The sea was rough again, just as it was yesterday. Davis obviously chose the site to pick up the roughness and roar of the sea, to buttress the story of Marlena's death. The sea had found her and claimed her. The gloom of the day. The starkness of the beach. The anger of the sea. The pensiveness of the figures walking. It would make superb footage—a great counterattack.

Kessler came in carrying a yellow lined pad filled with copious notes.

"As could be imagined," he said, "all the troops are in a state of shock. The telegrams have begun to swarm in. We've received about three thousand. Seventy percent are outraged and nasty. The other thirty percent are peptalks. It's been rough."

"And the papers?" He had asked Kessler to assign three of his best researchers to come up with position papers to determine the impact of the incident on the four major areas of the country—East, West, Midwest, South.

"They're working around the clock. We should get some feedback by tomorrow afternoon. The boys are good. They should give us the kind of input we'll need to get through the rest of the week. Oh, yes, I've contracted for the surveys."

Barnstable followed Kessler back into the house while I stood there alone watching Don and Karen continue their walk along the beach.

"Good soldiers," Henry Davis said from behind me. "I think she's fantastic!"

I turned around, looking into his intense, icy eyes, as they caught my look.

"I think the whole thing stinks," I said, expressing my contempt for him. I loathed him and our predicament.

"Yes, it does," he said, cool behind a stare that was both contemptuous and filled with envy. "All shit stinks."

It was frustrating as hell to find yourself at the mercy of someone like that. He was like a computer plugged into the mass media. "The ultimate prize," he said, smiling. "If you play in that big poker game, you've got to be prepared to bluff once in a while." I didn't appreciate his analogy. But it was more out of resentment than logic. He was right. He was right all the way down the line. Why had we let him take command if we didn't think so? And he was unquestionably assuming command.

"What's next on the agenda?" I asked.

"The father," he said. "I am genuinely worried about the father. We have no control in that situation. We lucked out with Bernhard."

Don and Karen returned from the beach in a state of irritation.

"The whole thing was silly—silly," Don said.

"How do you think I felt?" Karen said.

"With due respect, Senator," Davis said, "the important thing is how you will be perceived by the people who will view the footage, not how you both felt inside."

"It's really not necessary to go over that ground again, Davis," Don said. "I wouldn't have gone along with it if I didn't think it was right."

"Right?" Karen asked. "Right, you say?"

"Please, Karen. Cool it."

"I am cool."

Don went back into the living room and sprawled on the couch. We all followed. Barnstable hung up the phone and came into the room.

"We're really taking it from all sides. I've explained everything to Max Schwartz. He seems disappointed, but understanding. If anybody can hold the fat cats in line, he can."

"What can he say?" Karen asked.

"He'll say, 'Don't believe everything you hear.' He'll say, 'Have good faith.' He'll make an appeal to their steadfastness—I guess that's a good word."

The group of reporters and cameramen seemed to have thinned out. Some had certainly gone to drop their footage at the airport and would be back. The state troopers quietly continued to bar admittance—a fact for which we were very grateful. We all knew that the time was fast approaching when we could no longer hide from the world, although we were doing quite a good job of it at the moment.

Barnstable seemed tired now. He was showing his age. He sat down heavily in a nearby chair. Karen went back into the bedroom. Christine continued to type in the kitchen, and Kessler perched himself near the phone. Davis looked toward the water watching the last of the cameramen pack their gear and slowly straggle back from the beach, leaving in their wake the little yellow piles of Kodak boxes and the inevitable coffee containers, little white mounds of styrofoam strewn like snowballs along the beach.

XXI

The growing knot of reporters outside the beach house were loung-
ing, pointlessly it seemed, waiting for something to happen.
Information was sparse. There was no spokesman, only an inane
statement extolling the virtues of the girl who had drowned, or was
alleged to have drowned. Even that was a mystery, since there was
no body. Speculation was rampant. Ernie compared notes with the
other reporters and tried to get the time frames in perspective. This
proved illusive.

No one knew when the girl actually disappeared; they only knew
that the senator and his aide Lou Castle had reported the drowning,
or disappearance, or whatever, at around 6:00 A.M.

At about noon, a man who identified himself as Henry Davis,
an information man on the senator's staff, had come out and
talked to them.

"I'm sorry. There is no comment, absolutely no comment."

The reporters began to harrass him. He stood his ground, said
nothing for what seemed like five minutes, and then began to arrange
a picture-taking session which was to take place along the beach.

"All we want to know is what happened," Ernie shouted above the
din, his entreaty lost amidst the noise. Two policemen carved a path
for Davis to return to the house. Then the TV and still cameramen
began to pack their gear and proceed under police supervision to the
beach for what was billed as picture-taking only.

For two hours now, Ernie had played this charade. Everything, it
seemed, was deliberately vague, ambiguous. What exactly was going
on? He looked at his watch. Before long he had to call Chalmers.

At 12:15, the police chief came out, his tanned and leathered face
impassive as he was engulfed by reporters. The TV and still camera-

129

men scurried from the beach. Flashbulbs popped. The police chief
blinked and, speaking in a flat, barely audible voice, outlined what
we had waited all morning to hear—the girl's body was found. It
appeared to be that of Marlena Jackson. He gave the time sequences.

"You mean the senator waited eleven hours to report the girl missing?"

"The doctor's report fixed the time of death at about 7:00 P.M."

"That's eleven hours," a reporter shouted.

Chief Bernhard did not comment.

"Has the body been claimed?"

"Not yet."

"Has next of kin been notified?"

"Yes."

"Why did the senator wait eleven hours?"

"Where is the body now?"

Chief Bernhard cut off the questioning and pushed his way to
his car.

Ernie watched the car speed away. The reporters were confused.
Should they follow him? Should they stay here?

Ernie tried to piece the facts together. It was a maze. He stood at
the edge of the police barricade and watched the photographers take
pictures of Senator and Mrs. James on the beach.

Apparently there was no question of murder, Ernie reasoned. He
shuddered. The police chief seemed honest, very low key. But why
didn't Senator James just simply come out and tell it like it was?
Why all the hocus-pocus?

He spotted Charlie Hershey, the *Chronicle* man, in the band of
straggling photographers coming back from the beach. A twenty-
year *Chronicle* man, Charlie was strapped front, back, and side with
photographic gear.

"What do you make of it, Charlie?" Ernie asked. Hershey was a
sour man who rarely smiled. The younger reporters always
approached him tentatively.

"Snow job," he replied.

"I don't understand," Ernie said. It was always better to appear the wide-eyed innocent, for Hershey, like all old Washington hands, took his cynicism seriously.

"Games, man."

"Like what?"

Hershey seemed exasperated. Ernie knew it was a pose.

"It's a set-up. We know it. They set it up. We do it. They know the editors want pictures. They give us pictures. It's a game."

"Who wins?"

"We both win."

"You make it sound so simple."

"It is."

"Do you believe that this black chick was out here for a working weekend?"

"Jeezus."

"What's that supposed to mean."

"It means," Hershey said, "that you are a naive asshole."

"Will he get away with it?"

"Have you any doubts?"

"I don't know." Hershey flipped the used film into his pocket and began to move away toward his car. Ernie walked beside him.

"Really, Charlie, how do you read this? We're getting nothing." Ernie knew the query would have the desired result. Hershey stopped and turned to him.

"I just take their pictures."

"That's not what I asked you."

"Okay." His eyes crinkled in a half smile while his lips stayed tight. "We get paid to snap pictures. They stage it. We snap them. Frankly, I don't give a damn what happens to them. But you asked me for an opinion. The guy got caught—that's all there is to it. He's damned good at having it his way; otherwise he wouldn't have got where he is. This one's a charmer. He'll play to his strength. And he's a tough player. His objective now is to make you believe that he didn't shack up with this girl, that he didn't get scared out of his pants, that he's really a cool guy under all this strain, that he's fit to be president of the United States."

"And people are supposed to believe that?"

"That's his business."

"And our business is to tell it like it is."

"Have fun, kid." Hershey turned and got into his car. He shook his head, gave Ernie one last look, and gunned the motor.

Ernie watched the car pick up speed and pass out of sight. He got into his own car and began to search for a telephone. He had to drive halfway down the beach to find one. Then he discovered he didn't have any dimes. He drove a few more blocks and found an open grocery store. The James story was, of course, the main topic of conversation is this semideserted resort town.

"Some goings on," a woman behind the grocery counter said.

"I need some change."

"If you ask me, that woman was here for immoral purposes. That Senator James with all his nigger-loving ideas, no wonder this happened. It always does." The woman pushed some dimes across the counter.

"Thank you."

Ernie reviewed his notes before entering the phone booth at the edge of the beach. He was put through immediately to Chalmers. He told him all he had been able to find out.

"The key points are these. Was the girl a weekend shack-up or perhaps an ardent love affair? And why did he wait 11 hours to report her death?" Ernie said.

"What's the speculation?"

"That the senator slept with her. His wife didn't come out until later. It was a foursome—the senator, the Jackson girl, his administrative aid, Lou Castle, and his secretary, Christine Donato."

"What's their story?"

"Apparently they've issued a statement about a working weekend."

"Do you believe it?"

"Are you serious?" Ernie was confused.

"Of course, I'm serious."

"Why go to Rehoboth for a working weekend?"

"Why not?"

"Why not take along the wife?"

"Is there proof?"

"Proof?"

"You heard me. I'm an old police reporter. Is there proof of intercourse? Has there been an autopsy?"

"Not so far."

"Then there is no proof."

"No, there is no proof."

"Now to the next point. What's the story about the eleven-hour lag?"

"No explanation."

"What do you think?"

"I think that there was panic, then calculation. I think the man was scared."

"Hey, Ernie. Are you out to get this guy?"

Ernie took the receiver out of his ear and looked quizzically at the ear piece. Was he hearing things?

"You asked about speculation."

"I just want to be sure, that's all," Chalmers said. "I don't want to jump to conclusions."

"It's just that everyone is acting strangely."

"I can see that." There was a long pause then, as if he were talking to himself. Chalmers said, "I've tried to get through to him, but the damned line is busy. Can you get him a note or something? Tell him to call me."

"And the story?"

"I'll put you on rewrite. We'll write it from here."

"Shall I stick with it?"

"Of course, but keep me informed. And try to get him to call me."

When Ernie finished giving the facts of the case to rewrite, he closed the door of the telephone booth and walked to the edge of the sea wall. Sitting down on one of the railroad ties that formed the barrier, he let his feet dangle above the beach. The horizon, although clear now, was devoid of movement. In the distance a lone ship, a single dot, trailed a faint plume of smoke.

The conversation with Chalmers had unnerved him. Was he being naive? he asked himself. He was frankly frightened by the dangers of naiveté, of being too trusting, too open. Was it possible that he was jumping to conclusions? He, above all, did not wish to see the senator lose credibility with his natural constituency. But what good was a constituency if it felt itself manipulated, used, lied to. That was the whole point of it. He had the distinct impression—hell, it was more than an impression—that Chalmers, whose preachings on objectivity were one of the paper's great sources of élan, was actually trying to protect the senator.

So he wanted proof. More than likely there would be no proof. But what made him feel so certain about his own speculations? Who was he to read these events so suspiciously? Maybe his own conclusions were faulty. Maybe Hershey's view had swayed his own. After all, the facts were sketchy, ambiguous. And the senator did represent all the right things, all the good things, all the compassionate things. He could galvanize their movement. He could lead them, all the good people, the put-upon people, the harassed people. Better he than that pedestrian phony of a president with his platitudes and pious words. How he must be gloating over this one. And even if Senator James was guilty of panic or drunkenness or self-serving calculation, weren't they human traits, human failings? Hadn't he been taught that politics in America is the art of the possible, that compromise could be a virtue if the desired ends were always the goal? He tried to put himself in Senator James's shoes. My God, what do you expect the man to do? Get up before those reporters and admit his sexual encounter, then acknowledge his panic, apologize and get on with it? That's exactly right! That's what the movement would expect of him. Tell the truth. It's those stinking lies, those solemn ambiguities, those oblique answers, those calculated, rehearsed strategies designed to confuse—these were the main objections that the movement would have. There was only one way. It need not be fanatical, overzealous. Just tell the fucking truth, man, the truth, the whole truth.

He felt refreshed by his thoughts and excused Chalmers his obvious attempt to influence him. Chalmers, like himself, must be hurt by the senator's predicament. You couldn't blame him for attempts to help. But in the long run, Ernie felt sure, Chalmers would play the game by the right standards. He had only to present it in the correct way, the honest way.

As he sat there, lost in thought, his peripheral vision caught an uncommon sense of movement down the beach from the direction of the beach cottage. It was a kind of vehicle, moving swiftly. He strained to focus, putting a hand over his eyes to shield them from the glare. It was closing fast, leaving little puffs of sand in its wake. Soon it was almost abreast of him, speeding at a fast clip. He was able to make out the huddled figure of Senator James in the beach buggy.

XXII

It was Chief Bernhard who called to tell us about Marlena's father. They had apparently intercepted him and escorted him undetected to the basement of the hospital on the edge of town.

"It's quite obvious that we've got to see him," I told Don.

"And then get the hell out of here," Barnstable said.

Don sat immobile on the sun porch watching the sea. He stirred when he heard us talking about Marlena's father. He got up and came back into the living room.

"The moment of truth," he said.

Davis and Christine were working together in the kitchen. They, too, joined us in the living room.

"I've arranged it this way," Davis said. "Simon has acquired a beach buggy and has rented a car. A small plane is standing by at the airport, although I'm worried that the press might catch us there. Simon told the pilot if he mentions one word to anybody, the flight is off. We've got to get out of here without having any pictures taken. The beach buggy will pick up the senator, Mrs. James, and Lou at the edge of the beach and meet the car at the area of the beach near Dewey. I'll call Simon to get directions to the hospital. There may be press snooping around there, but we'll have to take that chance."

"I wonder what kind of a man he is," Don said, ignoring the logistical arrangements. Christine went to the phone and began to arrange the getaway.

"You've got one assignment with that man, Don," Barnstable said. "No autopsy. Above all, no autopsy."

"That's his prerogative."

"Yes, it is," I said. "And your downfall." Don was acting strangely again. He seemed to be swinging back and forth on a pendulum of uncertainty, one moment lucid and commanding, another moment withdrawn, reflective. Unfortunately, there was no avoiding this confrontation with Marlena's father. Chief Bernhard knew this. That's why he had called. The man had rare insight. Don got up and went into the bedroom to freshen up. Karen was already in the bathroom preparing for departure.

"We'll take care of all the packing," Christine said. "We'll go back with you, Jack."

"Above all," Barnstable said, "he's got to rest tonight. We'll have a staff meeting tomorrow."

"That's when we can work on the California speech," Davis said.

"What speech?"

"The one you must make to your constituency."

"You really think that's necessary?"

"Quite essential."

"Why?"

"There has got to be a public explanation. It is demanded. Somewhere down the line, you've got to appear in a controlled environment and make 'The Speech,' the expiation. It is absolutely necessary to complete the circle. That is, after we've gotten over this next hurdle. Marlena's father could really ruin things."

"In many ways."

The ball was in his court. It wasn't simply trembling in mid-air. Mr. Jackson held our fate in his black hands. He had an arsenal of options open to him. He could demand an autopsy, insist that foul play killed his daughter. He could make wild statements, accusations, reveal the affair, not that he knew, but he was close enough to his daughter to surmise. Above all, he could make it a racial issue, although race was totally extraneous to the situation. Suddenly, by this bizarre act of blind fate, an obscure Philadelphia mailman held the career of the country's most promising senator in the balance. That sounded like a headline in some True Confession farce. Perhaps he could be bought?

As if he had read my mind, Davis answered the question.
"We couldn't offer to buy him off. It would be suicide, adding the possibility of bribery to the arsenal of the enemy. This is where we, as they say in space, lose contact. We're out of it, on the other side of the moon. Jackson could hurt us badly."
"And if he does?"
"A whole new set of options. We'd be thrown for a dramatic, perhaps irretrievable, loss. You get into the fuzzy area of defensive denial. That's impossible. You can't win. At that stage, you can just hope public boredom sets in—a great equalizer, public boredom. But it might be too late by then. The record would be made. And a record is retrievable around election time."
Don had tried to make himself look reasonably presentable, although his face seemed ravaged. Karen emerged with her sunglasses on and a kerchief over her head. Outside, the press slouched about waiting for something to happen, cameras ready. It was three o'clock now. Time seemed to move slowly. The press formed a laconic tableau as they waited about in groups. Cameramen were lying on the ground napping.
Dodging reporters was a skill acquired with years of practice. It was agreed that four of us—Don, Karen, myself, and Davis, the inevitable Davis—would make the hegira to the hospital.
Barnstable stood out on the screened porch searching the horizon for the beach buggy, which had to keep a safe distance.
"There," he said. "It's out there. Can you see it?"
I could barely make out a speck in the distance. The beach was deserted except for the speck.
"Well, I guess this is it," Barnstable said. "The great escape." He tried to smile. Instead, his eyes began to water. He turned away to recover himself. Don put a hand on his shoulder. He stiffened and turned.
"Okay. Time for the diversion," he said, recovering his composure. "As soon as I open the front door—split!"

We sped over the beach toward the water. Then, where the surface hardened, we ran parallel, watching the beach buggy suddenly tear toward us in the distance. In a moment we were in it, huddled together and speeding toward the extreme end of the beach. The wind whipped at our faces, forcing us to arch our heads.

Looking backward, watching the summer house recede, I saw it as an episodic finish, a movie dissolve, the end of a chapter where the words do not quite fill the printed page. It dissolved into a new scene, a new chapter. Too much has already been said about how unreal it all seemed and how dreamlike. Perhaps it was because the events were so out of sync with the rest of our lives. Divine Providence. I caught myself forming the words over and over, then remembered how the words had been planted in my thoughts earlier in the day, only to rest there and repeat itself, intruding. Why had all this happened?

The operation was miraculously efficient. A car was waiting for us at the end of the beach. We all piled in with Kessler at the wheel. He gunned the motor and moved the car swiftly through deserted streets. All beach resorts out of season are eerie—the houses have mantles of ghostly emptiness, as if all the people had just died.

Slouched against the side of the back seat, his hand on the safety strap, Don was somber. He had retreated into himself. Karen's face was impassive behind her glasses. Thankfully, Davis was also silent, sensing the need for soundlessness.

Kessler drove the car to an alley behind the hospital, obviously carefully researched, for as the car nosed slowly into the alley, a door quickly opened, the car came to a halt, and, as if on command, we knew we had to hurry through it.

XXIII

Chief Bernhard, his face as impassive as ever, met us in the corridor. The hall smelled of disinfectant. I noted that he had somehow dispersed his police cars outside the hospital so that they weren't noticeable. Two of his police guarded both ends of the corridors. He led us to a wooden bench, which bore the eloquence of time on its rubbed and carved surface.

"He's in there with the body, Senator," Bernhard whispered. "I would strongly suggest that you keep Mrs. James outside."

Don nodded and motioned to me with his eyes to follow him into the room. Karen, who had heard the whisper in the silence, slumped against the fading, dull green corridor wall. Davis sat on the bench, crossed his legs, and began making notes on a pad he had taken from his pocket.

We found ourselves in a room that was stark white and overlit. We had to squint to put it in focus. It was devoid of any furniture, except a rolling cot on which was stretched out the sheeted body of what must have been Marlena. Beside it stood a small greying black man, his head bowed, his two hands clasped around a colorless hand of the dead girl extracted from under the sheet. Viewing him from the rear, one could see that he had not had time to change the bluish grey mailman's uniform, which, shiny with much care, was now creased, adding a further forlorn dimension to the pathetic scene.

I found myself swallowing hard, trying to tamp down the cry that was swelling in my chest, making my lips tremble. Don, whose reserves had depleted, could not contain himself. He made a sound, surely involuntary and primeval, like the cry from some monstrous cat that had caught a rake's teeth in its entrails. It was one long gasp, shattering in the starkness of the room. The greying black man gave a frightened start and turned.

His face, like some eroded riverbed, was parched with grief. The tears had ceased to come, but the eyes were heavily veined and red. He looked intensely at Don. He recognized him instantly. His lips curled slightly in anger, and then tightened, as he suddenly ripped the sheet off Marlena's torso.

She was a ghastly sight, her features distorted by her struggle against the sea to maintain her life. Her body, which once glistened like polished Swiss chocolate, was greyish, the color of chalk marks on a blackboard. The man's reaction was a bad sign, I remembered thinking. But the sudden shock of viewing the body and the man's uncommon act of anger seemed to have a calming effect on Don. It came to him as a relief, like a summer storm perhaps, fulfilling his need to be punished.

The anger was shortlived. The black man tenderly placed both of Marlena's hands against her chest and replaced the sheet.

"My little girl," he said, his voice strangely serene. "My little girl." He was not a big man, but stood erect, with that rare dignity of pride and age that one occasionally glimpses in men treated badly by life. One could see at once where the resoluteness of his daughter had come from.

"I can barely face you, Mr. Jackson," Don whispered, his words coming in fits and starts, almost like gasps. The black man had turned back to his daughter's form and had bowed his head once again.

"I wish I could share the intensity of the pain with you, Mr. Jackson. My own pain seems so meager beside yours."

Don's words came almost as a litany. "I've searched my mind for some logical explanation. Nothing I can think of makes any sense. One moment she was there, filled with life and beauty, and the next, gone beneath the sea. We tried to save her, Mr. Jackson. God, we tried. You must understand that. We tried."

The black man turned. Would he have understood if he had known that in trying to save his daughter, we, too, nearly died? Was it important for him to know that? There was no softness in his veined eyes, only hatred. Even the grief seemed less powerful than the hate.

"I despise you, Senator," he said quietly.

"I know," Don said. "Whatever explanation I might give you, I was the instrument of her death. I know that. I also know that I will not get your forgiveness."

The black man stared at Don, his eyes moist, his lips pressed together, reaching within himself for control.

"Marlena was—was a jewel," Don said, hesitantly at first, growing stronger as he chose his words, conscious of the care he had to take. In my view, he had passed the moment of greatest weakness, like a broken field runner who has shrugged off the last tackler. Perhaps it was the visibility of death in Marlena's ashen face—its finality. Marlena was gone—irrevocably. She was an inanimate stick of rigid bone and lifeless skin that lay on the table before them. Her beauty, her youth, her spirit had disappeared beyond the surface of the sea, and what was left was the clear blue flame of grief. Don straightened and stood before the black man. Perhaps he was saying to himself at last, "I did not kill this woman."

"It was a ghastly accident, Mr. Jackson. Your daughter was my friend."

The black man turned again to the body. His shoulders hunched; his head was bowed slightly.

"My little girl," he said. "She was a gift from God. She was the world." He turned again. Tears rolled down his cheeks. "Can there be no joy in this world for me?" It was the perennial cry of loss. "You cannot understand, Senator James," Mr. Jackson said. "She was born to fulfill the meaning of black destiny. This was a special person."

There it was, that sense of peoplehood and blackness that Davis had feared. If he invoked that thought, if he dwelled on that idea, there was danger ahead.

"She was a special person," Don said. I could see emerging the ever-present mark of the professional politician, the master of the right word, the right inflection, the correct platitudes, the product of endless days and nights of meetings, testimonials, campaigns, and, yes, eulogies.

"Her mother died when she was seven. I raised her. There was always the two of us. I was proud of her."

"I, too, was proud of her, Mr. Jackson."

He shook his head with contempt.

"She told me she loved you. Love—what is that word? Love with a honky. Always, this romantic love brings nothing. I told her that what to her was love was to you just a philandering with a nigger girl through the back door. And now she's dead for it."

"Mr. Jackson," Don began, his voice firm and unwavering. "I admired and respected your daughter. Her death is a personal disaster for you of unfathomed proportions. I know that, and nothing, absolutely nothing, I can say will soothe your pain. But I want you to know that I grieve for her, too. I grieve for you and I grieve for me. In the context of my life, her death is a personal disaster for me as well. I would have given anything to spare us this agony. But her death is very real, Mr. Jackson, a very real thing, and, whether we like it or not, it must be faced."

Somehow, the strength of Don's conviction, so straight-forward and simply stated, had a profound effect upon the black man. His eyes searched helplessly about him. I brought a chair from a corner of the little room, and he sat down.

"Yes," he said. "It must be faced, and I cannot accept it."

Don put a hand on the man's shoulder, poised, it seemed, to comfort the man in an embrace.

"Mr. Jackson," Don said. "I have something to say that must be said. I know that the moment is totally inappropriate. I also know that you may have no comprehension of what I am saying—" The black man raised his head and looked at Don.

"Senator, I am not stupid."

"I'm sure of that, Mr. Jackson."

"I understand what I must do," he said, quietly. "I intend to bring my daughter's body back to Philadelphia, and just as soon as I can, I will bury her next to her mama. I have no wish beyond that. My life is over, without meaning." He shook his greying head. "You needn't worry, Senator."

On the surface, it appeared as if both men had reached each other across a void. But there was a certain lack of specifics. It was obvious that Mr. Jackson had no thirst for revenge nor did he plan any deliberate acts to embarrass or otherwise hurt Don. But a man whose daily experience was to bring mail through did not have a real understanding of the nuances and subtleties of the media world. Even as I watched the black man, crushed, his small, tight body drawn into a knot as he sat on the chair, his head slightly bowed, looking aimlessly at the floor, silent and grieved, I was ticking off the possibilities in my mind. His very abjectness could be made an issue of formidable proportions by the television camera. Certainly, the racial angle could be devastating if he chose in his intelligent and articulate way to put it across. This was a man of substance. He was not the stereotype who ate into the black man's aspirations like lye reacting on human gut. I was certain that the business of the autopsy was moot. This man was not going to let his daughter's body be mutilated. I felt compelled to put these thoughts into words. No one could expect this man to understand procedures of this nature. I looked at Don. His face, although drawn, pale, and thinner—even the lines around the eyes had deepened—had a firmness that reassured me. He was tough, this man James.

"Mr. Jackson," I said slowly. I hoped my voice was modulated to the perfect tone for these circumstances. "There are problems ahead." I hesitated, looking at Don. He nodded assent. "There will be all sorts of attempts to draw innuendos—bad pictures." There, I was condescending again, to a man to whom spotting condescension was a religion. "Attempts will be made to distort the truth. There will be little we can do to stop it, at least at the beginning. People will say terrible

things; people will assume things about—your daughter's character—
and that of the senator. You will be outraged. You will be deeply hurt.
Few, particularly in the press, will be kind. There will be some rather
disgusting sentimentality. There will be pictures of your daughter
everywhere, old graduation pictures; it will be cruel—very cruel."

I paused and waited for some reaction. I could see the thick top of
his greying head. He did not lift his face to me.

"I do not believe that you wish to compound the madness that
will follow. But you must understand, our enemies are very clever.
They have a formidable arsenal. They know how to play on human
emotions. They know how to arouse interest. They can use you to
hurt us. They can use you to hurt your daughter's memory."

I knew it before the words were out. I had goofed. He lifted his
head and looked at me with contempt.

"What do you care about my daughter's memory?" He looked at
me searchingly. "Who are you, anyway?"

"I'm Lou Castle. I hired Marlena. She was my friend."

He nodded. She had told him about me. I could tell from the
man's reactions that Marlena had talked about me favorably. Hell,
we liked each other. She probably rated me in the colorful character category, talked about me with a smile. I guess I am a kind of
comic figure. The image stood me in good stead here. I followed
up my advantage.

"What I'm talking about is keeping Marlena's memory from
being insulted. You see, we do care about her; we care about her as
our comrade and friend. Marlena would understand exactly what we
are talking about. She knew. And you can bet she'd understand what
the implications of this situation are all about."

"What is it you want me to do, Mr. Castle?" the black man asked.

"Do not talk to the press. Avoid conversations with any third person who might be tempted to talk to the press. Don't give the press
any pictures of your daughter. Bar the press from the church.
Remain silent. Above, all remain silent."

I did not mention the autopsy. There was no question in my mind that he would never allow that to happen. What was there to find out from his point of view? He knew of Don's relationship with Marlena. He was not a fool. Don had remained silent. Twenty years of beating the ball around made the game one of instinctive moves. Like a tennis match. He knew when to lob or run to the net. He knew when to step back into rear court.

Already my mind was working on our next confrontation with Jackson. I wished Davis were with us. We'd get a picture of Don and the old man at graveside. Don, looking comforting and contrite, dripping with compassion and understanding. I saw the picture in my head. I hoped it would be raining.

"If there is anything I can do, Mr. Jackson," Don said, "anything at all, please, please let me know."

The black man turned his face upward again. Tears streamed down his cheeks.

"I want my daughter," he whispered. "All I want is my daughter. Oh, God, give me back my daughter." Grief had engulfed him. He was beyond understanding now. He slumped against the wall and clasped his hands, rocking slightly, resurrecting the old Negro pain that had that special brooding futility of the black spiritual.

We stood over him a moment, waiting for him to recover. When he grew quiet, we left.

Karen and Davis were waiting. I drew Davis aside.

"I hope he listens," I said.

"That's essential. He could blow us right out of the water."

"I think he suspects that. He's not very much interested in us, though; but he knows we were Marlena's friends."

"Let's hope that's one obstacle hurdled. Just called in. Things couldn't be bleaker. Our so-called friends in the senate, the unannounced three—" He referred to the three fellow senators who had geared up to fight Don in the primaries, Hopkins, Wilson, Mudd.

"—all crying tragedy, all being so damned solicitous. I can see them rubbing their hands. No comment from the president; I am told that he let a pool photographer in to snap a picture as he received the news. The clever bastard."

"Oh, come on, Davis. You haven't got a monopoly on all the brains in the business."

"Can't you just see the caption?"

"Let's face it; the president used to be an amateur actor."

"I guess he feels pretty good now. He just won his next term."

As they walked toward the entrance, Chief Bernhard handed Don a note. He opened it.

"Chuck Chalmers wants me to call," Don said.

"Good," Davis said.

"What does it mean?" I asked.

"It means," Davis said, "that doubt springs eternal in the human breast."

We ducked quickly into the waiting car and sped to the little airport on the edge of town, where we skirted the main entrance, turned into one of the runways, and came to a halt near a two-engined airplane, revved and waiting at the far end.

On the trip back, the sound of the motors and the events of the last twenty-four hours overwhelmed us with exhaustion. When we landed, I could barely remember we had been in the air.

XXIV

Ernie had made sure the car kept its distance. The streets were so empty, the town so small, that following the car from five blocks away was no problem. Even when suddenly there was no car to follow, he could sense that it had come to a halt somewhere near the old red brick hospital, the only building in a dead-end street. Deliberately, he passed the building, parked the car on an empty side street, and walked the distance to the hospital.

It was an old building, built perhaps thirty years ago, with narrow high windows, all still graced with old-fashioned pull shades. Over the high, wooden front doors was a sign engraved in cast stone: Rehoboth General Hospital. There was a parking lot along its side with a number of cars lined up neatly in two rows. Walking behind the second row of cars, stooping slightly to shield himself from exposure, he reached the rear of the hospital. There, two police cars were parked near a rear entrance marked "Emergency."

Ernie pulled his notebook from a side pocket; and, scribbling a note on the first empty page asking the senator to call Mr. Chalmers, he ripped it out, folded it, and wrote the senator's name along its front.

He could imagine the drama going on inside. Confrontation with next of kin, tears, recriminations, entreaties, the sad ritual of after-death. As a reporter, he had seen it many times. He had trained himself to be dispassionate. Sometimes, in the case of children, he had to fight back tears, but fortunately, he had been able to conceal his emotion while on the job. Sentiment interfered with objectivity. Later, after the assignment, he somehow was able to shake it off. It became cerebral, reflective. Then, finally, like a mysterious chemical reaction, emotion became an abstraction, nothing more than a comment on the human predicament. Death, after all, was a common experience. He had learned to accept it in all its unreasonable and illogical forms, its unexpected entrances and ridiculous guises. Had he become cynical? He would fight cynicism to his last breath. It was corrosive to the movement. Indeed, beside greed, it was the principal antipersonnel device. It knocked out the movement's members en masse, like an attack of dysentery—dysentery of the spirit. Between the moment of birth and death, there was life; and in life there was only truth; and if you loved the idea of life, then you must love the idea of truth.

He watched the back entrance from the line of cars until he realized that he had been seen by one of the policemen. He walked to the back entrance and identified himself to the policeman, fresh faced and officious.

"No press," the policeman said. "Orders."

"I'd like to speak to your chief."

"I said, no press."

A policeman by nature is an intimidating force, but Ernie had become wise in handling policemen.

"All I want is one word with him."

"Why don't you just beat it."

"Look, I'm a newspaper reporter doing a job. Just like you. I have no intention of moving." He could sense the young policeman's frustration. Unhitching his club, the policeman slammed it into his fist.

"I said, beat it."

"I would strongly suggest you don't use that club," Ernie said between clenched teeth. His heart beat heavily.

"Hey, Sam, cool it," the other policeman said. "I'll get the chief."

"You're a son-of-a-bitch," the young policeman said. "I'd love to beat the shit out of you."

"Don't be a damned fool."

Chief Bernhard appeared at the entrance. Ernie showed him his press card.

"I'm Rowell, *Washington Chronicle.*"

"So?"

"The story is in the public domain. All I want is to get the facts. I don't think you've been fair with us."

"What do you expect of me?"

"We're entitled to honest answers."

"You got honest answers. I gave you the facts up at the house."

"I'd like to know who is in there with the senator."

Chief Bernhard hesitated. He observed Ernie cautiously.

"The girl's father."

"And the senator and his wife?"

"Yes."

"Have they talked to each other?"

"Yes."

"What was their reaction?"

"You asked for facts. I'm not going to be drawn into interpreting these events."

"All right, then. Can I speak to the senator?"

"He doesn't want to speak to reporters. I feel I owe him that protection."

Ernie watched the stoic, leathered face, the cool, blue eyes, liquid but clear, in soft pouches.

"All right," Ernie said. "I have a note for the senator. Will you give it to him?" Ernie handed him the paper. The chief looked at it, and then took it and slipped it in his pocket. The chief started to move back into the hospital.

"Chief Bernhard," Ernie called. "It's just that this man, this Senator James, aspires to be President of the United States. Do you understand that? We can't just roll this story under the rug. You can't be a party to a cover-up. This is not just the senator's ball game. It's everybody's ball game."

The chief turned. A flush began to form around his jowls.

"We owe the American people the truth," Ernie said.

"The truth? Are you saying that I haven't told you the truth?"

"As far as the facts you've presented. But there are other things. Lots of unanswered questions." Ernie pressed on, knowing now that he had Chief Bernhard's attention. "Why did he wait so long to report the drowning? Was he having an affair with this woman? These are key questions."

"What difference does it make?"

"It's a question of integrity, of truth. Look, I'm not a judge. There's a lot at stake here."

"I have given you the facts."

"Look, Chief," Ernie said. "I'm not questioning your integrity. You've just got to see the situation in perspective. If we don't tell it like it is, a curtain will drop, and then we'll never know. The senator has resources. He can manipulate his story, he can bend it, and he can command huge audiences. I offer a counterbalance. Events move swiftly. We'll never again recover this moment."

"What difference does it make? What's one more bent story by a politician?" Ernie could see that the chief was sorry he said it.

"You mean the story is being bent."

"Son," the chief said. "I'm as tortured about this as you are. I have made my judgment. There is no crime here. As for the senator's career, that's really outside the jurisdiction of police business. I refuse to be tempted into interpretations."

"Christ, Chief, the issue is his fitness to govern."

Chief Bernhard scratched his ear and made what was to him an uncommon grimace.

"I raise bees," he said. "I have twenty-five hives. I spend all my spare time raising bees, collecting honey, watching their habits. All I want to do for the rest of my life is raise bees and collect honey. I know you'll think that's indifference, an obscure police chief in a small town raising bees. Bees are honest. I would prefer to live my life around honest things, like bees."

"What about people?"

"Bees are better."

"Haven't you got any kids? Don't you care about their future?"
He looked at Ernie. His lips began to move. No sounds came.
"In other words, you prefer to be indifferent," Ernie said, after a
long silence.
"That's about the size of it."
"It's wrong."
"It will take a little more living on your part to make that judgment." He looked at the note in his hand. "I'll see that he gets your
note." Chief Bernhard shook his head sadly turned, and was soon lost
in the darkness of the corridor.
"Now beat it," the young policeman said.
Ernie felt sweat in his palms. He wiped them on his jacket. He
looked at his watch. It was getting near deadline time for the first edi-
tion. He felt helpless. At the end of the parking lot, he found a telephone booth. He sat on the seat and looked at the dial, going over the
conversation with Chief Bernhard. What was nagging him? He seemed
to be overreacting. What was he really looking for? Why didn't he simply accept the bare facts and be done with it? Was it his own ambition,
the big scoop? Didn't every young newspaperman or woman yearn for
that one giant story that would make his reputation, make him famous.
Was it that kind of power he was unconsciously seeking? Like a film
clip, the white charger passed across the screen. He put the dime in the
slot and started to dial the paper. Before he finished, he pressed down
the lever breaking the connection. Instead, he dialed Ellen.
"Ellen."
"Ernie. I called the paper. They said you were in Rehoboth."
"I am."
"Quite a story." Her voice was warm, inviting. He remembered
making love to her.
"I'm having a crisis, baby."
"Animal, mineral, or vegetable?"
"No kidding. I think I'm being put on. I think I'm being vic-
timized."

"I don't understand."

"I don't either yet. I'm being frustrated by well-meaning men."

"Ernie."

"Yes, Ellen."

"I wish you were here."

"So do I."

There was a long silence. He looked out of the booth and saw two police cars rush past. Between them was another car and inside was the senator and his group.

"I'll call you later."

He hung up, opened the door of the booth, and walked back to the emergency entrance. A hearse was parked at the entrance and two men were wheeling out a sheet-draped body. A group of nurses and doctors stood silently. To one side was a small black man. He leaned against the wall. The back panels of the hearse were slammed shut. The doctors and nurses filed back through the alley door. Only the black man remained. The hearse sped off. He was alone now.

"Mr. Jackson?"

The black man looked at Ernie, his dark eyes red veined and swollen.

"I'm terribly sorry, Mr. Jackson," Ernie said.

The black man took a handkerchief from his rear pocket and blew his nose.

"They say she was a very wonderful person."

He had learned that flattery could penetrate grief, that flattery could offer solace. The black man nodded his head.

"I won't have to worry now," he said quietly. "I won't have to worry ever again."

"Did he at least say he loved her?" Ernie asked.

The black man slowly raised his eyes.

"He didn't even say that," the black man said. "They just used my baby and threw her away like a piece of unwanted clay, black clay."

"What will you do?"

"Bury my little girl."

Ernie tried to frame another question, but all he could do was watch the black man, bent and defeated, walk slowly to the parking lot.

XXV

It was the kind of bar replicated in every country of the world, near a busy port, sleazy, smelling of beer, cheap booze, urine, and the dried sweat of rootless men. Badly lighted, the interior seemed to complement the emptiness of the lives lined up against the bar, gnarled faces of bitter men who man the docks and ships of the world's ports. In one corner, two fat prostitutes nursed their beer and laughed shrilly.

"Mike's," the broken lopsided sign had beckoned. You couldn't see through the dirt-caked ancient storefront along the dingy back street of abandoned row houses, warehouses, and shipping offices. Don had insisted. Karen had shrugged in resignation.

"It's your goddamned life," she had said.

Davis was less resigned, especially since Don wouldn't reveal his plans.

"I just want to go somewhere. I want to fade for a few hours," he said.

"You're a public figure, Senator, with a public face. You'll be spotted. It will kill us." Davis, usually nonplussed, seemed on the verge of tears.

"Look," Don said. "I don't mean to be a son-of-a-bitch, but I've been through a bit of hell in the past twenty-four hours. If I don't just get away and think, I'll climb the walls."

I knew then that Don had finally gained full control again. He was measuring himself against the future, taking stock, calculating the odds. He had to work it out. We'd been down that road before together. Sometimes it was drink or just plain physical activity until exhaustion. Sometimes it was women. He needed to expend energy. Once he walked from San Francisco to Carmel. We were a hell of a lot younger then. Once he holed up with a Chinese prostitute for

157

three days in San Francisco's Chinatown. I can't remember what had set him off then, but he was always having terrible telephone fights with his father. Back in school, I would see him run around the track until he dropped while I dozed in the stands. Always, later, he would say, "Lord, I needed that."

I called two cabs from the little office at Montgomery Airport.

"Senator, I don't know what to say," Davis said. "I think it's pure madness."

"Don't worry. Where I'm going, no one will know me."

"I'll be with him," I said. Karen turned away in disgust.

"Let him go," she said. "They deserve each other."

She really hated me, Karen did. I guess I understood. Hell, I was closer to Don than she was. That fact was pretty well proven yesterday. Now it was being confirmed. Both she and Davis could see that Don would not be moved.

"I won't be long." He looked at Karen.

"I don't give a damn."

"I've just got to," he said. "You've just got to understand. I wouldn't be able to sit still. I wouldn't be able to talk. I just wouldn't be able to function."

Whether the explanation served any purpose or not, Don and I got into our cab and headed into downtown Baltimore. We didn't talk much, and we had the cab driver drop us at the fringe of the dock area. We roamed around for a while; then Don found what he was looking for. Mike's. It was a little corner of the refuse trap of life, a seedy little bar. Among the assortment of mismatched tables and chairs, we found a place in a corner. I brought double Scotches from the bar, suffering the strange looks of what seemed a hostile bunch. This was the kind of joint they called a "bucket of blood." Above the din, we could hear an occasional argumentative outburst, a curse shouted over some unknown irrational drunken dispute. Even the bartender, a fat, unshaven old salt type with a red face, scowled when he passed over the drinks. We were two strange fish swimming in another ocean. This was the other world. Don would not be recognized here. He downed his drink in one gulp and hit his chest as the booze burned its way down.

"Shit," he croaked, his face reddening.

The bartender watched his reaction.

"Rotgut," Don said. He stood up and moved to the bar.

"I paid for Scotch whiskey, buddy," he said.

The bartender looked through him, then spat, smiled, and pulled another bottle from behind the bar. He poured it out into a double shot glass. Don downed it in one gulp.

"Hit me again," he said. The bartender poured. Don threw a five-dollar bill on the bar. It soaked up some spilt whiskey. Turning with a contemptuous sneer at the fat bartender, he walked back to the table.

"Son-of-a-bitch," he said, as he sat down.

The bartender huddled with two men, sitting in a corner of the bar. Occasionally, he looked our way. Smiling, he gave me the finger. I didn't call it to Don's attention since it was obvious that Don was going out of his way to be offensive.

"Lou," he said, smiling. "We are in one hell of a pickle. One hell of a pickle."

"Well, that's one statement that doesn't need a response."

"It was seeing Marlena's body lying there on that table. Just a lump of useless matter. That's when it occurred to me. I didn't kill that girl. That's when the guilt died inside me. Death had come and snatched her. I did not kill that girl. Nor do I feel that I was the instrument of her death. That is neither cruel nor calculating nor rationalizing. I did not kill that girl."

"Who the hell said you did?"

"I said I did."

"When?"

"When I dived into that surf, Lou, I felt like a murderer, I wanted to die with her. I nearly did die. Not until I saw that body, that lump of useless dead flesh and bones, did I conclude that I didn't kill that girl." He stood up and moved to the bar again. The bartender, who had been observing us, straightened belligerently, and, without a word, poured another double Scotch, and contemptuously lifted two dollars from Don's wet pile of bills on the bar. Don came back, sat down again, and polished off the whiskey in a single gulp.

"I didn't exactly enhance my political career."

"That's for sure."

"I'm sorry that she died. She was a nice kid. But I didn't kill her. And I'm going to fight this thing. No matter what fire I have to walk through. No matter what hot coals I've got to pass over. I'm good at my trade."

"I'll buy that."

"From nothing. From shit. My father was a goddamned nothing, a turd. I was this much away from taking a shot at being president of the United States—the head motherfucker—"

"The head motherfucker," I repeated, downing the original shot of rotgut. It burned its way down.

"I will not yield to self-pity, Lou."

"I know, Don."

"When you're good, you're good. And I'm good."

"Yes, you are, Don."

"I refuse to feel remorse."

"Right on."

"Or guilt."

"No, not guilt."

"Only stupidity. I feel stupid, Lou. It was stupid to believe I could live a charmed life forever. It had to catch up with me sooner or later."

"I should have foreseen it."

"It's just that sometimes you get overconfident. Power! Success makes you overconfident. I felt that I could never make a mistake."

"We were careful, Don. It was just one of those things."

"I will not cry about it."

"No, Don."

"I will not let it defeat me."

He banged on the table. I knew he was getting drunk.

"I feel like jumping out of my skin, Lou."

He swilled down the remains of his drink, stepped up to the bar again, and banged down his glass. The bartender nudged one of his companions and stepped up to Don.

"Okay, buddy, don't make so much fucking noise," the fat bartender said, winking at his companions.

"Just pour it in."

"I don't have to serve you."

"He's looking for trouble, Charlie." It was one of the bartender's friends, a huge man, with thick features and tattoos crawling up his hairy arms. He looked thickheaded and mean, used to barroom brawling.

Don put up both hands, palms outward. He smiled.

"No offense," he said. "I'm not touchy. You don't be touchy. Just pour the drink." He said it with a snicker. The bartender shrugged and poured the drink.

"Very touchy bunch," Don said. The booze was taking hold. He was beginning to slur his words. I determined to stay sober.

"I'm going to lay off the broads, Lou. I'm going to be the soul of propriety. God, I loved the girls, Lou. All the pretty, wonderful girls. All the great bodies. Ah, joy of joys. I just got caught. That's my crime. I got caught. I humiliated Karen. The punishment doesn't fit the crime. Who knows? Maybe I'm just a guy whistling in the cemetery. Maybe I'm through, washed up."

He shook his head, then slapped one of my thighs.

"Do you think I'm through, Lou?"

"No, I don't."

"I'm not ready to quit yet, Lou. I'm ready to show the some character. I've got a lot of ideas up my sleeve, Lou. Believe me, I know their game. They may think I'm washed up."

"We're going to stick it out."

"Good old Lou."

"All the way."

He was beginning to get red on the tip of his nose, a sure sign that the alcohol was getting to him.

"They're gonna remember me," he said. "I wish the old man was alive today. That son-of-a-bitch. That bastard. When I was about six or seven he used to have these bum friends of his come to the house for booze and poker every Friday night. They were a bragging bunch. I used to be a gopher for the beer. They always drank boiler-makers. Pop had taught me his cheating system. I would watch and then give him signals, a wink for two pair, a finger in my nose for three of a kind, I'd blow bubble gum for a full house. A flush! What the fuck was a flush? Yeah, I'd touch my head. I can't remember the other signals. He was such a damn bastard. When he walked out, I wanted to go with him. I cried like hell." A tear started slowly down the corner of his left eye. "Hey, pop. Did I let you down? I'll do better next time, pop. I'm smart, pop, like you, pop."

"If you keep your cool, we'll weather this storm, Don," I said.

"This fucking country—," Don said. "This great fucking country."

"Great fucking country."

"You're a cynic, Lou, We're just in the middle of the revolution. Recognize it. The old America is as dead as Kelsey's nuts. Maybe Marlena's death is the Master's way of saying that the time is not yet come for me. I have this uncanny feeling, Lou. I should have drowned. I felt I was drowning. You saved me. Good old Lou. It's my destiny, my fucking destiny. That's what Marlena's death tells me. I've been saved for something. One day, Lou."

"One day, Don."

"I'm gonna lead this country. I'm gonna resurrect this country. We're sinking deeper into the mud every minute. We're a country of dying cities, without roots or direction. We've become a greedy little nation, and we're getting greedier, bloated, sated. That's my destiny, Lou. This country is on its knees, waiting for a leader. I'll lead the motley crew, all the bastards of the world, all the fucking left-outs."

I had never seen Don like this. His thoughts were embarrassing. He frightened me. I tried to credit it to the booze, but despite the slurring of the words, he seemed remarkably clearheaded.

"I'm just caught in the entrails of my own fantasy, Lou. And, unlike a hell of a lot of people, I know it. I want them to know that Donald Benjamin James lived here. Goddammit, I want them to know."

"That's a teenage American dream right out of the thirties," I said. "And I lost it just about the time World War II came along."

"I know you did, Lou. But I never lost it. By God, it's still inside me, and it grows every year. My whole life is geared to that idea. Why the hell not? Besides, I know this game. I know it and I'm going to prove to the world I know it. I'm going to show the bastards that I can rise above this. Let them think what they want. I am going to make them believe my story. How about that—make them believe me. Davis is right on the ball. Between you and Jack and me, we're gonna make them believe our story. Let them try to tear my heart out. I've got things up my sleeve they never dreamed about. Let them uncover every little floozie I've banged over the last twenty years and I'm gonna make them love me for it."

"I hope you do, Don."

"I know that, old Lou. Good old Lou. You and me, Lou. Someday we're going to run the whole fucking world, the whole fucking world."

"Sure, Don."

"We're gonna make the world remember us a thousand, two thousand years from now. Donald James and his old buddy, Lou Castle."

"What will they remember us for, Don?"

"I've thought about that, Lou. I've thought hard about that."

He pointed a finger at me and looked deep into my eyes. His were redder now, squinty with booze and exhilaration.

"We're gonna give this fucking country back its hope. We're gonna hypnotize them into getting back their hope. What are any of us without a dream? You gotta have a dream. I got a dream. You think I could have lived through the last twenty-four hours without a dream? And when they pack you into this life with such a short timeframe, if you don't have a dream, what the hell have you got?"

"There's lots of us walking around with nothing but dead dreams."

"That's the point. They're dead. You can't live without dreams, live ones. And nothing, nothing they can throw at me is going to stand in the way of keeping my dream alive."

As he talked, the bits and pieces of past conversations came back to me, the boyhood confidences, late-night talk across our college room. It was amazing how consistent Don's outlook was, even now, after all he had been through, in this crummy Baltimore bar, even now with the liquor talking, it was still there—the pugnaciousness and audacity. Only death itself could have cut it down. Marlena died and that was terrible. But that was yesterday. Tomorrow was the only thing that counted.

"I'd like to see the look on Mr. Plankwhite's face—," Don said, suddenly, a random thread plucked from an old suit.

"Who the hell is Plankwhite?"

"I fucked him good with my signals to pop. He always lost his ass."

Don laughed hysterically and banged on the table. Then, in a sudden deflection of interest, he stood up and walked to where the two fat prostitutes were sitting.

"My ladies." He bowed cavalierly. "Wouldst thou join my friend and me for some pleasant conversation."

The woman twittered. He threw twenty bucks on the table. The women looked at each other, and then at him.

"You a dick?" one of them asked. She had big spaces of lost teeth in her mouth, which was ringed with a thick, sloppy smudge of lipstick.

"A dick, a prick, a hard-on, an erect phallus. I am he."

The women giggled, got up, and joined us at our table. They were really raunchy looking, heavily rouged, beneath which you could see the stark white pallor of age and abuse. Both of them had dyed their hair a fading, nondescript red.

"I'm Molly," the one with the smudged lipstick said. "They call her Big Red." Big Red laughed, her three chins shaking like jelly. "Have you a red pussy, Big Red?" Don asked, winking at Molly. "Red and juicy," Big Red said.

Both women seemed to have soaked themselves in cheap perfume. It was stifling just to be near them. Their breath wheezed and sputtered.

"How do you like my lady friends, Lou?"

"Beautiful."

There was no dragging him away now. He began to fawn over the one with the smudged lips. He squeezed her tits.

"Hey, watch the merchandise," she laughed.

"How much is a peek worth?"

The women looked at each other.

"Two bucks?" She said it hesitantly.

"Just for a peek?"

"Okay, a buck," she said.

Don put down the buck. The woman with the smudged lips looked around her. The bartender gave her a tough look.

"Look, let's get out of here. Big Red has a place two blocks away."

"Are you afraid of the fucking bartender? I paid for a peek." The woman was confused.

"Look, I'll play with your cock under the table, but I can't do that; he'll kill me."

"I want a peek."

"Come on outside. I'll give you a peek outside."

"I want it here."

"Jeez, man. He'll kill me."

"Come on Don," I said. "Let's get out of here. This is crazy."

"I want my peek."

"Okay. Okay. Take it easy," the woman with the smudge said. She waited until the bartender was at the other end of the bar. She began to unbutton the top of her dress, revealing a huge mass of veined flesh. She literally lifted one huge breast out of its brassiere cup.

"You like?" she said.

"Now I want to suck it."

"He'll kill me," the woman whispered. "Please come on outside. I'm terrific. You can put it in my ass."

"Whoopee."

"I'm good. I'm really good. And Big Red's great. Aren't you, honey? Tell 'em how great you are, Big Red."

"I'll take you around the world. That's three bucks more. But I'm good."

"And if you tip her, she'll take you to heaven," the one with the smudge said.

"Will you drink my piss?" Don said.

"That'll cost you twenty bucks," Big Red said without hesitation.

I couldn't take it any longer.

"Don, let's get out of here."

"I don't want to leave these pretty ladies."

"Here's Big Red's address. Come on and meet us. He'll get sore, and then we can't hustle here any more. Come on, honey."

Don winked.

"Do you take American Express?" he asked, then enjoying the joke, fell back and rolled off his chair.

"Cut that shit out," the bartender said.

Don got up and sat down again.

"Come on, Don. Let's meet them outside. Let's all go to Big Red's house."

The thought of copulating with that mass of flesh literally made me nauseous. But I had to get him out of here somehow.

Don smacked his hand down on the table.

"Just great girls."

"The address is 203. Two blocks to the right. We'll be waiting."

Don leaned over the table and gave Big Red a wet noisy kiss on her cheek.

"You just keep that big, juicy, red pussy waiting for us."

The two fat prostitutes got up and flounced out of the bar.

"What was that all about?" I asked.

"Human garbage," he said, gulping down his drink.

Suddenly, Don stood up and threw his glass on the floor. It smashed to bits, and the noise it made turned all eyes in our direction. The bartender looked at us menacingly.

"Another double," Don said, stepping up to the bar.

"I ain't servin' you anymore," the bartender said.

"The hell you ain't," Don said belligerently. I grabbed his sleeve.

"Come on, Don. Cool it." He shrugged me away.

"What's with this guy?" the bartender asked, looking at his two cronies. The others, after a passing glance, turned back to their conversations. Barroom brawling was as commonplace here as the bad booze.

"Hey—," the big man who had spoken before said. "You hoid. No more. Get the fuck out of here."

"For Christ's sake, Don," I pleaded.

"I want a double Scotch," Don said, with drunken deliberation.

"Where did you guys come from?" the bartender said. "You look like a couple of fags. These guys will break you up and throw you in the bay. When I say no more around here, I mean no more."

"Listen, you fat turd," Don shouted. "Pour me another drink."

"He's really pushin' me," the bartender said to his buddies.

"Throw him out," someone shouted at the other end of the bar, squealing with laughter.

"You know, I'm gonna get to the other side of this bar in one minute and hand you your teeth, you fuckin' fag."

Things were getting mean. I stood beside Don at the bar. Strangely, he seemed to be sobering, egging them on, calculating his moves.

"You're a fat turd."

This finally set the bartender off. He walked the full length of the bar, ducked under the opening and made his way to a spot directly in front of Don. I tried again to pull him away.

"Leave me, Lou," Don said.

The bartender seemed smaller now that he had come from what had been a raised platform behind the bar.

"Now, what were you saying?"

"I said—" Don, with his sure sense of public reaction, looked around him. Apparently, he was winning respect among the customers. "I said that you're a big, fat, ugly turd." The bartender lunged; Don sidestepped, stuck his foot out, and tripped the bartender, who fell crashing against the tables, overturning two of them, and scattering empty bottles and glasses.

"I'll take him, Charlie," the big man said as he confidently planted himself in front of Don. He stood there, two heads taller, crusty, mean, unshaven, relishing the scent of blood.

"Don, for crying out loud," I shouted. I was on the verge of panic.

The big man was truly big, with that raw ugliness that afflicts a man to whom authority always means brute strength. He was totally confident of his physical power, which was accentuated, perhaps, by his bigness, his bovine face, his huge belly protruding over his belt. He looked as if he could crush Don's head between his two hamlike hands. Don stood his ground, spoiling for some action, bursting to use up energy. The bartender's friend was at least a head taller than Don, who stood coolly, unintimidated, cocky, his lips curled in a cool smile, cheeks flushed from the booze and excitement. All the faces in the bar—the lost empty faces of the sub-underground of womanless men—turned toward us.

"Now, what was you sayin'?" the big man said to Don.

"I called him a fat turd," Don said without hesitation, jerking his thumb back to where the bartender stood nursing a sore knee. "And you're a dumb shithead."

From where I stood it looked like a death wish on Don's part. Even then I knew that it was some kind of test Don had set for himself, a need to measure his life against fate. Hell, I'm no psychiatrist.

The big man lifted his right fist and started to bring it down on Don's head in a hammerlike motion. It never reached its mark. Don stepped back and with the point of his foot, motored by a full punting kick, administered a shot in the groin that was awesome in its power. The big man's face contorted in pain as he sank to his knees on the filthy floor, strewn with spittle and cigarette butts and broken glass. It was not enough. Don took the man's head in his hands and brought his knee full strength up against the man's chin. Then, in an act of violence that challenged my knowledge of him, Don hit the helpless hulk on one side of his face with every bit of strength and frustration and anger that his body could muster. It was as if all the hurt of the past days, of past years, had found its way into Don's fist. It was an awesome bone-crushing blow that left the man dazed and pouring blood from nose and mouth as he whimpered on the floor in pain. The scene seemed like a stopped moment in time: the patrons at the bar were stunned and silent; the bartender, openmouthed in disbelief, was frozen with a hand on his kneecap; there was a total absence of sound. Even the smoke refused to move. Don looked at the man on the floor, turned, and walked slowly out of the bar. I followed.

We ran. I could hear only the sounds of our shoes against the pavement, reverberating through the narrow empty streets. I can't tell you how long we ran. Perhaps it was only a few minutes. My chest began to burn as Don's lead extended itself. Finally, I stopped and leaned against a deserted storefront. Don came back and stood by me as I gasped for air. I could barely make out his features in the darkness, but I sensed that he was calm and sober—spent, but content. When I recovered, we walked slowly along the streets, found a cab, and in silence rode back toward Washington.

"Lord, I feel good," Don said.

XXVI

Karen explored herself in the mirror. Years of careful observation had etched a map of her face in her brain. She knew every fold, every wrinkle's history, every skin shade, and, more important, she knew how to use her creams and liquids and pastes to ward off and hold back the handiwork of time.

Now, sitting as she was in front of the half-walled mirror with its circle of vaudeville lights, creaming off the day's makeup, she could see the ravages of the lost battle. She ticked off the new sags around the jawline, the spreading crow's-feet around the eyes, the beginnings of crenulation along the throat, the general pastiness of the skin tone. She was a mess, she concluded. Looking deeply into her own eyes, was even more confirmation. That old fresh-faced California girl was gone, fixed in history only in old photographs and her mind's eye.

From the moment the little princess phone beside her bed had tingled its sad news, she had responded as someone walking in a cloud bank. She had taken four Darvons already during the day and now she was preparing to take another one. A sleeping pill on top of it might be too dangerous, she thought.

She was too strung out to think clearly. In general terms, she characterized herself as deeply hurt, but her feelings were so numbed by drugs that she couldn't be sure about the extent of the psychic pain, except that she was numb, beyond feeling. Self-pity, nevertheless, dominated what little emotion she could muster. The familiar "Why me?" clanged a litany in her head.

Perhaps at age twenty-five it would have been easier to accept, to shrug off like a bad cold, but with more than half the shooting match over, it was tough. Tougher than hell, because she had fantasized herself in the White House, had already begun to redecorate those gorgeously cavernous rooms, seen herself walking down the long curving staircase to the main entrance hall, gliding downward in a flowing, gossamer Paris gown.

It was the kind of fantasy that little girls have when they play with dolls. She recalled that safe, warm world in her father's house, the wonderfully green lawns stretching to the lake's edge, the birds chirping endlessly in the morning. It was a great pastoral dream on a shelf in her memory, a lost, irretrievable world.

Her father's hand, soft in the center, a bare roughness along the inside of the joints from tennis, was always a dominant image in her life. That marvelous hand that drew her on their long walks, along streets to infinity, to circuses and puppet shows, to toy stores and candy parlors and other places with sweet smells and happy colors.

What would he have said now? She knew! Betrayal is betrayal is betrayal. "Did I know?" she asked herself, asked her image in the mirror. Suspicion doesn't mean confirmation. Yes, she had been suspicious. Nights and weekends away from home. Surely, he could control himself when away. She acquiesced. The cause was everything. A political wife expects absences, like a navy wife. Perhaps even accepts an occasional clandestine sexual encounter. After all, men were different than women. Her sense of the erotic was not as highly charged as his. Dirty things just never turned her on. And she just couldn't bring herself to suck that thing, although many of her friends admitted that they did—some even said they liked it. It was disgusting. Maybe that's why he would step out on her, to get someone, some slut like that black bitch, to suck his thing. She shuddered. What was the world to think of her? Poor Karen, they would surely say secretly. Poor two-timed Karen. It was mortifying.

I had to be a wife, mother, friend, political ally, she thought. All those endless banquets, handshakes, smiles, speeches, trips. She had memorized three whole speeches and had gotten real good at making them. Smile here, Karen. Tell that little joke here, Karen. Raise

both hands here, Karen. In her sewing room, she kept thick scrap-
books of his career, their career; and sometimes going through them,
looking backward, it was totally unreal, as if everything that had
happened was to other people.

They liked being celebrities. She liked it, loved it, revelled in it,
wallowed in it. "My greatest political asset," Don would tell everybody. And she was. Karen Whitford, the all-American girl. You're
everybody's dream wife.

Then she knew with certainty what her father would have
advised. Leave him! In his life there was little truck with compromise. Word—"the word" was everything. Honor was the great,
numero uno virtue. You died for honor. You ransomed your soul for
honor. People said he was a right-winger, an ultraconservative. But
he believed in individual responsibility, a lost virtue in today's
world. Don's politics inflamed him.

"We built this country on individual responsibility."

"Technology has made it too big for the individual to cope. Only
joint efforts can pay off. The government must assume the total
coordination of this joint effort."

"Technology does not preclude individual responsibility."

They would argue long into the night.

"Bullhead" was Don's inevitable parting shot, but under his
breath. No one called Dr. Whitford a bullhead to his face.

Dad was right, because individual responsibility was supposed to
work for marriage too. Her anger rose in her. If only I were stronger,
like dad.

What did that girl, that—what was her name—Jackson, give him
besides a good suck? On top of everything, she had to be a Negro.
The whole world will feel sorry for poor little Karen Whitford
James. As for the great senator and that ass of a hanger-on, Lou
Castle—well, for one thing, the presidency will go down the tube.
What a chance he had! He would have whipped the president badly.
All the polls said so. And the boys were so proud of him. The boys.

He had never been a father to the boys; he was always away. She, too. She had tried to soften the blow, lied to them, told them not to worry. Lies within lies within lies.

Maybe now she had carte blanche to have an affair of her own. She had creamed her face and massaged the goo into the skin. After all, she also had her desires. It was just that they were different than his. I must be a shallow woman, she thought. I am a shallow woman. Why don't I have the same passionate nature? Self-doubt had now crept in with self-pity. One thing is certain, he'll be faithful now. He got caught before the eyes of the world. He couldn't step out of line again. That's a consolation. And he's still young enough to stick it out another five years. Maybe it all happens for the best. Tears began to well up in her eyes. "I will not cry," she said aloud. "Dad wouldn't like me to. Why don't I have more fight in me? I'm a sad, weak bitch."

She put on her nightgown and lay down on top of the covers. Where was Don now? He said he couldn't bear to come home. He needed to expend energy. Anything but be with me. It could be that she had failed him.

She dozed. Then she opened her eyes and Don was moving around the room. The sickly smell of alcohol was intense.

"You stink like a brewery," she said harshly. If only she could be more forgiving. She would try to be more forgiving.

"I had a few drinks."

She could hear him throwing his shoes on the floor, unzipping and dropping his clothes, leaving them where they fell. He lay back next to her.

"Well, it's been one hell of a day," he said.

She thought, "What does a wife say to a husband in moments like these?" If only he would turn toward her.

As if he had read her thoughts, he did so.

"I need you to forgive me," he said. But there was little conviction in his tone, as if he were saying it by rote, as if it were expected of him. Well, it was, she thought. She didn't answer him at first.

How did she fail him? He brought his body closer. The smell of alcohol was nauseating. She turned her face away. He whispered in her ear, "Forgive me. Forgive me. Forgive me." She could feel the hardness under her nightgown.

He pinched her buttocks. His breath came shorter, heavier. Her hand found his sex. She stroked gently.

"I am feeling something," she thought. "Why am I feeling something?" Her head moved down his chest, her tongue over his stomach and then her mouth was over his erect member.

"I am as good as anybody," she thought.

XXVII

"All in all," Davis said, "I'd say we're on our own ten-yard line and we'll have to punt."

He was not one to use sporting expressions. It must have been a line picked up from Barnstable, who was beginning to show the effects of the ordeal. His eyes were encased in black pockets. Don, on the other hand, was strangely fresh, his face again returned to its old look of balance. He appeared to have slept well and was now eating his breakfast with relish. Virginia, the maid, quietly poured their coffee. The morning papers were piled beside him, but he had not opened them. Davis, too, seemed fresher, alert, his ice-blue eyes as intense as ever. I was numb with fatigue, having twisted and turned all night, trying to understand the careening chain of events. My chest still hurt from last night's exertions. I noticed that Don's right fist was carefully taped, like that of a professional boxer.

"Must have bumped it somewhere," he said, winking at me, but putting an end to the subject. His spirits were extraordinary.

"Where the hell did you guys go last night?" Barnstable had asked.

"Walked around. Had a few," I said, hoping that Barnstable would drop the subject.

"It was a dumb chance," Barnstable said. "It was dangerous."

"Forget it."

"Were you recognized?"

"No," I said.

"Where did you go?" Barnstable tried again.

"Stop worrying. I wasn't recognized."

The bloody face of the man on the floor of the bar came back to me. What must the man be thinking now? How could he know that by an accident of fate, he was a victim of forces beyond his comprehension, beyond his own daily rounds, a foil for some-one else. Who was this man? He was merely a sacrifice. It was a cruel trick to play on this man. Oh, shit, why am I getting so damned philosophical?

"Leave it alone," I said. Barnstable pouted, repressing his anger.

"Okay, gentlemen," Don said. "Where do we go from here? I'm ready now."

Davis stood up. He was neatly dressed in a grey suit, dark tie, white shirt—a fastidious man, totally absorbed. He had been with us eight years, a smart-assed kid straight out of USC, always con-trolled. He had that uncanny ability to orchestrate well in a small group. Hell, he was always the best salesman in the room, articulate and unflappable. I envied this quality in him. When not doing his thing, he was a pretty cold fish, completely nonsocial, stuck to him-self. I had never seen him with a date.

"The options are narrowed," Davis began, standing up and remov-ing the cover on a large art pad. He rested it on a countertop and held it up for all of us to see. He was energized by all the strategies he had worked out in his mind. I know he must have worked all night. The man was indefatigable. On the top of the page he had written in magic marker, "Options." Below that, "1. To make 'The Speech.' " "2. Not to make 'The Speech.' "

"In order to evaluate these options," he said, "we must first reach a basic conclusion. One, we are no longer a contender for the next Democratic presidential nomination." He looked around at us. Acceptance was obvious. I saw Barnstable shake his head. He had the most to lose. He was older. We could wait. "Two, the credibil-ity factor, while shaken, is not completely gone. To most of the sen-ator's hardcore supporters, the roots of credibility remain. Our opponents will always be our opponents; the rest, the vast middle, our basic election target, are probably ambivalent—although we must assume that at this moment in time, many have taken strong pro and con positions, which, in my opinion, time will dissipate.

And three, the crowd mind is, thank goodness, quite fickle, and subject to manipulation. One device is the television speech. Such a speech has risks." He turned the page. "More options: One, we could botch the job with lousy presentation—unbelievability, bad wording, poor emphasis, bad makeup, bad lighting, inferior technology, and the rest. Murphy's Law; Anything that can go wrong goes wrong. Two, we could misread the timing; or, three, an outside event, some cataclysmic, natural disaster could throw the whole thing into a cocked hat. Believe it or not, the fact that we're still front page is a tremendous plus. People will want to listen. I believe we should make the speech, and make it in California at your mother's home in Carmel. There is something reassuring about a mother's home. And, certainly, I needn't go into the political importance of doing the speech in California."

"Suppose we do nothing?" Barnstable asked. I was just on the verge of asking the same question myself.

"I was coming to that." Davis flipped the page of his art pad on which was written, "No Speech Option." 1. Time-passage—our ally. 2. Crisis of believability.

"The shortest thing on earth is the human memory, someone once said. People will forget. The coals will be harder and harder to stoke and raise fire. Should we leave it alone? Batten down the hatches, lower the mainsail, and hope for the storm to pass?" His metaphors were insufferable this morning. I guessed it was because he was thinking about it hard last night and wanted to sharpen his arguments.

"There's a lot to say for that," Don said.

"Yes, there is," Davis pointed out. "But then we leave no record of denial. I think we've got to have that. Four, ten, twenty years from now we'll need it. Senator, the record—it haunts a politician, and no matter what you do or say in your political career, this episode will be your sword of Damocles. It will hang over you forever. It will never go away. Someone will always be dredging it up. There could be books written about it, articles in exploitation magazines and the

Sunday supplements for years to come. Some definitive statement must be made by you, publicly, aggressively, bravely."

"What you're saying is that no matter what happens in the future, I'll always have to run first against the record of this—episode."

"Exactly. I don't think we have any options on that one."

"But will they believe me?"

"I don't know," Davis said. "How can we be sure? But one thing is certain: whatever you say, most of the people must be willing to give you the benefit of the doubt."

"What doubt?"

"Doubt about your—fitness. Let's face it. Regardless of how the media reports the events, certain lingering doubts remain. Did you have an affair with the Jackson girl? Not that this is crucial. This is not England. You're allowed your sex here, providing it hangs out there in the clouds somewhere. It's only when the public validates it that it assumes negative political significance. If sex were a political danger, we might as well close up Washington. All we have to do on that point is deny it. Everybody might turn to each other and wink, but that will be the end of it, except for hardcore purists who won't support us anyway. The real problem is the eleven hour delay. This is where we have to finesse things. That's the point that's sticky."

"How do we attack it, in your opinion?" Barnstable asked. He seemed agitated, building up a hostility.

"Well," Davis said, "obviously I opt for the speech."

"I say," Barnstable said, "that we simply lie low. We're sticking our necks out, besides the expense. Why go through something as chancy as this?"

"We need the record," Davis replied quickly. "We've got to plant this doubt in people's minds."

"But will they believe it?" Don persisted.

"Some will. Some won't," Davis said. Don rubbed his taped hand against his chin.

"What do you think, Lou?" he asked.

"We're pretty well damaged as it is, Don. I think you've got to do something. There's also a hell of a lot of fence mending you've got to do inside your own structure—the staff, the contributors, even your three buddies in the senate, one of whom will most likely get the nomination, whoever he is. I feel for him. No matter what, he hasn't got a chance in hell. Christ, Don, I don't know. I'm inclined to go."

"Jack?"

"I wish I had a sure answer," Barnstable said sadly. "Maybe I'm just getting too old for this game." His self-pity was showing.

"Christine?"

She was sitting quietly in the corner, her inevitable steno pad on her knees.

"I appreciate your asking, Don. It's over my head. I go wherever the ship goes."

Don looked into his empty coffee cup.

"Do you think I should ask Chuck Chalmers? I got a note to call him."

"He'd be flattered," Davis said. "He's a powerful man. The *Washington Chronicle* can be a heavy gun in anyone's arsenal."

"What should I tell him?"

"Tell him exactly what you told the police chief," Davis said.

"You think he'll buy it?"

"He'll want to believe you," Davis said. "He'll buy it. If he does, then ask his advice."

"Suppose he gives me advice that I won't take—like not making the speech."

"Tell him it's a matter of conscience. Liberals go for that word," Davis said.

"You're such a leering cynic, Davis," Barnstable said. "I still say, don't make this speech. It's too much exposure. You'll have to tell an outright lie, a whopper. It'll come back to haunt you."

"There's no proof," I said.

"I'm afraid to say 'conscience' now," Barnstable said. "A lie is a lie."

"It's a white lie," Davis said.

"Just a little white lie," I sang.

"There really isn't a better option," Davis said, taking command again. "I've already got the setting planned. Your mother's place would be perfect. Might even take an opening shot of the rugged hills around there. And the sea. The mysterious forces of nature. I can hire out of San Francisco and bring in a good crew. It'll be expensive as hell, but well worth it."

"How's the old bank balance, Jack?" Don asked.

"We've got enough to cover, but that's about it. I still think it's crazy." He was seething.

"It'll be a rough two days for you, Senator," Davis said. "We'll also arrange a meeting at your mother's place with Schwartz, Basil, and Hammond."

Don made a grimace of derision.

"Let's face it, Don," Barnstable said. "They're the moneybags. If you can't convince them, you'll have one hell of a rough time convincing anyone else."

"I'll convince them," Don said confidently. He was right. The fat cats were easy. Feed them flattery. They soaked it up like a sponge.

"Then, there's Marlena's funeral," Davis said, "the day after tomorrow. We've got to have a good turnout for that. Fellow workers. All of us. I can assure you that will be one of the best-covered funerals in the country."

"I can't see why we have to go to the funeral, either," Barnstable said angrily. "All we should do now is just lay low—like gangsters. Just shut up."

"But it won't go away," Davis said.

"I just don't agree with it."

"Christ, Jack, it's a simple act of human decency," Don snapped.

"Human decency?" Barnstable said. "What's all this got to do with human decency?"

"How people perceive human decency," Don corrected. "It's a simple act of kindness, okay?"

"It's a charade," Barnstable said testily. He seemed suddenly out of place.

"Come off it, Jack. We're talking politics, image. We're not discussing moral questions."

"Yeah, Jack, what's eating you?" Don said.

He looked at each one of us.

"I guess I'm tired," he said, retreating. "I've been at it too long."

"Of course, we'll be at the funeral. That makes good sense," Don said. He smiled.

Don's cool optimism was infectious. I began to feel good about things for the first time since yesterday morning. Lord, it seemed like a century since Christine and I went walking along the beach. Well, why not? Confidence seemed to well up in all of us again. All was not lost, after all.

Davis grabbed the phone and began to arrange time on the California stations. We'd have to pay for an all-California hookup. The networks would carry choice quotes free. A good network news director would carry long excerpts from the speech. Davis, always the pro, would alert them in time to pick up a feed. The speech was to be on prime time and last no longer than five minutes, in just enough time for a network feed for the eleven o'clock news in the East.

"Okay, Christine," Davis said abruptly, "into the study. Let's take a crack at a first draft. I'd suggest you call Chuck Chalmers, Senator." They went into the study and closed the door.

"Well, Jack," I said. "What do you think?"

"I don't think anymore," he said, bitterly. "Because if I did think, I'd get the hell out of this racket. I wish I could be as optimistic as the rest of you. But the odds against recovery are staggering. Maybe I'm old fashioned. But how dumb do you really think the American people are? Pretty dumb, I guess. To tell you the truth, Lou, it's way over my head. Davis is in control now, like some scavenger. The media man. He's in control now. I'm like Christine. I guess I go where the ship goes."

"Come on, Jack. Hell, cheer up. It's all part of the game."

It was hard seeing this loyal workhorse down in the dumps, while the rest of us were buoyant. But Jack was pushing sixty, and he knew that time was as much his enemy as it was Don's friend.

At that stage, I don't believe I was too introspective. Events were occurring faster than I could absorb them. Yet there was something that had begun to nag at me, something indefinable, something I was fighting back within myself. I really don't consider myself a very important character in these events. There's something so terribly blunted in the way I perceive things. It was as if my feelings were gone—no passion, no compassion. It was as if I were strapped into an electric chair with all those electrodes in my head and on my hands and legs, and when they pulled the switch I wouldn't die because the electric current wouldn't hurt me. Because I couldn't feel anything. I felt fear. I know I felt fear last night in the bar. But that's where it seemed to end. No feeling beyond fear. Was I unique? Hell, no! There must be millions like me who have lost the power to feel anything—love, hate, anger, indignation—nothing. Worse than that, I had no destination. Don was at the tiller and I was on the deck, a listless crewman. I didn't have power over my own destiny. But who has? Even a controlled force like Don James was the victim of an enigma, of the mysterious power of the ocean. Maybe we could manipulate man's technology, but the fucking oceantides had got him anyway. I said to myself: Hey, you're Lou Castle. You know your role: Don's friend. His old roomie. Damon and Pythias. Bread and butter. Don't go and get reflective on us. That's no way to act. He didn't kill that girl. There it was. Even Lou Castle was saying it. The old goddamned guilt tugging at Lou Castle's sleeve. You're damned right he didn't kill that girl. Why the hell weren't we both Catholics? We could get it off our chests the easy way, in a dark cubicle talking to a faceless man.

XXVIII

A reporter is a hunter, Ernie knew, and all true hunters develop instinctive maneuvers, intuitive machinations. Just as man adapts to his environment and develops strategies of accommodation, Ernie moved with the surefootedness of a deer in the forest.

In the end he had agreed with Chalmers about proof or, at the very least, a kind of corroboration. He could not bring himself to believe that the great Charles Chalmers could prostitute himself, the newspaper, his vision.

The truth could be viewed through any prism. Every good reporter knew this. The light could change the angle, distort the image, but in the end, the prismatic illusion dissipated. And even when all light failed, the truth was there to touch. Preconception was always dangerous. The model could be wrong; the prefabricated matrix, a bad fit.

Chalmers was simply goading Ernie to produce the truth, absolute truth, or at least to discover a set of facts leading to a single logical, unalterable conclusion.

Even now, Ernie could feel his role of hunter, as the blood scent taunted his nostrils and urged him to the kill.

The drive back to Washington was tiring. His mind raced around on a track of white heat. His spirits ranged from unbridled elation to adject depression. He believed he found, in the almost mute evidence of the grieving father, all the proof he had needed. But intuition, feelings, sentiment could be deceiving, expecially to a reporter. What he needed was concrete, dispassionate proof to satisfy Chalmers. Piecing together a played scenario involving two adults in a sexual encounter seemed reasonably simple for an experienced reporter. Something literally exuded from the pores, antennae sharpened, sixth senses operated. Clues were everywhere.

The core of the issue was not the sexual encounter itself, but rather the calculated moves to deceive, to manipulate the public. The so-called proof was merely trivia. So Senator James was having an affair with a black girl. Hardly a startling act in itself. How did that affect his ability to govern, his concept of political leadership, his beliefs, if he had any, in ethical principles? That was the wheat. He was in search of the chaff.

Senator James's office was a beehive of studied moves. People moved around the reception room of his office like cheery automatons with smiles pasted across their mouths. Doors to inner offices were closed. A bright-eyed woman sat at the reception desk clicking away at her typewriter, crisp and busy. Undoubtedly the order had come down to look crisp and busy. Four staff people sat in the reception room: the receptionist and three others, two women and a man, a black man. All seemed preoccupied and intense.

"May I speak to someone in charge of the office?" Ernie said, humility oozing. He identified himself haltingly, searched for his press card, conscious of acting out the mannerisms of the unslick, the inarticulate. It was the standard investigative device to get people to put down their guard.

"I'm terribly sorry, Mr. Rowell," the girl said, aggressively sweet. "No reporters are being seen."

"Yes, I can understand that," Ernie said. "You see, I'm just looking for someone who could tell me a little about Miss Jackson."

"So sad about Miss Jackson," the receptionist said with sincerity. Then adding quickly, "She worked for the committee. The committee office is down the hall."

"Did you know her?" Ernie asked.

"Oh, yes," the girl said. "She was a wonderful, a fabulous person."

"So I understand."

"A really fabulous person."

He looked at the girl, knew she had been programmed in advance, but took the plunge anyhow.

"You think she was having an affair with the senator?" he said, certain he was being heard by everyone in the room.

It washed over her like burning lava, bowling her over with its swiftness.

"Mr.—"

"Rowell."

"I really think that you're being rude. How can you be so rude at a time like this?"

"I'm sorry," Ernie said, retreating. He had watched the three other staff people in the outer office for effect. Only the black man had stirred perceptibly. He could almost see the man's ears cock.

Afterwards, he had gone to the offices of the committee. There, his interviews were more businesslike. They wouldn't let him speak to the clerks. He would have to come back. Only the committee's executive director would see him. The man was loquacious, casual, but skillfully guarded.

"You know how it is when you're finishing up a report," he said. "Hell, it was extremely important to the senator. Let me tell you, these birds have to write legislation based on that report that will affect our educational process for generations. Marlena was a key person in its preparation. It was very proper for her to be there, very proper."

Ernie listened carefully, hoping for an echo, a hint. There were plenty of those, but no fresh leads. The executive director was too deflective, dwelled too much on the report, the nonessentials. Ernie wondered if the man really thought he was being convincing, if he felt satisfied that he was outwitting him. He would probably tell his boss, "Reporter from the *Chronicle* was snooping around. I sent him packing. He was a nosy bastard."

"Come on," Ernie said, deliberately reassembling his features, erasing the humble bumpkin look. "Are you seriously expecting me to believe that horseshit? All I want to know was how long the affair was going on. What kind of a girl was Jackson? Everybody in town knows your senator would fuck a wall. Stop this bullshit."

The man feigned indignation, a favorite ploy of the obvious liar. "You guys always making something out of nothing. Anything for a story."

"We're not going to print your bullshit."

The man turned white. He was the perennial bureaucrat, his job on the line. He was undoubtedly wondering whether he had said anything, even the slightest hint of something quotable.

"Forget it," Ernie said, taking him off the hook. "Just show me Marlena's desk."

He took him to a back room and pointed to a cluttered desk in a corner, piled high with publications and memoranda. There was a picture of Mr. Jackson on her desk, his face shiny from too much flash, the face without a trace of the dignity he had seen in person. Casual photography was not kind to a black face.

Ernie started to touch the desk.

"Please, Mr. Rowell, I've showed you the desk. There's little to be learned from it. The fact is that we all respected Marlena. You'll find very few people who had anything bad to say about her. She was brilliant and dedicated."

"And beautiful."

"Yes, she was beautiful."

All he had wanted was to get the feel of her environment, to put her in context. He knew that despite her death, she was a trivial actor in the upcoming events. She had said her lines, had done her gig, and then had exploded, her remains scattered, like confetti, over everything. His focus remained narrow. He hadn't the patience to go through the whole staff learning about Marlena Jackson's character or ambitions. He felt guilty about it. He was not doing the sidebar feature on Marlena Jackson, the why's and wherefore's of her life, the momentous event of her death. That was another story, perhaps, for another time, another place. A Sunday supplement piece, perhaps. The kind that always started with a question: "Did she know that her death would change the course of history?"

He tried a few questions on some members of the staff as he departed. They were tight-lipped, banal, and finally insulted when he probed deeper. One girl called him a "dirty bastard."

"Only filth. That's all you guys are interested in. Only filth," she said.

He could understand their feelings. But the method was essential. He had made sure that each person had heard his name. Feedback would come. Sexual secrets were impossible to keep on the Hill, where the starfuckers were as thick as Indians in an old Western and carried their scalps on public display like badges of honor. The result of all this probing wasn't even worth more than a paragraph buried deep in the story like a mine. He turned and, without an acknowledgment or good-bye, left the office.

Walking into the cafeteria, he filled a cup of coffee at the counter, paid the check and sat down. His bones ached. He sipped deeply. In his mind, he began to write his story, toying with leads.

"Every philanderer has a nightmare fantasy," one began. "There is a moment in life when the vectors of disaster interconnect. It happened this week to Senator Donald James," another began. "Last weekend Armageddon came to a golden knight," went another. They were all too conclusive, too damning, too unfair. He would have to think about it. His mind was too tired.

"Was it conceivable that he was wrong?" he thought. Tiredness had brought doubt in its wake. He waited until the coffee was lukewarm, swallowed it down to the grounds, and stepped up to the counter for a refill. It was then that the voice intervened.

"I'll pick you up in front of Union Station—" the black voice said. There was no escaping the inflection. "—in twenty minutes."

He knew without turning that the voice was directed at him. He nodded, filled the coffee cup, and walked slowly back to his table. The man's back receded as he moved away. It was the black man in the reception area of the senator's office. "Paydirt," he thought. Judas had shown himself.

Looking at his watch, he let five minutes pass before he finished off the second cup. He moved swiftly out the door of the cafeteria, through the corridors into the street.

It was almost his first bit of acquired knowledge of the Washington scene. The army of blacks that worked for the government had a built-in underground, an infallible communications system, like prisoners in a penitentiary. They cleaned the huge government buildings, emptied the trash bins, polished the brass, served the food. Wherever leaders moved, blacks moved in invisible battalions, a fixed part of the scene, like the gold frames on the oil paintings of the celebrated which graced the walls of the offices of the high and the mighty.

He walked quickly now, monitoring his time as he approached the station, the Greek temple monument to the Iron Horse. The symbolism seemed so appropriate. They couldn't recapture the truth and purity of the Hellenes and so they copied their buildings instead. Reaching the cavernous entrance of the columned building, he stood at the curb, a beacon for the black man to navigate towards. He did not have long to wait.

It was a big, nondescript, white Buick, old and dented, its grill smashed. The man opened the door. He got in quickly, and the car lurched forward.

"I'm Pierce," the man said.

He was youngish, a scraggly black moustache sprouting valianty over thick Negroid lips. His hair was in the natural style. The eyes drooped slightly, long eyelashes curving over the lids.

The car cranked up and swerved in a sharp right into North Capitol Street, then right again into the colorless jungle of Northeast Washington, a section long abandoned by the Whites, now decaying like forgotten fruit. In the security of the endless black neighborhoods, the car slowed.

"She was jazzing the honky," the man said, the accent and idiom in exaggerated street-nigger dialect. Ernie remained silent. The black man looked at him bitterly.

"She was jazzing the honky, man," he repeated. "That nigger bitch." He opened the window and spat.

"How do you know?"

"I seen 'em."

"Where?"

"Mostly in that cat Lou Castle's pad over in Southwest. I'd bring 'em messages, packages. I'm a messenger. Once I seen her naked in the bedroom with the big man. They closed the door. She knowed I seen them. But they never paid me no mind. Not this motherfuckin' lackey nigger. He laks his jelly roll, man. And nobody rolls jelly like a nigger girl." He paused and lit a half-smoked cigar.

"Don't you like the senator?" Ernie asked.

Pierce was silent for a moment. He chewed on his cigar. "He a good man, good man. It's that uppity Jackson woman. All the time so high. Nevah talked to me. I ain't dirt."

So there it was, Ernie thought. Simple jealousy with a racial base. "Anybody else know about this?"

"Besides Mr. Castle, Miss Donato, few more people."

"Like who?"

"Doorman maybe at Mr. Castle's. Maybe Marlena told some people. Lotta jazzin' goes on up on the Hill."

"Why are you telling me these things, Pierce?"

"Ah got my reasons."

Ernie felt foolish pursuing the obvious. Here was the classic inferiority complex, the bane of the black male, sharpened by frustration. He understood. Senator James had ripped off one of their women. If the girl had been white, there would be a different set of reasons. Betrayal had no racial base. Confirmation would come from others. He was sure of that. He wanted to tell the man that his malice, his revenge, was nothing really, a small useless fire giving no heat. But jealousy, compounded by frustration, was a strong enough motive. Soon, he was certain, he would find a snakepit of other motives. Girls whose loneliness sapped their compassion. Bitter older women who fantasized that they too might park their shoes at the foot of the senator's bed. Ambitious people to whom Marlena was a threat. He would spend this day of penance on the Hill, and he would hate every minute of it.

He felt certain that this was the kind of "proof" that Chalmers really wanted. It seemed so pointless, somehow. Only a healthy helping of self-delusion would deflect the truth. It was a valid point in the story even as speculation. The denial was pure sophistry, cynicism of the highest order. Why was he pursuing this make-work?

The black man dropped him off at Union Station. Without a word, he got out and walked back toward the Capitol. He knew he would find an endless chain of witnesses to corroborate the story.

XXIX

"Chuck—this is Don James."

"Great to hear your voice, Don."

"Good to hear yours. A friend in need and all that."

"How are you bearing up?"

"Under the circumstances, I'd say fair to middling."

"And Karen?"

"Middling."

"What are you going to do?"

"There's only one way, Chuck. I'm going to tell it like it is."

"Don, you know you don't have to tell me anything. After all, I am a reporter."

"I know, Chuck. I also know that this blows me out of the water as far as the nomination is concerned. God, how I wanted to take on that bastard in the White House. Well, I guess I made his day."

"I'm sure of that."

"Chuck, I hate to disappoint all the vultures, but it's not the way it looks. You know me well enough to know that the worst piece of strange sounds pretty good to me. But not this weekend. We really went out there to work. The whole thing was a fluke. One rotten fluke. The damned tides were vicious. She was right at the edge—and poof."

"Frankly, Don, I really don't think that's important. But how in the name of hell did you allow yourself to wait so damned long before calling for help?"

"Chuck, Lou and I nearly killed ourselves trying to save that girl. Christ, they had to pull me out of the water. I thought I was finished. I was out. I was actually out. If you've ever been confronted with a circumstance like that you'd know that it's difficult to act rationally. I had to assemble my thoughts. I had to get it together."

"I understand. But why so long? That bugs me. I could see two, three hours at the outside, but eleven. That's the tough part."

"We searched up and down the beaches. We thought maybe the tides would roll her back. You don't lose hope so fast in situations like this. Chuck, she was a wonderful girl, a fine person. I've talked to her father."

"What was his reaction?"

"He's destroyed. What could I tell him? We're all going to the funeral. It's sad. The whole thing is sad."

"I know, Don. I don't quite know what to say. It's too damned bad. We'll just have to put up with another five years of that fascist animal in the White House."

"Don't be so pessimistic. The Democrats could surprise you."

"No, Don. You were the man."

"I haven't given up, Chuck. I'm going to fight this thing. That's one of the reasons I was so anxious to talk to you. I need some advice."

"Shoot."

"I'm thinking of going on television in California. I've got to tell my side of the story. I've got to make a record of it. There's too many ambiguities about this incident. I know the time lag thing will haunt me. But that's what happens when you're in the frying pan. Besides, nothing a politician says is wholly believed, anyway. There has actually been some hint that I murdered the girl. Can you imagine?"

"Yes, I can imagine. Let's face it. You've got passionate enemies."

"Then I've got to explain this business of no immorality, no sex."

"That will be a tough one to swallow."

"You're too cynical, Chuck."

"You mean logical. I know you, Don."

"It's either that or hang up my cleats."

"I suppose."

"I'm fighting for my political credibility, Chuck. I've got my constituency. I owe them. Look, it's one hell of a responsibility. I'll need their patience. I hope they'll be able to wait five years. I hope I can tough it out."

"I guess you haven't much of a choice. Your Democratic competitors are a bunch of assholes—gutless."

"What do you think, Chuck?"

"I don't know, Don. I'm not sure."

"You know how a politician's record keeps popping up."

"No doubt about that."

"The truth always wins out in the long run."

"Yes, it all comes out in the wash."

"I'm a victim, Chuck. A victim of fate. I simply will not let fate defeat me. I believe in my sense of mission. I believe in my political posture. And frankly, Chuck, if I may be immodest, I think there are lots of people in this country who need my political viability. The poor, the outs, the minorities, the victims. Maybe they'll understand. But I think I owe it to them to try to make them understand. Or should I roll over and die? There has got to be a voice on the other side, a strong voice."

"It's worth a shot, Don. And let the chips fall where they may."

"I hope to hell they believe me."

"I always say that if you tell the truth you'll be believable. That's the way we run this goddamned paper."

"Thanks, Chuck. I'm glad I asked your advice. Keep your fingers crossed."

"You know how I feel."

XXX

"Let's try it from the top again, Senator," Davis said.

"My fellow Californians. The tragic events of the past weekend have, as you know, received quite a lot of attention in television and newspapers. Judging from the letters, telegrams, and telephone calls that I have received from you, my constituents, I felt it only appropriate to explain to you this tragic episode—"

"Strike 'explain,' " Davis said. "That was one word that was bothering me. You're not explaining. That smacks of justifying. I don't trust the word."

"How about 'outline'?" Don asked, pencil poised.

"Yes, that might make sense," Davis agreed. "Try 'outline.' That's more—"

"Honest," I said.

"—outline to you this tragic episode."

"Too many 'tragics,' " Davis said. "Gilding the lily. How about, 'to inform you directly about the events surrounding the accidental death'—?"

"That's even better," Don agreed. "Yes, I like that."

" '—to inform you directly about the events surrounding the accidental death of one of our most dedicated staff members, Marlena Jackson, a woman of rare intelligence, wit and charm. Miss Jackson had joined a group of our staff people for what is quite commonplace in Washington, the 'working weekend,' to complete the 'Report on Minority Education,' a project of the subcommittee of the senate on education, of which I am privileged to be chairman—' "

"Are you sure we're covered on that, Don?" I asked. "It came as a surprise to see it in the draft. Christine, I didn't think it was finished."

197

"Absolutely," Christine said. "On Friday, I asked Albert Barker, the subcommittee executive director, to give me a copy of the draft. I actually packed it in the senator's briefcase. I hadn't remembered it until Davis, here, began dictating. There are all sorts of people who could substantiate that fact."

"But did he specifically assign Marlena to work on it with the senator on that weekend?" I asked.

"No, not specifically," Don said. "But I do have some prerogatives as senator. Also, and this is the clincher, Marlena had a great deal to do with the report in a substantive way. I'd say we're covered."

"All right," Davis said. "Let's continue."

" 'This report is one of the most important documents ever undertaken dealing with this subject. It brings together all the arguments and alternatives which we, in the Congress, must come to grips with if we are ever to arrive at a sane way to improve the quality of education in an environment that offers equality of opportunity.' "

"Good," Davis said. "I like that. Very statesmanlike. As long as we don't get into specifics."

"How can we do that?" Don said. "I haven't even read the damn thing."

"I better read it quickly," I said. "Especially after what you're going to say about it."

" 'We in California know what it means to enjoy our beaches. The simple pleasures of tossing a ball around and jogging along the water's edge is one of the true delights of the seashore. You all know how much I love sports and exercise. I've always believed that the way to clear one's mind for further work was through these means, and I encouraged such activity among my staff.' "

He paused. "You know, I like that." He went on.

" 'Miss Jackson, along with the others, joined us. If ever there was a moment that one would wish to eliminate in one's life, it was that moment when Miss Jackson, by some inscrutable act of pure chance, slipped along the water's edge, and, again, with the intervention of fate, found herself swept into the tide. It all happened so quickly. It was as if the ocean had fingers which suddenly gripped her and dragged her into it.' Do you think it's dramatic enough?" Don asked.

"A little purple, perhaps. But the way you say it, I think it sounds very sincere, very probable," Davis said.

"You don't think it needs even more drama. It seems too matter-of-fact."

"It sounds fine."

"I want them to believe it. Because it's true."

"What's that got to do with it?" Davis said.

Don paused and shook his head.

I had a suggestion, scribbled hastily on the back of an envelope.

"How about something like, 'One moment she was there, full of vigor and energy, and another moment she was fighting for her life in an angry sea.' "

"Great, Lou. Terrific. Let me put it in."

"I agree," Davis said. "It gives a more vivid picture, a scene of tragedy, the struggle, life and death."

Don finished penciling it in and continued.

" '—My administrative assistant, Lou Castle, and myself, quickly jumped in after her. Both of us, products of the California shore, were strong swimmers. Ladies and gentlemen, I have never in my life been so close to death. (I'll look them square in the eye right here.) The tides were beyond conception in their strength. I am thankful to God that I am alive, but deeply saddened that all my efforts, all of the efforts of Mr. Castle, were not enough to save the life of this fine young woman. As I told her bereaved father, we tried and failed. When she went down below the surf, she simply disappeared. We never saw her alive again.' "

"I think that's wonderful," Davis said. "Now if only you keep the delivery on that level, it will be perfect."

"God, I feel sorry for that girl," Don said.

He continued: " '—That is the simple truth. You, my constituents, are entitled to know this directly from me. I would not be here today unless, in my judgment, it were not absolutely necessary to dispel the confusion about this episode. After all, it does involve your senator. You have a right to know the facts without benefit of other interpretations by the middlemen of the press, radio, and television.' "

"Doesn't 'middlemen' sound too harsh?" Davis asked. "It seems hostile. I mean, there's no point in getting the press down on us."

"I think maybe you're right. How about simply striking everything after 'interpretations.' They'll know what we mean."

"I'll buy that," Don said.

" 'But most of all, you have a right to know that there was no immorality involved. Miss Jackson was a woman of the highest moral character. Any attempt to cast aspersion on the conduct of either Miss Jackson or myself is false, and, I might add, insulting to me and my family.' "

"Instead of 'false,' " Davis said, "how about 'simply not true.' I wish I could give you a logical reason for the change. It just sounds so much more sincere."

Don made the change without argument.

" 'I have been your senator now for nearly fourteen years. My principal consideration has at all times been the wishes of the people of California. I believe in this country, in its promise and its dreams. But all of us, yes, all of us, are victims of the vicissitudes of fortune, accidents of fate. They come from out of the blue, a kind of misguided missile from a cosmic force too illusive to understand. The simple fact is that, by the same random selection that snuffed out the life of Marlena Jackson, I have been spared. One cannot accept such a reprieve from death without a resurgence of devotion.

" 'Therefore, I have only one objective now, to get on with the unfinished business of this great country, to vote my conscience on those matters that profoundly affect this and future generations. These are critical times.' "

"Beautiful," I said. The guy was good.

"When you say that," Davis said, "emphasize strength. Perhaps you could narrow your eyes. I'll have the cameras come in close. You've got to look like the Rock of Gilbraltar."

" 'We had chosen a beach house for our worksite for two reasons,' " Don continued. " 'The first was that it was away from the distractions of Washington and yet only a few hours' drive from our homes. The second was that it enabled us to refresh ourselves along the seashore and take normal relaxation, between sessions of work on the report.' "

"I wonder if we need mention who gave us the beach house?" Don asked.

"I'd rather not. Why insert another personality if we don't have to?"

The beach house had been lent to us by a neighbor of Don's in Washington, who, with his family, was touring Europe. He was also a bit of a swinger, although he had quite a respectable façade. Even though he would know how to field any inquiries, I agreed that it was not necessary to inject another personality into the speech.

" 'We had put in ten hours the first day and starting again at 6:00 A.M., we began another long day of work which lasted late into the afternoon. At approximately 4:00 P.M., I adjourned the working session and suggested some physical relaxation along the beach—' "

"Strike 'physical,' " Davis said. "I didn't quite catch that in the second draft."

"These are critical times," Don practiced. "I'll emphasize 'critical.' These are critical times." He grimaced. "Do you think I need more material here to accentuate what I mean, like threats from abroad, inflation, energy crisis."

"I doubt it," Davis said. "It'll look too much like you've set up a straw man. Too much like the president's method. Too hollow. Just make the statement and forget it."

Don nodded and continued: " 'My wife, who sits by my side today, with my mother in her home, is weathering this episode with the same devotion—' "

" 'Devotion.' 'Devotion' seems to mean that they are sticking with you through thick or thin. That's the wrong word. We need one that says they've been put upon and are bearing up, but that they know you are telling the truth."

"You're right. I hadn't noticed that," Don said.

"How about—" I looked at the copy of the speech in my hands— " 'join with me in sending condolences'?"

"Yes," Don said. "I think you're right. Even the reference to wife and mother is a bit heavy."

"It's pure corn," Davis said. "But desperately needed—"

". . . 'my wife and mother in whose home I am delivering this message join me in expressing the deepest sympathy to the family of Marlena Jackson. Thank you and good night.' "

"I think it's fine," Davis said. "But there is one thing that has me disturbed. Do you think it needs a black reference? We did it in the earlier statement."

"I don't know," Don said. "I thought of that as I was talking, but rejected it. I think it's an unneeded complication."

"I doubt if there's any political mileage in it," Davis pointed out. "It's probably inappropriate."

"I think any time you call attention to her blackness, you hurt yourself," I said. "There are too many people who just hate blacks. Someday you might need those rednecks and nigger-haters."

"You're probably right, Lou."

"My own view is that intercourse with black women is acceptable, has long been acceptable as a kind of good old Southern tradition. My rejection of the appellation is because we've characterized her as being brainy, body-less. Let's just forget about skin color."

"Now we've got to work on delivery, Senator. I think you'll do the dramatic parts with great feeling. But you've got to guard against overplaying your hand and giving it too much slickness. I wish you could memorize it, but that would be leaving too much to chance. I'll work out the technical details so that you can read it from a crawl or cue cards."

"I'll have five hours on the plane to practice it."

Christine went into the study to type the final draft. Don slouched in his easy chair and scratched his head.

"I hate to ask," he said, smiling, "but how the hell are we doing out there?" He had deliberately avoided reading the newspapers.

"You really want to know?" Barnstable answered. He had sat watching us silently without comment. He was seething with anger. We all ignored it. You could read the sad news on his face.

"No, I guess not."

Barnstable had already given us a kind of summary. Nasty letters, telegrams, phone calls. Reams of newspaper copy with innuendo piled on innuendo. Davis, to his credit, had foreseen all this as the first wave. It was, literally, only innuendo, not fact. Vagueness dominated. Nobody could pin down anything more than suppositions. The police chief had apparently continued to be tight-lipped. And none could penetrate Mr. Jackson's grief. There were no witnesses. Reports were reduced to careful speculation. The political columnists had a field day. Though they were unable to assess the long-term impact on Don's political career, most of them agreed that he was out of the contention for the presidential stakes this year. Who didn't know that? Eaton and Nevins went so far as to write his political obituary for all time. Finished, they said. But that wily old fox Antwerp was not writing him off so fast. True, he had written, the American people were a bunch of middle-class hypocrites, but they were ready to be told what to believe, and, Don, as the columnist pointed out, had always been, "a master of the media." That's cynicism for you.

"Who gives a shit what any of them say?" Don said, slipping further down in the easy chair. "We'll play it one step at a time."

XXXI

Don's Chevy Chase house sits on a rise surrounded almost entirely by trees, accessible only by a sweeping driveway which approaches upward, winds past the front of the house, and dead-ends into a wall with barely room for cars to maneuver into the garage.

There is no sidewalk on the street, only a low wall that stretches along the frontage of the property. At dusk, the inevitable knot of reporters and photographers still kept their vigil at the foot of the driveway. Montgomery County police manned the cordon, letting through only those who had been cleared in advance.

The rest of that day was taken up by preparing the final draft of the speech and putting the senator's office staff to work getting the California trip confirmed and preparing the technical details of the broadcast. All day long, messages had been relayed that Senators Hopkins, Wilson, and Mudd had wanted urgently to speak with Don. We all knew what they wanted. The three had, in the folklore ways of Washington, made themselves available for the Democratic nomination. Publicly, of course, they all denied it. Apparently, most political strategists were in agreement on that one point of reticence. Don't start the active seduction scene until the girl is salivating and ready. Just stand there with the bulge in your pants and wait.

Hopkins, Wilson, and Mudd, like Don, were not amateurs in the political game. Hopkins, a World War II hero, had parlayed his notoriety to the senate from Oklahoma. He was now fifty-six, had learned to discipline his drawl in places where the drawl was not an asset, and had put together a solid organization that could provide strong coverage in the South and Southwest. Wilson was older. He had made two unsuccessful nominating runs before, but couldn't get it out of his system. Running for the presidency had become an addiction. He had one enormous failing. He talked too damned much, and, although he was popular with special interests such as labor, the blacks, the Jews, and others who formed the core of the liberal establishment, he could not quite shake the "flannel-mouth" image. He was from Michigan. Mudd was a Virginian, a middle-of-the-roader. Lincolnesque in appearance, with a great capacity to put away booze. He was the most entertaining speaker in the senate. Besides, he and his family were the tobacco people from Virginia and he had a personal fortune of astronomical proportions. Even jaded Washington had a special place in its heart for the super rich.

All three felt the need to speak to Don, and all wanted to do it separately. Like vultures, they had smelled blood and knew that Don's political carcass was ripe for the stripping. When the speech had been disposed of, the matter of the senators had to be dealt with.

"Their strategy is obvious," Barnstable pointed out. "They've written us off as an acceptable candidate. They also know that we've had to make the same decision. Now they need our people, our know-how, our money sources, and your tacit support, although they wouldn't want it to be made as a public commitment. They're going to fish like crazy for those who would be expected to be our delegates. What they don't know is that none of them can win."

"Hey, Jack, you can't tell a politician that. He always thinks he can win, even when he's being a realist." Don smiled.

"If you can't see one of them without the other at this time, you'll be starting a Donnybrook within the party."

"Individually, they're great guys," Don said. "We've had great times together. That Hopkins—he's insatiable. But when it comes to the presidency, that's a whole different ball game. They'd cut out their mothers' hearts and eat them if they thought it would get them the grand prize." He said it as if he, himself, was indifferent to the possibility. "If I know those boys," Don said, "they think I'm pretty broken up personally about all this. That's because that's the way they would react. They probably think I'm contrite, unable to function, and that I've holed myself up here to weather the storm."

"And that's what we want everybody to think for the time being," Davis said.

"How they must pity me."

"In that case," Davis said, "why not see them? Invite them all here tonight at the same time and don't tell any of them that the others are coming. They won't tell each other, and by the time they get to the driveway of your house, it will be too late. The reporters will all know."

"Great, Davis," Don said, slapping his thigh. "The mountain comes to Mohammed. That ought to start the political stocks moving up again."

"Unfortunately, not high enough, Senator. Just one little rung. It will make it appear that you are the kingmaker. That you're pulling the strings. It would make a great show of strength. They're going to be mad as hell at you, though."

"Yes, they will be. But the bastards will know I'm not dead yet."

Senator Virgil Mudd was the first to arrive. He kissed Karen and went into the den, where Don, Barnstable, Davis, and I were sitting. Don tried his best to look abject, but there was an unmistakable twinkle in his eye. I poured Mudd three fingers of Bourbon.

"Well, you bought it, Don. It was one bitch of a coincidence. I sympathize, my friend. I do sympathize." He drank his whiskey, downing half the glass in one gulp.

"You live by the sword and you die by the sword, Virgil. I just got caught, that's all."

Mudd sat down and spread his big body across the couch. He was a marvelously expansive man, with great charm and feeling, always the courtly Southern gentleman.

"I really appreciate your seeing me, Don." Both men looked at each other. They had worked together for fourteen years, jockeying themselves carefully into the right position. Both had their brain-

trusts, their strategy meetings. They knew all the nuances and subtleties of the game. Unfortunately, before Senator Mudd had time to
proceed with his expected pitch, the doorbell rang, and Karen
admitted Senator Billy Hopkins. He was boiling mad. He pecked
Karen on the cheek and strode angrily into the room.

"God damn it, Don, it's bad enough about this fix. We're all real
sorry it happened, but why did you have to embarrass us like this?"
He looked helplessly at Senator Mudd. "Virgil, it was a damned
lousy trick."

"Cool off, Billy. We've been had. Just sit down and enjoy it. You
might as well expect Sam Wilson to be bobbing in at any time now."

Wilson appeared on the scene in a more philosophical mood.

"For a fellow in as much political trouble as you, Don, you sure
got your crust."

When they had all arrived and had been helped to drinks, Don
got up and paced the room for a moment.

"I'm going to fight this thing, gentlemen. I know I'm written off
for this trip, and I wish all of you lots of luck. I feel pretty lousy
about what happened, as you all must know. But I intend to use
every angle to keep myself alive for the future. Politics is my life, as
it is yours."

"It's a damned shame, Don. You know we would have supported
you down the line," Virgil Mudd said. "We could have unseated that
son-of-a-bitch in the White House."

"Anyone speak to him today?" Davis asked.

"I did," Billy Hopkins said. "He was chipper as hell. You know
him—old true blue, Mr. Clean. There's a man whose public morality is
worse than the worst alley cat, while privately he's a bloodless turnip.
It's quite obvious that his chances have improved after all this."

"Do you think he'll be able to hold together his constituency?" I
asked. "You know his credibility is worn pretty thin."

Wilson looked about the room. He was the oldest of the group,
heavy-set, grey, with scraggly eyebrows.

"Will it upset you, Don, to talk blunt talk?"

"Not at all. That's what we've been doing for two days."

"I think his constituency not only will hold together, but as of this morning, it's a hell of a lot stronger. Your own strength, Don—the young people, blacks, all those flaming knee-jerk liberals have got to feel somewhat betrayed now that their hero finds himself with his presidential hopes shattered. As for the wavering middle, the fickle center, they'll go back to the president stronger than ever."

"That's our analysis," Don said crisply. "The breaks of the game."

"Recoverable, Don. You're young enough to recover."

"We think so, too," Davis said.

"Brave man, Don," Virgil Mudd said. "If anyone can do it, I guess you can. You've always had the advantage of us in your ability to charm the pants off a snake. When I first heard the news, I said to myself, 'Virgil, but for the grace of God, there goes you,' and I tried to picture the way I would react. I know one thing. I wouldn't be putting up such a brave face to my friends. I'd be holed up drunk somewhere, commiserating with my navel."

"Virgil, once you've lived in the nightmare that you've always thought you were about to have, it's a hell of a lot easier to endure it," Don said.

"It must be. But what really floors me is that I thought I'd find you contrite. And here you are cocky."

"I think it's wonderful," Wilson began. "I, too, thought I'd find you lower than a snake's asshole, and here you are bright-eyed and bushy-tailed, besting us with your usual public relations coup and spitting into the wind. We all look like a bunch of vassals come to pay tribute to a feudal lord. But now comes the question of reality. With you out, Don, we've got to decide how much fight it's all worth."

"A bitter primary could be a disaster," Davis said. "It has got to be a tough haul for any one of you. In my view, a primary fight could cost each of you about $20 million apiece. The election itself, three times that. With the president looking good, he'll raise all kinds of money in a walk. You'll have a tough time. Money is the ball game."

"I know," Mudd said, refilling his glass. "It's staggering."

"I don't think we need a lesson in realism," Hopkins pointed out. "We all know the risks, the hardships, the frustrations; and we don't have to sit here and articulate why we'd go through the fires of hell to shoot for it. The question, it seems to me, is that of expedience. Don is out of the race. We're afloat for the time being. Which way do you move, Don?"

"Stay neutral," Barnstable said. "Stay out of it."

"Don, you and I have been through a hell of a lot together," Hopkins said. "I wish to God, someone else had gotten into this mess. I would have gladly stepped aside. You know it. There was no real contest for the nomination. You had it in the bag. We were just playing around. Right, Virgil? Weren't we saying to each other just two days ago, Don was in. We couldn't muster enough strength between us to beat you."

"We did talk about that, Virgil," Mudd said. "I figure it would cost the family about five mil in the primaries to even put up a decent fight, and even then I'd lose."

"No contest, Don. It would have been no contest."

"Look, Don. We're big boys. You've got two choices. Back one or none," Mudd said, a rosy glow beginning to spread over his cheeks.

"Back none," Barnstable said angrily. He was losing his cool again.

"Take it easy, Jack," Don snapped.

"There's no percentage in it for us," Barnstable said. "Let's not dismantle our organization yet."

"Dismantle," Hopkins piped in. "Barnstable, your candidate is finished. You know it. I know it. Don knows it. None of us created your situation. We sympathize with it. It's a goddamned shame. But you knew what you were doing. Don't be self-righteous. We're in public life, too. If you stick your neck into a compromising noose, don't always be sure you're going to pull your head out before the hanging."

"Maybe from your point of view, Don," Wilson said, "we look like a pack of vultures ready to eat the body; but let's face it, you are presently washed up. Now the question is, can you do us harm by helping or hindering us? One of us is going to be the party's nominee. You've built an organization, a terrific organization. You've got great fundraisers, good advance people. This has been your business. I know why I came here today. I want your organization. So do they. So what's wrong with that?"

"Nobody is asking for special favors," Wilson said.

"The hell I ain't," Hopkins shouted. "Don, you and I have been friends for a long time. One of us has got to get the nomination."

"No question about that," Don said quietly.

"This is nuts, absolutely nuts," Hopkins said. "We should be meeting privately. This little joke of yours, Don, has got to backfire. We might look like a band of jackals now, but, at least, we have some credibility."

"No need to insult the man, Billy," Virgil Mudd admonished.

"Well, he has insulted us, you know. This whole staged event has been a lousy trick."

"Oh, come, off it, Billy," Mudd shot back. "Don has enough trouble on his hands without our problems."

"He sure does."

"So let's be gentle."

The undercurrent of bickering seemed strangely out of place. While Don had been the front-runner, there was more cordiality, more camaraderie. In politics, as in real life, yesterday's heroes were gone with the wind. Don sensed this.

"You don't have to humor me, gentlemen," he said with an attempt at affected dignity.

"You're not being humored, Don," Virgil Mudd said. "You're simply being told that reality has closed in on you. In the language of politics, your credibility gap is a mile wide. The only help that any one of us would want from you at this point is your organization, not the corpus delecti. That's not worth much at this point. I hope you don't mistake what I am saying to you for cruelty, Don. You know me better than that. You could stay in the background. Share in the fruits, so to speak."

"I understand perfectly the parameters of my position," Don said. "But I am still a member of the senate."

"And you'll have your hands full staying a member of that august body."

"I don't think so, Virgil."

He was learning the hard way that his political currency had suffered a big drop in value. Davis motioned me aside.

"Don't let it worry you," he whispered. "We've bested them. To the public, it'll still look like they've come crawling to Don for endorsement and help. They know it, too."

"I think they're being rough on him."

"They're going to eat their words."

Virgil Mudd poured himself another drink and held it up to the light. He shook his head and laughed.

"I'd put a gun to my temple before I supported any one of these creeps," Barnstable shouted.

"Gentlemen, gentlemen," Wilson admonished.

"For crying out loud, Jack," Don said testily.

"I wouldn't blame him," Hopkins said. He could be cruel. "He's lost his reason for being, Don. He's finished."

"Bastard," Barnstable hissed.

Barnstable was, indeed, on the verge.

"We're all under a strain," Don said.

"I can imagine," Mudd said. "Except that the whole business is unreal. After all, Don, what did you really do wrong? Nothing. It could have been any one of us in the senate of the United States, that worthy deliberative body. How many of us are closet queers, or compulsive masturbators, or transvestites, or alcoholics, or practicing God knows what kind of degeneracy. Someone once said that if you took us all as a profile of ambitious, most likely venal men, you'd come up with enough to make Krafft-Ebing look like he was writing the adventures of the Bobbsey Twins. But the people, whoever the hell they may be, prefer us as models; so we dehumanize ourselves. And when I go into the hinterland of the great state of Virginia, I hide the booze and suck cloves all day long. And, worse than anything, I don't give a damn that I do it. I tell myself I'm doing the right thing."

"Maybe it's better that way," Wilson said. "Maybe if we revealed the human side, it would be worse."

Well, they were revealing their human side now. It's amazing how philosophical those politicians get at times of crisis, like people sitting around at a wake. No discussion of the issues or the nitty gritty of the legislative process, obsessed only by the way other people observed them, judged them.

The talk droned on. It went round and round. There was no point to it. Everyone in the room knew the verdict. Don was just catching his breath. He would support no one until a winner was in sight.

I looked at Henry Davis, his blotterlike mind taking it all in, planning strategies, bits and pieces of public statements floating through his head.

XXXII

Who the hell was Henry Davis, anyway? It was one of those corrosive cranial itches that defies attempts at tranquility until, like an overripe pox, it explodes in the mind, and you had better find out who the hell Henry Davis was, simply to keep your mental equilibrium. The explosion took place in my bed as, unable to sleep, the events of the past few days raced through my mind.

After hours of this, it became apparent that one force dominated all of these events. This force was the mind of Henry Davis, which had us bobbing without gravity in the wind tunnel of his self-generating energy. It was like passing a kind of landmark every day of your life, never noticing it. Perhaps it is a tree or a house or a sign or a storefront. Then, through some mundane set of circumstances, there it is imprinted on your consciousness, dominating the daily round. First, there is the sense of wonder in that you've never noticed it before. When that passes, all you ever do is notice it. You pick at it, explore it in your mind's eye. It becomes an obsession within an obsession.

It was in that way that I suddenly noticed Henry Davis. And, once that door was opened, my mind began to travel back through the maze of my memory, to every encounter I ever had with him. I hired Henry Davis eight years ago, a skinny kid out of the University of Southern California. We assigned him as one of a group of advance men for Don's second statewide campaign. I couldn't remember a thing about his background other than the college from which he had graduated as a political science major. Lord save us from political science majors. I knew he had never married, and, although I saw him almost daily, in dozens of working situations, I didn't know a damned thing about his life.

The overriding thing about his personality was the sense of organization that he appeared to have. Even his physical make-up seemed calculated. It was an impression of control that was so dominant and which I now knew I envied. He was a man of no wasted motion. That was it—no wasted motion. Like a Laser beam with total concentrated energy, he had burned his way through all the heavy layers of bureaucratic protection that swathed Don, to become, as of this moment, the central force in his political life, in our lives. It was he who was pulling all the strings. It was we who dangled waiting for the deftness of his touch to force our movements.

It frightened me to discover that I couldn't get a fix on his character. I couldn't photograph him in my mind. He was an apparition. That's the kind of a thought that gives you goose bumps at night. But I had never seen him in what I can describe as a human situation. No drinking. No smoking. No panic. No sweat. No girls. He was never sick. He was always simply there, observing. No wasted motion. Henry Davis had made the study of Donald James his life's work in a far more objective way than any of us—Barnstable, Christine, myself, even Don himself. Davis had, undoubtedly, been through "games," simulating Don's present situation as well as who knows how many different combinations. Like the simulated battle situations that are the delight of the military mind.

No confirmation needed. Politics was simply a big roulette game for paranoiacs. And we were presently following Davis's system.

There was something, though, that even Davis had missed, even Davis could not know. He could not get into Don's mind, could not see that Don would only follow the game plan if he perceived himself in the called-for-role. As a central actor in his own drama, Don had to believe in his role to make the whole act operational. At the moment, it was Davis who best articulated the "role"; and it was Davis currently in the director's chair. And who the hell had either the will or the justification necessary to resist him?

Besides, you knew that Davis enjoyed the exercise. Why not? It gave him the power he secretly longed for. And yet you knew him to be totally immoral, without guile. You knew this because he never questioned motives once an act was recommended, making judgments solely on what effect they would have on people's minds. All means were weapons. The end was "the goal." Goals never changed, only means. Strategies were everything. There was no spontaneity, only calculated response. Put a penny in the slot and you always got what you wanted from the prize-strewn gum machine.

I envied him his bloodlessness.

The most disturbing thing about my discovery of Davis was that it revealed something that I thought I had lost years ago—my moral indignation. Now that sounds like a lot of horseshit, I know. It used to be called 'conscience' by my generation. All this deliberate manipulation of the public, that sad, dumb glob out there in whom all real power, nevertheless, is supposed to repose, people who are thought to be masters of their fate through what we call participatory democracy; all this glorification of the people, the fucking people. It made me sick at heart to see us use them to cash in on their witlessness. Strike that! That's what they're out there for—to be used, to be seduced, like an innocent victim to be fucked and refucked. The day I get soft about that fact is the day I quit politics.

But don't despair. Pangs of conscience are an occupational hazard in my business, like black lung. The attack of conscience passed with the coming of dawn and two stiff Scotches, which I downed standing by the window and watching the sun come poking through the low Washington skyline. I don't know why I was angry, but I was angry. I knew that I didn't have the balls to stand up and fight, largely because I didn't know what I would be fighting for or against, except some vague abstraction that made me feel that somewhere deep down in my shiftless and ever-expanding gut, there was a faint but flickering flame of purity.

Of course, that was exactly what gave Davis the edge. He was far more practical on how to skillfully maneuver his sloop through the political shoals, a nautical expression he would hardly understand.

The California trip was, as all of Davis's logistical packages, a monument to logic. Three seats were booked on a TWA first-class 747 to San Francisco for Barnstable, myself, and Karen. One seat of the three was taken in the name of Senator James.

The objective of his strategy of deception was to dodge the press. Davis briefed us.

"The senator will leave with Lou in the back of the car under a blanket."

"Like cops and robbers," Don said.

"The rest of us will leave in one car soon after. I want to move quickly down the driveway. If the press has done its homework, it will have picked up the flight booking out of National. Schwartz's Lear Jet will be waiting at the Friendship Flying Service hangar at the Baltimore International Airport. It will take us to Carmel Airport. Bob Brogen will pick us up and take us to Mrs. James's house, where everything will be set up and waiting for us to tape the show."

"Will Schwartz be on the plane?" Don asked.

"Unfortunately, yes."

"You mean, I'll have to listen to his nonsense for five straight hours?"

"Four and a half," Davis said.

"The man's a bore."

"He's the best fundraiser we have," Barnstable said. "We need lots of bores like him. Hell, he was nice enough to lend you his plane. He's promised me that he'll stand by you through thick and thin. The least you could so is to be friendly to him. He's already raised three million dollars for you with lots of promises for more."

"God knows what he's promised everyone," Don said.

"The promise is always implied," Davis said. "That's the way it should be. You wouldn't want a quid pro quo. It would one day come back to haunt you."

"I know," Don sulked. "It's such a goddamned trial though. You have to take a lot of shit from a bunch of ignorant slobs."

Max Schwartz was a simple man. He had made, from the most humble beginnings, upwards of $50 million in oil and real estate. And, yet, if he were shrewd and hard-driving, it never showed through what appeared to be a very sweet and humble exterior. His home on the topmost hill of Beverly Hills was overflowing with both rare works of art and more than one hundred plaques given to him, "for humanitarian service," meaning money, by both religious and help organizations throughout the country. His gluttony for plaques and publicity was well known, and most times he was humored and pampered, but satiation eluded him.

When it was apparent that there was no place more to go in charitable causes, expecially since he was "honored" to the point of embarrassment, he took a fling at politics on his own, running in a senatorial primary in California at the same time that Don made his run for that office. To come out tenth in a field of ten after investing $2 million of his own money in an astonishingly inept campaign in print and television was a blow that shattered even old Max's ego, but only temporarily. One TV spot was a pan of all the plaques on his wall, with a deep voice booming high-blown prose, describing each honor ad nauseam. After that spot was shown, the joke around the California political jungle was that the final campaign windup gimmick would show Max walking all the way to Catalina Island followed by the heads of all the organizations who had ever given him a plaque, culminating in being met at the Catalina pier by JC himself, who would congratulate him and make a brief supporting statement.

A joke to everybody, including his wife, Max, nevertheless, could be induced to raise huge sums of money. His only tangible reward was to be—like the proverbial Jewish mother caricature—needed. Don was reminded to call him at least once a week, and when he came to town the senator was always available for dinner. It seemed a small price to pay. Until now. For Max, at last, was really needed and, of course, would rise to the occasion armed with vats of psychic chicken soup.

The "escape" to the airport was remarkably simple, partly because the ranks of the reporters had thinned considerably. As Davis had predicted, the story was losing its momentum nationally. It was still on page one, but reduced to speculations and inconclusive ramblings gleaned from rummaging around Rehoboth and interviewing the locals. The young policeman to whom we had reported Marlena's disappearance finally got his picture in the paper, although none could pry a word out of him. There were some political vultures screaming for investigating the circumstances of the drowning, but these came mostly from Delaware politicians, noted for their holier-than-thou stance, which made it impossible to take them seriously.

Barnstable's staff had prepared a compendium of newspaper clippings and television comments, Xeroxed neatly and bound together in a red cover, marked "Confidential." Don wouldn't read it, but I couldn't resist seeing it. Like the country itself, the coverage was split down the middle on the basis of political persuasion. The more conservative media reveled in implied licentiousness. The more liberal media seemed restrained, more "factual" and classically journalistic. God knows how many editors and desk men were biting hard on their pipes, while pencils, like surgical knives, sliced skillfully at over-extended prose. If you knew how to read the stories, you could almost see the stitches, as the liberal news surgeons patched their stories. The conservatives, on the other hand, gloried in the blood of an impaled Senator James. You could almost see the intestines slithering like a barrel of snakes along the butcher's floor. The important point was that the media had shot the whole wad right at the beginning. Follow-ups would lose their bite as the so-called facts dissipated into thin air. Our policy of deliberate vagueness had begun to pay off.

There were photographs of Marlena, cap-and-gown pictures from her college yearbook that made her look featureless in the third-generation newspaper reproduction process. The summary, written by Al Simon, at the end of the report read, "The study of these clips cumulatively reveals a complete lack of objectivity on the part of most reporters." Who didn't know that!

XXXIII

Max was waiting for us at the plane's gangway. He embraced Don, who accepted it stoically.

"We're going to fight this thing, Don."

"Right, Max, all the way."

The second car was right behind us. Max embraced Karen. Then he shook hands all around, and we were whisked into the plush interior of the Lear jet.

There was a certain ritual connected with all relationships involving Max Schwartz. He was an insatiable sponge for compliments. It was the staff of his life. Don performed it admirably.

"I want you to know, Max," he said, so that all of us in the interior of the cabin could hear it, "I don't think any of us can ever forget your generosity to us in this hour of our greatest need. We'll know who our friends are. And Max, we know you're our friend."

Tears welled in Max's eyes. He was an emotional man. In varying degrees, all the so-called fat cats were cut from this mold. Their hobby was politicians. They never asked much. They had everything money could buy. All they wanted was to be looked upon as insiders. They always exaggerated their own importance to their friends, anyway. And their friends were not people who could dispute them. It was simply a game of one-upmanship.

The seats of the jet were arranged easy-chair style. Don sat between Davis and myself and began reading the speech. When we were airborne, Davis took a paper from his jacket pocket and thrust it on top of Don's speech manuscript.

"Schwartz is essential to keeping the fundraising apparatus intact. I recommend that you use this opportunity to persuade him that you are a victim of circumstances. Make him come up with the notion that he must fly around the country in your name to convince others that they must stay with the team, that we will ultimately recover from this setback."

Don read the note and handed it to me. He knew all about Max's basic sentimentality. Switching seats, Don sat down beside Max and held his forearm in a comforting gesture.

"Max, I want to ask you one question," Don said.

"Anything, Don."

"You've read all newspaper reports. Without my giving you my side, I'd like you to tell me what tentative conclusions you've made. Now I know this is a tough question, but it's important to both of us that you answer it accurately from your point of view."

Max looked at his fingernails and swallowed deeply. His hesitation was enough of a clue to his answer. He also looked around to see if Karen was far enough from earshot. She was dozing in the far corner of the plane. Max bent low over us.

"I think you were having a party and there was—there was an accident."

It was extremely painful for Max to say this. Don shook his head and feigned injury. He was particularly good at that expression. It had served him well in many a debate and would come in handy during the next few days.

"I want you to believe this, Max."

"If I'm wrong, tell me."

"I'm being hanged for a crime I did not commit. This does not mean that I am as pure as the driven snow. I've outlined in my speech in my hand the real story of last weekend's episode. Only my closest staff has seen it. I am going to show it to you, Max, because I know you are a great and compassionate human being." Max seemed to puff up like a blowfish.

"Here, read it." Don thrust the speech at him, winking at me as he did so. He looked at Max's face as he read the speech.

"Do you think people will believe me?" Don asked when Max had

finished reading. His eyes were filled with moisture. He pulled out
a handkerchief and blew his nose.

"I don't know about other people, Don, but I believe it."

He grabbed Don's forearm again and squeezed it. He was reveling
in his role.

"Do you think you might be able to tell our friends that you
believe me?"

"Of course, Don. I won't let you down."

"I know that, Max."

Throughout the plane trip, Don worked busily at his speech,
underlining words for emphasis. At times, he lay back and dozed,
thinking who knows what thoughts. His strength had returned. That
was apparent. But there was another quality, a texture intruding into
my observation of him. Or, perhaps, it was in the way he was moving
through these events. I couldn't get a firm hold on my own feelings
about him. It was just an indescribable tugging. Something about
him was different, or getting different. It was like those little toy
kaleidoscopes made years ago. You turned the rim of the lens and the
colorful designs rearranged themselves into something else. Don
seemed to me to be rearranged or, at least, rearranging.

Davis was busy going through a huge pile of Xeroxed papers. I sat
down beside him at the seat Max had vacated.

"Letters," he said. "I asked for a sample of letters. We've got them
collated into 'Total Support,' 'Total Rejection,' 'Questioning,'
'Hate,' and 'Crank.' "

"What's the score?" I asked.

"Support and rejection are about fifty-fifty. The hate letters are
running high. They haven't calculated it. Here's a typical one."

I looked at the carefully written copy. "Dear Senator: I am a con-
stituent, a God-fearing woman, who has raised a family and given
three sons to serve in the armed forces of our great country. I want
you to know that I think your actions are a total disgrace to the
flag, the worst part being your being in bed with a goddamned

nigger. You and all your pinko commy friends can all go to hell. I
won't vote for you ever." I took another one from the pile. This one
was even more explicit.

"It's one thing to fuck around with black action. It didn't change
your luck, did it? I hope they throw you out of Washington, you
cocksucker." Some were more intelligent. All professed varying
degrees of distress and confusion. One theme seemed to dominate all
the letters: betrayal. How could the senator do this to them? After a
while, the letters got boring. Don had no interest in them at all. But
Davis, like a tiger, was reading every one of them in the pile on his
lap, making notes, and carefully refiling them in their place within
the pile.

The flight was smooth and quiet as the Lear knifed through the
sky on its westward journey. Karen stared quietly out of the window,
deep in herself. I hadn't thought much about Karen since we
returned from Rehoboth. After her initial outburst, she seemed to
have stabilized, holding herself together, probably with tranquiliz-
ers. Karen was always big on pills.

I must admit I didn't feel bad about Karen. Occasionally, when
our eyes met, it was I who turned away.

Swiveling around, letting my vision wash over all the figures in
the cabin of the plane, I saw us as a traveling road show, about to do
our gig on the Coast. Everyone but Davis and I dozed.

"It's all a dumb dream, Davis," I whispered. "I think we're all
whistling in the cemetery."

"I don't agree. I think we're coming out of this thing with
great success."

"I'd like to know why."

"Two reasons. We're in control of the scenario and the lead actor
is functioning with skill."

"You really believe that you can hoodwink the people."

"We're not hoodwinking. We're just repairing a breach in our
image. Hell, in retrospect the breach is not that tragic. The senator's

liberal credentials, his carefully worked-out posture over the past twenty years is impeccable. A personal peccadillo doesn't wipe out the record. He's just acting out every man's nightmare. I'm not panicked anymore. And I don't think the senator is."

"You're so damned cocksure about everything, Davis. God damn, I've never seen anyone so cocksure."

"If you look at it like a science, if you use the scientific method, you move on the basis of certain theoretical conclusions. Move X will almost always get an X reaction. Move Y will get a Y reaction. We look at the options and make the moves, X, Y, or Z. The trouble with you and Barnstable is that you consider politics an art form."

He was insufferable, this man Davis.

"You really think you're a fucking genius, Davis."

"Not at all. I just know my product. I chose my product. You didn't choose me. I knew I made the right choice years ago. This little setback had me concerned, but I think now we're over the hump."

"What do you want, Davis?"

"Just what I have, Castle. Just what I have."

We sat down in the airport outside of Carmel. Don had to be awakened from a deep sleep.

XXXIV

The president closed the last page of the news summaries, placed them carefully in a corner of the desk, leaned back, and lit a cigar. He puffed a few times, letting the smoke drift easily into the shafts of bright sunbeams that darted through the great bay window. He liked this time of the morning. Everything was orderly, muted. People had not yet begun to pollute the day, to fill air with their discharges, the obscene rumblings of their comings and going, the clack of their voices.

The hands of the antique grandfather clock jerked perceptibly as the hour moved inexorably onward toward seven-thirty, the time when Baum, his chief of staff, would arrive and the day would be staked out minute by minute, the time doled out like precious chunks of bread.

Picking up the milk china coffee cup with the presidential seal emblazoned, obtrusive and regal, along its side, he sipped carefully, sparingly, with measured movements. He allowed himself three cups of coffee a day, at precisely the same moment every day, all before 2:00 P.M. Any deviation in this schedule set his mind going when he knew it must be shut off, like a timed spigot at precisely midnight, when the last chime of the last hour struck in his bedroom. It was all conscious, practiced, studied, this measurement of himself, by time, by distance, each block of energy programmed.

Spartan training, he acknowledged. Self-discipline. It was his ultimate weapon, his personal strategy. Let them indulge their weaknesses. He'd outlast them all. Now Senator James, that arrogant young bastard, had gotten his comeuppance. His problem—he couldn't keep his cock in his pants. He could feel the beginnings of a joyous shriek gnaw at his gut, wanting to come out. He felt it go off in his mind, a kind of wild hysteria of relief that could be indulged silently with equal release as if it had roared out of him like a jet screech.

Again he had bested them. Like a tennis game. He had waited for them to make a mistake, playing the easy lobs, the well-timed response, waiting, hoping that they'd show their mistake in whatever form—a ball bashed impotently into the net, an overshot, a missed step.

He had watched the flock of vultures circle overhead, the latest leader, this man James, his curved beak itching to sink its points into his flesh and tear him to pieces. Now they were dispersed, routed, and he could for the moment go on about his business.

If they only knew, he thought. You climb through the excrement and come to the top of the dung heap and you fight to stay there, while they lap at you from all sides, all juiced up with hate at the smell of your blood.

No one knew, except those that had been there before, and even their perception of the office was no longer valid. There was no way, no way to totally predict and control the fate of the ship of state, not yet. Technology boggled the brain.

They all talked like computers, an endless liturgy of inputs, scientific pep-talk. Boil it down, he urged. Boil it down. Let the mind absorb it. Give me options. Simplify! Give the essence. He always strove to get the essence. Then he would trust to his instincts. Hadn't his instincts carried him this far? True, not every decision had been a winner. Around every corner was an unforeseen factor. The economists with their gobbledygook. The generals with their double talk. The social scientists with their bleeding heart garbage. One would think that with all the money spent on research, all the time wasted on talk, that they would give him foolproof alternatives. How could you trust any of them? You had to be a genius, to have a mind that absorbed facts like a sponge. His instincts were far more accurate. He had more confidence in his instincts than in all the

warmed over bullshit. Where had it gotten any of them?
Bureaucratic functionaries.

Even their intelligence reports seemed somehow incomplete, full
of holes. If they had their way, we'd wind up like automatons, programmed to surrender to the least common denominator. He wondered if they would, in the end, appreciate him. Would they know
how he labored to save them from the bleeding hearts who wanted
to take all the incentives out of America, to make it impossible for
men like himself to rise to the top level. Over my dead body, he
shouted inside his head. If only they had let him use his instincts
completely. Only from up here, from this oval office, could one really understand the flawed system. They promoted impotence with all
their checks and balances. How was he to act for them, to keep them
free, to prevent their self-delusion? He'd shown them how tough he
could be. Let those jackals yap at his toes. He'd ignore them.
Someday they would come to believe him. History would vindicate
his instincts.

He'd molded together an unbeatable combination of real
Americans. All that remained was to make them understand. James,
that moral degenerate, had shown the country what he was made of.
He knew what America needed. Moral leadership. Trim the fat off
our minds. Get down to the nub. He had come from pioneer stock.
We hadn't built this country by shilly-shallying around.

What could that son-of-a-bitch James do if he ever got to this
desk? All that rabble that would crawl in beside him. The blacks.
They could barely go to the bathroom by themselves. Labor. All they
wanted was more fingers in the pie. Bleeding hearts. Pinkos.

James and his ilk would destroy America, the real America. They
are the real enemies, and they won over the media. But despite it, he
would win, as he had always won. This James incident proved it.
The moral degenerates would always lose. Someday they could thank
him for saving America. James was a threat, a goddamned demagogue. Human garbage.

He looked out of the window into the rose garden. The forsythias along the edges had just begun to bloom. Soon the rosebuds would pop, and each day they'd put a bouquet on his desk. He liked to smell the roses in his office; the faint perfume seemed to tranquilize the air.

With all its constrictions, he liked being the president. He had climbed the highest mountain. Not bad for a poor kid from Binghamton, New York, whose father had run a grocery store. Everything seemed so simple then. Not bad. Hey, mom, I really slipped it to them.

Now with James out of the way, he could admit to himself that he made some bad decisions. But only because he had to bend, to compromise. After his reelection, he would owe no man. He would be free to move ahead, to take a firmer grip. He'd rely on horse sense, the same horse sense that had brought him to the presidency in the first place. He'd use his will, his instincts.

He'd make them pay.

XXXV

Mrs. James lived in a small California-style house with a fine view of the craggy rocks and white surf of the Pacific coastline. In the distance the sea was visible and sparkling. Davis quickly began a non-stop instruction to the director on how to proceed with the speech.

"I want this to begin with a long shot of the house from the beach. Send the trailer down below and let them shoot a sea shot, near the rocks, then pan upwards until you hit the house, closing in on the picture window. I want you to capture all the anger of the sea and roughness of the landscape."

"Do you think the sea might be too reminiscent?" Barnstable asked.

"Not if it's what we're trying to make the villain in the piece," Davis said. His remarks needed no further explanation. The sea, nature, the mystic force.

"I'd better hurry," the director said. He went outside to instruct the people in the videotape trailer. The lighting crew continued to work while three of us—Davis, Barnstable, and myself—huddled around Don as the makeup woman skillfully applied the grease and powder to Don's face in careful strokes. She stepped back occasionally to survey her work. Outside, the inevitable reporters had arrived to begin their never-ending vigil. A scruffy bunch, they had the same hang-dog look of reporters anywhere. What a forlorn looking lot. A crowd of the curious swelled the ranks outside. Four or five very makeshift placards could be seen. "We support our senator" was the dominant theme. We knew it was Brogan's handiwork. He was in charge of our San Francisco office and had met us at the airport.

"We've already put the speech on the crawl, Senator," Davis said. "Watch your eye contact. It's got to look like it's spontaneous. Try not to squint. We're going to do a run-through, maybe two. I'm worried about the sound. I want it as clean as possible."

Unflappable as ever, Davis outlined the schedule. Both Jack and I felt totally useless as we stood there listening to the smooth flow of Davis's instructions. He had thought it out to the last detail.

I looked about the room for Karen and Mrs. James. They sat side by side in a corner of the room, bewildered by the activity around them; both were silent. Mrs. James was a woman in her late seventies, well preserved, with a face that duplicated her son's balanced bone structure, even in aging. She wore her white hair parted in the center, which accentuated the similarity of the two sides of her head, like segments of an unblemished oval. Even during our college days, Mrs. James had always been cool, distant, even with her son, as if they both shared some dark secret understanding that needed no articulation. She, like Karen, knew her political role, although to Mrs. James it seemed to flow as the natural course of events.

She had always felt she married beneath her, and, as far as I knew, had barely spoken to Don's wastrel father after their divorce. Don had described her many times as a bitch, and he never did quite become free of her tyranny. As for Karen, she hated Mrs. James with vigor. The two women hardly ever spoke, although they knew their public role as political props, a role which they were scheduled to perform today.

Throughout the process of preparation, the makeup, lighting, testing, the technicians crawling over the little house with their meters and intercoms, Don was totally relaxed. He was uncommonly pliable as he went through the paces, just as a thoroughbred might coolly do his workout the day before the Derby.

Schwartz and other contributors who had met with him sat at the kitchen table in another part of the house talking quietly. Don had greeted them all warmly on arrival. They savored their roles with relish. This was really inside for them. The press would describe them, perhaps, as close friends, although they did enjoy the political appellation, "fat cats." There was lots of currency in that.

When the makeup woman had finished, Don motioned to Davis and myself to follow him into his mother's bedroom. He started to get undressed, then stopped abruptly and sat on the bed.

"A number of new possibilities are running through my mind," he began. "In the first place, I've begun to believe that we've become victims of a kind of defeatist philosophy. And maybe, just maybe, it's come about because of my own feelings of guilt. After all, what the hell did I do wrong? I've done nothing illegal. Why should I just sit back and wait? We're programmed and financed to make this fight for the nomination. What the hell can I lose? Besides, four years from now I could be dead. The opportunity is now. The time is now." He got up and looked into the mirror. "I feel strong. I know I can do it."

Davis, who had listened without expression, followed Don's movements with his ice-blue eyes.

"A politician can only build from a base of reasonable credibility. Yours is presently shattered."

"I'll make them believe me," Don said.

"In the long run I think you will," Davis continued. "But right now, things are too raw. We'll have to come up with a series of exercises that will establish your credibility again, bit by bit, like a finely orchestrated piece. You can't will people to believe you."

"I just don't believe it, Davis," Don said. "Don't you understand, I feel I can do it. That's part of the game. You have to feel it. I know they'll believe me. You know my speech style. I could have them raid the treasury if I roused them enough. And who can use television like me? Name one other person in public life who can get on the boob tube and make them believe. Compare that to the president. He can't make his own mother believe him.

"What do you think, Lou?" Don asked.

How was I in a position to judge? Yes, I'd seen him sway large groups of people. I'd seen them shouting from the rafters. I'd seen a

statewide poll immediately after a statewide television performance.
Don did, indeed, have that precious commodity, charisma.

"You've got balls, Don." That's about as far as I had the guts to
commit myself.

"You're goddamned right."

"I calculate the odds as presently against," Davis said. For the first
time I could see him angered, his eyes flashing, his lips pursed in a
tight line. "Senator, don't let self-delusion limit your grasp."

Don exploded.

"Self-delusion! What the hell do you think I am? Some puppet to
be programmed, like a wind-up doll. I'm human. I bleed. I feel.
Don't tell me about self-delusion."

"Senator, in my opinion, you are presently too vulnerable. Your
credibility is suspect. Aside from the strong strain of strict morality
in the American people, there are whole states dominated by
Christian fundamentalism. There is also the fact that your case is
built out of thin strands indeed. You philandered. You panicked. It
took you eleven hours to act intelligently. This is the brutal truth."

I could see Don begin to seethe with anger. He fought for control,
then banged his hand down hard on the dresser. When he spoke, he
did not turn around.

"Who the fuck are you to judge me?"

Davis looked at me. He was suddenly anguished and a trifle
helpless. He knew he had gone too far; the truth hanging out
there like that had been overpowering.

"This is not a judgment," Davis said quietly. "This is the truth."

"The truth," Don boomed, turning. "What do you know about
the truth?"

"Senator, all I can do is give you options. It's your job to decide
among them. I say you'd be hard pressed to win now. Aside from
your own vulnerability, just think how your opponent can use this
incident against you now."

"That fascist creep."

"Name calling won't beat him."

Don looked at Davis.

"You turd," he said. "Why am I listening to you. It's not your career. What the fuck difference does it make to you?"

Davis ignored the question. We both knew it made one hell of a difference to him. This was his obsession, to be at the epicenter of power in his own way.

"Why don't you both get the hell out of here and let me think."

When we had closed the door behind us, I shook my head.

"He's frustrated. He'll get over it."

"Megalomania," Davis said.

"Just frustrated."

"Megalomania," Davis repeated. "It's probably an absolute requirement of a successful politician."

"How do you think he'll go?"

"I think he'll run."

"Will he lose?"

"Badly."

"Will he be finished forever?"

"Nothing in life is forever." He turned and walked away toward the door.

"Whom the gods destroy, they first make angry," Davis said, before closing the door behind him.

I went into the living room and looked about the little stage set that Davis had created, with its warm homeyness, the view of the rugged cliffs in the background, pictures of Don's two sons. It was a set filled with the symbols one would expect to find in a loving home. Mrs. James sat stoically in her place with Karen, her eyes glazed and indifferent to everything around her.

It was like a war; everyone was waiting around for the big offensive to start. In a corner of the room, I saw Jack Barnstable, tired, disheveled, slumped half-dozing in the chair.

"He just blew up at Davis," I said.

"I'm too tired to think about that just now."

"I wish I could be."

Don came out of the bedroom. He was neatly groomed, a sprayed gloss on his salt and pepper hair, the beige makeup heavy on his face, giving him an air of unreality, like a body made up for display in a coffin.

He sat down at his designated seat in the middle of the set, the lights went on, and the adjustments of the lighting began with the director's voice booming over the speaker, dominating the room.

Don, like the pro that he was, followed the directions to the letter, glancing occasionally at the black and white monitor near the crawl machine. He looked at his mother and Karen and smiled.

"Here goes nothing," he said.

"When that camera light goes on, Mrs. James," it was the director's voice. "Don't flash a smile. Just keep the slightest hint of a smile fixed on your face so that the camera will not appear to simply turn you on mechanically."

Both women nodded.

"Now let's do a run."

The crawl began. Don spoke quietly into the camera, reading the speech, looking solemn, appropriately stern, the maligned, put-upon man striking back with dignity. While he was reading the speech, Karen got up, found her pocketbook, and reaching into it, pulled out a pill vial. She popped two in her mouth and returned to her place. It had all happened so fast. But the movement had deflected my attention. Then it had dawned on me. Karen's glazed look was more than that. She had deliberately drugged herself with God knows what. He stared at her. She was pathetic, lost in a subdued fog. I wondered if it would come over on the tube. The black and white monitor revealed little.

Walking outside to the studio trailer, I went in. The director sat before a bank of small color screens, firing instructions. Davis stood behind him, watching, making suggestions.

"Don't start to move in until he says: 'I believe I owe my constituents,' " Davis said. "Also, a little more side light. There's a
slight shadow on his nose."

The cameras were not on Karen. I would have to wait for the pan
shot. When the camera finally moved, it caught Karen in a blank
stare, drugged and out of it.

"She's taking some kind of pills," I whispered to Davis.

"I noticed that. I've cut down on the pan time." Then he said loud-
er, to the director, "See if you can get her to smile." The director
boomed his instructions. Karen smiled wanly. "It's good enough."

"If it's really bad, we can edit her out. We've got a few minutes
time lag before the tapes have to go."

I decided to stay in the studio. The director gave the signal to get
ready. Then he pressed the start button and the tapes began to roll.

Don looked cool, refreshed, and handsome. Sincerity beamed out
through the screen. Who was that man up there on the little screen?
There he was, showing his greatest asset. He spoke quietly, sticking
to the letter of the speech. He approached the end.

"Any implication of immorality on the part of myself or Miss
Jackson is utterly false. I have no doubt, though, that there will
be those who imply otherwise, whose own sense of cynicism
will raise doubts. Against all this innuendo and speculation
there is only one defense—the truth. In the end there is only
the truth."

The words were expressed with directness, with modesty and
humility. It was a masterful performance. People had to believe. It
had to be effective. Then Don paused, smiled, and looked directly
into the camera.

"He's not on the crawl anymore," Davis observed quietly.

"Here it comes. Keep the camera static. I don't know what he's
going to say."

The director barked out the instructions to his two cameramen.
"And keep the cameras off the women. Come in tighter."

"There are those," Don began. His look was calculated to show the audience that this was an obvious departure from the text. One could tell by the eye contact. Don was literally peering through the tube. "—who see my political career damaged beyond repair by the strange tragic events of last weekend. There are those who would write me off as a viable candidate for the presidency. By all standard political measures such judgments might be correct. But these are truly, as Thomas Paine once said, 'the times that try men's souls.' For we stand at the abyss. Will humanity win over repression? Will our cities sink into final irreversible decay? Will our blundering and lack of vision lead us to the deep forest of nuclear annihilation? Will the vast majority of people in this country ever have a chance to have a say in creating the kind of world in which their children can grow and prosper? Will there ever be true freedom and justice in this great country of ours as our founding fathers envisioned it? Or shall we abdicate our God-given right to create a society that will root out repression and thwart those men who view power as an end in itself?

"I say we cannot allow these men to destroy us, to allow our way of life to disintegrate, to allow the cynics and doomsayers to take control. We must not ever again allow our political system to be controlled by men whose compassion and sense of justice is suspect. That is why, whatever the consequences, whatever the weapons that will be used against me, I will not shirk from my responsibility, from the leadership role that my supporters expect of me. I believe in my destiny. I believe in my mission. I know that this will be an uphill battle. But I also know in my heart that the truth is on my side. I therefore offer my candidacy for president of the United States on the Democratic ticket. Many problems lie ahead. I am fully aware of them, but as a matter on conscience, of honor, I have determined to rise above the petty accusations of small minds and follow wherever the truth leads me. Thank you and good night."

The camera zoomed in, caught a tight shot of Don's face, then the director punched off.

We stood silently looking at the blank set.

"It was stupendous," I said. I meant that. Don's words were charged with emotion.

"I think he really believes it now," Davis said.

"What do you think the reaction will be?"

"Demagoguery has great appeal. But lots of people will see through it."

"How could they?"

"Now you're suffering from megalomania by association."

He was a snotty bastard, that Davis. I walked back into the house. Don was surrounded by Max Schwartz and his friends.

"Fantastic."

"Great."

"We're with you."

It was, of course, the litany of sycophants.

"Shall I run it back, Senator?" the director's voice boomed over the speaker.

"No. Not necessary. I've said it all. I don't wish to see it."

He broke through the know of well-wishers and walked over to me. He was ecstatic, warm, and flushed.

"What do you think, Lou?"

"You and me, Don. We'll tough it out." We embraced. Tears welled in my eyes. God, I loved that man.

"I was sitting there looking suddenly into that lens. It was just then that I finally made up my mind. I wanted to crawl into their heads and make them believe. Make them, Lou. You know what I mean."

"You're damned right," I said.

"We're going right to the top."

"You said it, baby."

Davis came back into the house. He had recovered his usual aplomb. Barnstable was a new man, revived, as if he had just had a transfusion of adrenalin.

"Let's get to work," he shouted. "Get me to the telephone."

Karen, still in her chair, was glassy-eyed. Don's mother was smiling and proud. She embraced her son. As they embraced, Don looked at Davis, who had already begun to take notes.

"Well, Davis, what do you think?"

"We have lots of work to do."

"Right."

"We've got to go to Marlena's funeral in Philadelphia tomorrow."

"What an ordeal!" I said.

"There is no escaping that one," Davis said.

"I guess not."

XXXVI

It bugged Ernie, like an itch you couldn't scratch, like a pinprick in some unspecified spot. It was like a kid who had just eaten the chocolate, with the brown liquid stickiness still at the edges of his lips.

"Did you eat the chocolate, kid?"

"No."

"But I see some of it still on your lips."

"There's nothing there."

"You just licked it off."

"No, I didn't."

"But I saw it."

"You're mistaken."

Ernie shook his head. How do you unravel that? He was annoyed with himself. Is it important to know or even believe that Senator James did indeed sleep with that girl? Who gives a flying fuck about that? And the delay in reporting the drowning. An intelligent person could accept an honest explanation. There was apparently no violation of the law. It seemed such a simple equation.

He tried to imagine himself in the senator's shoes, tried even to assume the intensity of his ambition. The options were few. Admit the philandering. Don't admit the philandering. In the absence of proof, why admit it? Because, you dummy, this is below the line of the acceptable national standard. You just don't go around screwing strange women after you make the marriage contract. If you do and get caught, then you have abused the contract, have abused your word. You lied. You cheated, that's why. And once you start cheating on your word, it becomes a never-ending maze, a coverup.

Aha, but there is an acceptable standard of lying. You cheat on the marriage contract. You deny it. Sexuality is a strong drive. What

harm is there in it? The contract is archaic. Cheating on a spouse has
the precedent of history, from time immemorial. It has the authority of common usage. But what happens then to the moral question?
You break your contract. You break your word. That is immoral. He
remembered deciphering his college course in logic.

He was lost in the tangle. The fact is that the American people,
in politician's terms, votes, don't like to know that their presidents
are sexual cheaters. They don't want to see the photographs. Hell,
the guy is human. Accept his frailties.

As for the delay, after the first half-hour anyone would know the
girl was gone. What was the point in waiting? Was he searching for
the body so that he could bury it somewhere, burn it and sprinkle
its ashes into the ocean. Why not? What harm would that do? After
all, if you're going to begin to suspend moral purity you might as
well go all the way. No, the chances were that all that time was needed to put together the alibi. Of course, the longer you waited the
more you needed an alibi.

So what was he all exorcized about? What was annoying him?
Perhaps it was the sense of betrayal. Senator James was the great
white hope. He was going to lead us out of the clutches of the mad
power centers, the big money, out of the web of greed and disillu-
sionment that has gripped the American experience. He's just a
plain old weak-kneed, scared human being like the rest of us, and
that was the story that ought to be written.

But this television performance. It was an exercise in sophistry
that made everything that went before pale beside it. It was fraud
incarnate, a lie of gargantuan proportions, the work of a
demigod. He felt almost physically ill as he watched the senator
perform. And yet the tone was convincing, the words ringing
with indignation. The man should have been a Shakespearean
actor. Hell, he *was* a Shakespearean actor. What poise. What subtlety. What sense of nuance. His skill at his craft was awe-inspir-
ing. He was dangerous.

He had seen the reaction on Ellen. They had watched it in his apartment, sipping Scotch sours. The evening news had played the entire segment.

"I think he's fantastic," Ellen said, after the breathless pause, that clutched in the throat, when the handsome image had faded.

"You believed him?"

"No, but I don't think it matters."

"It doesn't matter that he lied."

"They all lie."

"That doesn't make it right."

"What would you want him to say?"

"The truth."

"He was great. That's all that matters. He stands for what's right."

"How can you be so sure?"

"I feel it."

"Feeling is thinking at the subconscious level."

"Ernie, why do you have to intellectualize everything."

"Damn it, Ellen, you can't tell me what he stands for."

"Of course I can." She thought a moment. "He stands for young people, us. He stands for really trying to make a better world."

"A liar stands for nothing."

She reached over with both hands and held his head.

"You're the most marvelously unspoiled man I ever met." She kissed him deeply on the mouth.

The truth is the truth is the truth. He had been down this street a thousand times in his mind and in the actions of his life. Unethical means do not make ethical ends. What could this man James do for this country?

Perhaps—was he being trivial? Wasn't this, after all, a little white lie, something to be winked at, passed over, like a harmless wart on the tip of one's nose.

Now he was rationalizing. It was a simple conclusion: the man was not fit to be the leader. What was the function of a president, anyhow?

To inspire us. To expand our awareness. To lead us into ways that will make a better, stronger people, a more aware country. Instead, what was he? Just another bullshitter, covering up some petty meaningless peccadillo with an elaborate façade of platitudes and lies.

He softened, started to reach out and pat her hair, then checked himself.

"Ellen, I'm not putting you down. I just don't understand how you can be indifferent. When I say 'you,' I mean the collective 'you.' I've actually been walking around in a fucking vacuum. Maybe it's me? Am I so thickheaded as to believe that what this man has done is dangerous?"

"Oh, shit, Ernie, they're all like that. The president is worse. In fact, he's the worst." She sat up. "As a matter of fact, if you really pressed me, what does it matter at all to me? I'm Ellen Kay. I'm me and that's all that counts, to know me, to be me, to understand who I am. And to give the good things in me to my fellow human beings."

"I must really be out of it, Ellen," he said, sitting down beside her again. "Either that, or everybody around me is so damned narcissistic that nothing, absolutely nothing, is getting through."

"Why is it so important?"

"Because of its effect on our lives. Believe me, Ellen, if you really comprehend it, it gets down to basics, right down to the nitty gritty of our own personal lives."

"That's pretty obvious," she said acidly.

"I really feel that I'm talking into a cloud. It's not you, Ellen. It's Chalmers, filtering the truth through the *Chronicle* like he was some godlike censor. The subtlety of it is astonishing. And that pitiful black man, who sees it only through the lens of his grief. And Pierce, the Judas, who sees it through his jealousy. And Hershey, who sees it through his cynicism."

"And you, Ernie?"

"Who sees it through my own anger. Damn it, Ellen, why can't I be objective?"

He watched Ellen now nestled in the crook of his armpit, leaning back, staring into space. It was incredible, the power of it. Even Ellen was not immune to their manipulation, a reasonably intelligent, self-aware person. He admitted to himself that it was a narrow frame of reference, but he could feel that there were millions out there like her, millions who could accept the DBJ con job.

Releasing himself from her, he stood up, paced the cluttered room, with its piles of books on tables and floor. It looked like Stonehenge.

"My God," he said. "Why doesn't it make you angry?"

She was startled by the suddenness of the words.

"Angry?"

He wanted to make her understand that it was not a personal thing, but that proximity to him had simply made her a foil, a representative of so many out there.

"I mean the man—him—" He pointed to the television set, "just got off the tube—he lied to us. He gave us a snow job. Christ, Ellen, he's not selling soap. He is on his way to being the fucking president of the United States. He will hold in his hands the largest concentration of power over our lives. How can you not be angry?"

He knew that all the pent-up frustrations of the last few days were bubbling upward like a volcano, and he also knew that it was his ferocity, not the meaning of his words, that was making an impression on her. She had curled up on the couch, with her limbs under her torso, as if for greater protection.

"Its becoming an obsession," she said. "I'm no punching bag."

He lay down beside her and held her close, kissed her, felt her stir beside him. She unzipped him, drew down his shorts, stroked him exquisitely. In turn, he rolled down her panties, moved them down over one leg, spread her wide and let her guide his prick into her deeply, feeling the warmth and softness of her body engulf him. He moved in slowly, feeling the ecstasy rise in them both as she responded. Then came the moment when all thought ceased and the cosmic mystery of the evolutionary force became urge, then need, then release, as the convulsion of their mutual orgasm washed joyously over them.

"How does this fit in on the scale of your priorities," she said deliberately, a bit too soon, before euphoria had come. She was clever, he thought appreciatively, but her words had only reinforced his view. He refused to intellectualize it, since he was neither confused nor dominated by his sexuality as she was by hers.

Later, when he was alone, he pulled out his typewriter and jammed a piece of paper into the roller. It is a story that must be written, he argued. Like all journalists, he had been writing it all along, working it out in his mind, groping for objectivity, turning the facts over and over again. He stared at the blank paper. Could he make it subtle enough to pass through Chalmer's critical appraisal? Should he pander to Chalmer's prejudice. Wouldn't that be engaging in the same detestable, manipulative practices the senator used? He could be straightforward and simple. "Senator James is a liar." He could start it that way. Too raw. Too emphatic. He had to win them first before his accusation would have any credibility. Damn it, the lie itself was not the most important part of the story; it was only the linkage, the clue to the manipulative process. The essence of the snow job was in the method, the delay, the news control, the thought process that went into the planning, the speech, the nuances and subtleties, the shots of the sea splashing over the rocks, the equally craggy face of his mother, the brave show of his wife, the technical proficiency of his organization.

Finally he began to write the story. Picking away at it on the typewriter, he knew that his objectivity faded with the same conscious movement as a dissolve on a movie screen. He knew that he could not be objective, that he was writing from the vantage point of his generation, of the standing target which had weathered another spray of shot and would not, could not, be upended.

He wrote all night.

XXXVII

"I can't publish this," Chalmers said. "You've quartered the man and left his carcass hanging from the ceiling."

"The man is constructing a defense of half-truths. He's manipulating us," Ernie said. "You know it and I know it."

"I think you're judging him too harshly," Chalmers said. "Anyway, your position is not to be a judge. You're a reporter."

"If he can get away with this, he's potentially dangerous."

Chalmers sat back in this chair and looked out of the glass-walled office into the huge city room.

"I think you've pushed it too hard, Rowell. This is a hatchet job."

"Mr. Chalmers, you can't have it both ways. I know you favor the man's basic politics, but what's good for the goose is good for the gander."

Was he stepping over the line? He was coming very close to insubordination. Chalmers paused, tamping down the hot coals of an explosive temper.

"Ernie," Chalmers began. He could tell that his editor—youngish, greying, with the trim Ivy League look, the Brooks Brother blue shirt and slant-striped tie—was mustering his considerable resources. Ernie knew he had reached him at last, had finally stripped off the veneer of calm objectivity that had been so carefully fabricated and used to propel him to his present position of power. He was annoyed at himself for having found him out, as if he had deliberately slashed the canvas of a superb painting.

"It's a great responsibility to run a newspaper like this." Chalmers smiled, another proven tool of his persuasive arsenal. "We cannot be the repository of all wisdom. Certainly I cannot be. But I do know that we, our political institutions, the whole fabric of our freedom,

249

are endangered by the man in the White House. There has got to be
an alternative to him."

"And James is that alternative?"

"I know this is difficult for you to understand."

"I don't think so." Ernie said. He wished he had not been so belligerent. Chalmers blanched, but let it pass.

"James, himself, is not important," Chalmers said. "But he is a
polarizing influence, a genuine power force, able to bring together
those who believe that social change in the context of justice is necessary now, before power is concentrated in the hands of fewer and
fewer people. I tell you that man in the White House is going to
consolidate his power beyond anything we have ever seen. I have
made him a lifelong study. He thrives on opportunism. He panders
to all base prejudices." Chalmers stood up and brought his hands
together, fist in palm, angry. "That man has got to go."

"But Senator James, Mr. Chalmers has just proven that he, too, cannot be trusted. I don't see a particle of difference between him and the
man in the White House."

"There is a difference, Ernie. Why can't you see that?"

Ernie knew what Chalmers was saying.

"Mr. Chalmers, where there are no ethics, no honesty, there can never
be good leadership. That's all I'm saying. Senator James is not ethical.
He's a liar. He's a cheat. His real expertise lies in manipulation."

"Of course it does, Ernie. That's the point. He has the ability to
get himself elected. Without that, he would be nothing. But in getting elected, he would have a constituency that would exercise a control, a point of view that would be healthy for our country. I think,
I truly believe, that the man, the person, is less important than what
he represents. In fact, that, in my opinion, is about the best we can
ask for. I'm being pragmatic. Young people—"

"Here it comes," Ernie thought.

"—young people don't easily grasp that the first law is what's do-
able in the environment of contemporary events. Now, I'm not put-

ting anyone down, certainly not the people of your fantastic generation. There is no such thing as a pure politician, and no matter what
you say, there never will be one. And this story here," he waved
Ernie's manuscript in front of his face, "implies that a politician
must be as ethically pure as the driven snow. Let he who is without
sin cast the first stone."

Ernie listened with the deep look of attention, but his mind
was racing elsewhere.

Chalmers had begun to work himself up. He appeared in need to
rationalize his position, to explain to Ernie, almost to beseech him.

"You see, Ernie, we're dangerously close to repression. If the president wins the next election, he'll have four years to subvert us. He'll
put his men everywhere. He'll build an empire that will last far
beyond his constitutional term. I see it coming. They're all asleep
out there. The only man who can crystallize the forces that can prevent such a takeover is Donald Benjamin James. Don't you see, man,
a paper like ours, which represents a similar point of view to the
Senator's, can destroy him politically. What does it matter if some
rightwing conservative sheet prints a story like this? Who will
believe it? In our paper, it will be taken as gospel. We cannot destroy
this man."

"But my story tells the truth."

"Only from your point of view."

"It is the truth. And you know it is the truth."

"It's exasperating," Chalmers said.

"Let me ask you a question, Mr. Chalmers."

"If it'll help you understand, I'll answer anything."

"Do you believe the senator's denial?"

"Of course not."

"Then how can you cover it up."

"I don't intend to cover it up. I intend to ignore it."

"That's just as bad. In fact, it's worse."

"Not considering the options. How do you get rid of the president?"

"There's got to be other men."

"Name one."

"It's not important. The president is only dangerous if you have lost all faith in the system. If we haven't any self-correcting institutions in our society. If we have no ethical men, then to hell with us. We'll go the way of Greece or Iberia or Rome."

"Pie in the sky," Chalmers said.

Ernie could see that he was getting testy now. He also knew that his own moment of truth was coming and with it a rush of all the old images, the white charger down Main Street, the great sea of human touching that he found in Woodstock, Hank Petrucci's funeral, the still-standing target. He felt it begin to wobble, felt the press of the bullet against the very middle of himself, felt the giving way—

"There must be something wrong with me," Ernie said, "I haven't got the capacity to persuade you. I truly believe that you are wrong. If the truth can destroy a man, what good was he in the first place? We need leaders for whom the truth is a goal, a weapon to be used to root out the lies, all the false pretense—"

"You amaze me, Ernie. You absolutely amaze me."

"How so?"

"You're so—so overzealous. So naive. You want to be a martyr? Who the hell are you to set yourself up as the final judge of what is true and what isn't true?"

"The man's a liar."

"A harsh judgment."

"If it was a question of the other side, the president, you'd have a fleet of reporters looking under every rock."

"Hell, Ernie, you know I'm right about the president."

"I'm as frightened about his potential actions as you are."

"So you agree."

"There may be a hundred different ways to observe some phenomena. Maybe a thousand. Maybe a million. But, Mr. Chalmers, there is only one truth. In the long run, the truth is irreducible. Start excusing one lie, and more have to follow."

Chalmers got up from his chair and stood looking out the window into the city room.

He peered into the huge room. More than a hundred reporters, editors, photographers, copy boys, clerks, and secretaries worked feverishly to reduce the day's events to words, to perception, to analysis.

"This newspaper is my life. The responsibility is heavy, Ernie. You don't know what it means to carry such a burden."

Ernie watched him. What the hell was he struggling with? It all seemed so clear. He let it pass. He sensed that Chalmers was at war with himself, in need of talking it out. The editor was not interested in dialogue.

"The point is that all men are frail. Someone has got to protect the weak. There are larger issues that must be considered. You'll find that out when you grow older. You'll be more tolerant, accept more frailty. Everyone has an Achilles' heel. Even you, Ernie."

"The truth is still the truth, Mr. Chalmers."

"Ernie," Chalmers looked at him fiercely, "why can't I make you see it? This whole business is a compromise. All life is a compromise."

Ernie thought, "Is this the time to make my stand? Is this the time to put my own life on the line and put principle before expediency? Cop out! Make out!" Chalmers' self-righteousness was goading him over the brink. He hadn't intended to be Horatio at the bridge. He was frightened now.

"Forget about personalities, Ernie. Look at the larger issues. Unfortunately the system makes it impossible for us to choose between saints. The men we get to choose from have already made their compromises. If we demanded perfection of them, there would soon be no one to choose from."

"It's not a question of perfection, Mr. Chalmers. Ethics. Standards. Those are the real issues. If we demanded perfection, then maybe we'd get it. Instead, we get ignorant men, illiterate in most things except mass manipulation. Experts at mass hypnosis. We should put our trust in intelligence, in knowledge and honesty. If we used that as a yardstick, we wouldn't get the Jameses, or men like the president; we'd get Jeffersons."

Chalmers was silent. He looked out at the city room again.

"You'll be convinced only by experience."

"Nothing will convince me."

A telephone rang on Chalmers' desk. He picked it up, answered perfunctorily, and then hung up.

"Ernie, I haven't really got time to give you all the reasons why I am rejecting your copy. But it's my decision to make. I'm rejecting it. I'm sorry you don't understand."

Ernie felt a lump grow in his throat. He knew his hands were shaking, and a hot flush bathed his neck in sweat. I'm not heroic, he told himself. He had worked hard to get this job, in small town papers, then New York, and now, right into the heart of the matter, where he wanted to be. A film of tears muddied his vision. He swallowed hard, fighting back the tears, tears of rage and impotence. "I think you're full of shit Chalmers," he said, conscious that it had come out as a screech. "Who are you to make judgments about truth? Who are you to tell people how to think? You're the same as they are." Then tears obscured his vision of Chalmers and he could only turn and leave.

XXXVIII

Get out of Philadelphia before ten, the adage goes, or you'll never get out again. There is something so desperately colorless about this town, so enormously soul chilling that it seemed a perfect setting for the funeral of Marlena Jackson. Dark clouds hung low over the city and a cold drizzle added to the gloom. The Lear jet, thankfully without Max aboard, had traveled through the night fighting a strong headwind. We checked into an airport motel about 4:00 A.M., and staggered out into the morning at 8:30. We had hired a car. Now we listlessly crawled into it, still tired, suffering from jet lag, looking the worse for wear. All except Don. His recuperative powers were, as usual, beyond human comprehension. He was cheerful, energetic; and yet, there was none of the normal banter and light talk that might have accompanied a trip under different, normal, circumstances. Karen, who had barely spoken, seemed immersed in a deep state of depression. We had left Barnstable and Christine on the Coast to take a commercial flight back to Washington.

Back at the office, the staff was apparently working at a feverish pace to keep abreast of how the press and television stations were reacting, capsulating the information and feeding it to Davis, who was, undoubtedly, on the phone all night. From all initial reports, he reported as they drove, the television speech was well received, very well indeed.

"Apparently the liberal press is willing to give us the benefit of the doubt. There are skeptics, of course, but they've been blunted. The *Chronicle* had an interesting editorial."

"What did they say?" I asked.

"In a nut shell—patience and absolution, a kind of 'there but for the grace of God' piece. It was very compassionate, very understanding."

"Good old Chalmers," Don said. "A truly fair man."

"We'll owe him one on that one." Davis said. "Kind of narrows our options. He won't let us move too far over to the right."

"We'll cross that bridge when we get to it," Don said, looking pained as the car rolled deeper into the depressing greyness of the city.

All in all, Davis's report indicated that Don was indeed getting the benefit of the doubt. Some opposition papers were stubbornly indifferent. But, in general, the prognosis was guardedly optimistic, according to Davis. Even that conclusion seemed a concession by him. What we were seeking from the beginning appeared to be coming to pass, perhaps sooner than expected, a plateau from which we could build upward. God, I'm beginning to sound like Davis. Upward to where? To credibility. To believability.

The church where Marlena's funeral was to be held was one of those converted synagogues abandoned or sold by the Jews on whose turf they had been established. Then the blacks had come co-opting the cavernous structures for their own gods. The Stars of David, unerasable, were visible on the stained glass windows. The church, appropriately, considering the decoration, was called the Zion Baptist Church. Davis, who had carefully traced the route on a road map before we had left, maneuvered the car through the crowd of mourners which spilled over beyond the sidewalk in front of the church. The police were working hard to keep away the curious onlookers who had gathered, as if on signal, across the street from the church. Don was hunched in the center of the back seat, hiding his head from view. This was, indeed, the last ordeal, the last chapter in the nightmare, the obligatory ending.

Faces, black and white, peered through the car windows, searching for Don. He was, after all, the superstar of the funeral.

"Goddamned faces," Don said with irritation.

"It's the last major hurdle, Senator," Davis said as his eyes searched the crowd. "It simply must be done. It would be perceived as callous to have stayed away. Unfortunately, we have no control, except over ourselves."

That meant, in Davis's shorthand, control over facial expressions, posture, dress, words and aspect, the emphasis on aspect was essential. Appear the way you want to be viewed. Be your own media.

Finally, someone recognized Don and pointed into the car.

The crowd, like some liquid mass of heated molasses, shifted its position to get a good look at him. Davis jumped out of the car, opened the back door, and Don followed him into the rain. The Philadelphia police made their way to where we stood and wedging ahead of us into the crowd, brought us slowly into the church. Flashbulbs popped like flickering matches in a dark arena, blinding us momentarily. The catcalls of the photographers came at us from the din. Don's face was somber; Karen was somnambulistic. The four of us took our places in the middle rows of the church. People turned and gaped. We were a conspicuous white glob in a sea of black faces.

Mr. Jackson sat in the first row opposite the closed coffin. We could only see the back of his grey head, short cropped and bowed. The mood, both physical and spiritual, was black, with the especially bleak grey costumes of the black mourners enveloping the gathering like smoke.

"We've got to get a picture of the senator with Mr. Jackson. It would make a great study shot at graveside," Davis whispered. All photographers were being kept outside the church although I spotted at least two taking nonflash shots of the scene and, when they could, the senator's face. Suddenly, the organ music stopped abruptly and the pastor mounted the pulpit. The church was stilled for a moment. Then, like a Greek chorus, black voices erupted individually at intervals. Each was like some primeval cry of pain.

"Lawd."

"Oh, Jesus."

I found myself trying to picture Marlena's water-corroded body within the closed wooden coffin. What had happened to us within the last few days was so beyond the periphery of our understanding, that even this funeral seemed like something one might have stumbled upon by walking through Alice's looking glass. What the hell were we doing here?

The pastor's words droned on. It was difficult to make out what he was saying. The idiom was different, the inflection foreign to my comprehension. I felt sorry as hell for Marlena, sorry for me, sorry for all of us. I wanted to cry. I wanted to cry for myself mostly. In spite of the urge, no tears came.

The congregation burst into song, the old spiritual, "Go Down Moses." It washed over us like molten lead, burning my skin. Was this the time one questioned the meaning of one's life? I felt a shock wave of self-pity. They would piss on my grave. Who would? Who would even take the trouble to make the acknowledgment?

And what would they do on your grave, old senator, boyhood friend, fighter against fate, a chosen person. You who sit there so stoically, holding yourself together with what extraordinary cement. Would a lone horse come clumping down the street, the clickety click of its horseshoes echoing in the hushed tunnel of people? Would your body bump along in the caisson, pulled by six matched stallions to lie in state in the rotunda, enshrined, immortalized by historians, your name on the world's lips? And all the flags at half-mast!

Was that what Don was thinking now? Does each person imagine his own funeral at someone else's. His face revealed nothing of his thoughts. Somewhere along the line, ambition, a kind of madness, had staked claim to him. It was a madness. I knew that now. What did anything matter beside the vision, with appropriate sound effects of the clickety click of the lone horse in the hushed streets and all the flags at half-mast? God, I want them to remember that I was here, that I came this way once. Could I be superimposing my own misplaced ambitions on his? Was this what kept me locked into his shadow? How many of us walk in the shadow of other men? The sun never streaks across our forms to throw a moving shadow of ourselves along the pavement. All power to the king. God save the king. Thank you, Mr. President. Thank you, Lord on earth. Smile your favor upon me. All make way. His lordship comes.

Marlena, Davis, Barnstable, Karen, Christine, and all of us, dead and alive, were nothing, in the face of his all-engulfing, all-powerful ambitious fury. All things were justified. No, he did not kill Marlena. Only after her death did he kill her, by denying her existence as a loving person, as someone who felt and hungered. Nothing, nothing at all, must survive in the wake of his ambition, a politician's sad, sick, frenzied, awe inspiring, cymbal-crashing ambition.

I felt anger. I felt shame. But I knew that I had long ago lost the will to rebel. I could find no options. Self-loathing is such a destructive emotion. There was nothing left but to dismiss it, tamp it down, like the earth that would soon over Marlena's coffin. Who would know I ever came this way?

Suddenly we were standing up. Six black pallbearers slowly carried the coffin through the center aisle followed by the abject figure of Marlena's father. As he passed our row, he raised his head, his eyes flickering in angry recognition beneath his grief. Then the coffin passed and Mr. Jackson moved out of the church.

"That man hates my guts," Don whispered.

"Wouldn't you?" Karen said quietly, a trifle loud. It was the first time she had spoken all morning.

"I really feel for that man," Don said.

"You feel for nobody." It was Karen again.

"Cool it, Karen," Don hissed.

"You bastard," she said. "You filthy bastard."

Don looked at me helplessly, raising his eyes in an attitude of exasperation. It was obvious now that Karen was not in control, on the verge of hysteria.

"Karen, this is not the time or the place," Don whispered.

"I hope you rot in hell," she said. Her energy seemed suddenly spent by the anger of her outburst. She sank back into silence.

The procession filed down the aisle, emptying out row after row in disciplined fashion. Don managed a faint smile to faces that turned toward him. As our row filed into the procession and into the entrance, flashbulbs began to pop. The crowd surged around us once more. We were carried forward slowly by its momentum. In the street, the rain was falling in a steady mist. The crowd had grown during the service. People were hanging out of the windows waiting to get a glimpse of Don. I noticed that he had tried to grab Karen's hand in the crush, to pull her along. She twisted free. Her lips were tight.

The police had left our car parked along the curb. When they spotted us, they formed a wedge again, shoving people aside, as they led us to the car. We got in and locked the doors while the police kept the area cordoned off.

It was a strange scene. Our car was jammed in a sea of people and cars, like a dust speck in an air bubble. Curious faces bent down trying to get a glimpse of us, poking their heads under the elbows of a tall policeman who stood in our field of vision.

"We need a picture with the senator and Mr. Jackson at graveside, preferably with Mrs. James—"

He didn't get a chance to finish.

"Can't you just keep quiet," Karen said, exploding. "Can't you just stop talking. I'm sick of it all. I'm sick of this whole thing." She began to sob hysterically, her shoulders shaking. Don tried to hold her as I tried to shield her from the view of the crowd.

"Come on, Karen," Don said. "Just hold on."

"Bastards," she sobbed, beating her fists into her knees. "You bastards."

I saw Don's eyes in the rear view mirror. How was he measuring the scene? To the spectator, perhaps, a grieved woman. Was she a friend of the deceased? Who would suspect she was crying for herself?

Don's face had become ashen.

"Karen, this is nonsense. You've got to pull yourself together. A lot depends on it." His appeal sounded genuine enough.

"You are all bastards," she cried again. The pounding on her knees had ripped her stockings.

"Goddamn it, Karen," Don exploded, "cut this shit out and cut it out right now." He grabbed both her wrists and held them in a tight grip. She helplessly tried to release herself. We knew he was hurting her. Her face became distorted with pain. She screamed. He held a hand over her mouth. "You'll ruin me, you goddamned bitch," Don shouted. Then, he released one of his own hands and slapped her hard in the face. The shock of it quieted her as she slumped backward in the seat whimpering. I could see his red fingermarks spread across her cheeks.

"Do you think anyone saw that?" he asked.

"I'm afraid to think about it."

"Let's get the fuck out of here."

"I think the procession is forming up ahead," Davis said.

Don reached for Karen's pocketbook, opened it, rummaged through it, found the vial of pills, and spilled two into the palm of his hand. He forced open her mouth and popped them in. She swallowed hard.

"Now just relax, will you?" he beseeched.

She said nothing, closed her eyes, and laid her head back. Tears moved haltingly out of them from the sides of her eyelids. Don pulled out his handkerchief and wiped them roughly away.

Finally, the way was cleared, and the car, waved on by police, was slipped into the moving procession.

"It sure is lousy weather," I said, breaking into the long silence.

No one responded.

By the time we reached the little country cemetery, Karen was sitting up again and surveying her face in the mirror.

"Do you feel better?" Don asked her.

"I'll never ever feel better, Don."

"I'm sorry about that, Karen."

"So am I."

It was embarrassing to listen to this interchange, for it was obviously the last turning point in their marriage. It was something you sensed between them. From here on in, everything would be strictly business. The charade was over.

The television crews, cameramen and reporters had already arrived, assembled nearby, jockeying for position as our car turned into the rusted gate of the cemetery entrance. We hesitated before opening the door, waiting for Karen to put a comb through her hair and reapply her makeup. The rips in her stockings would barely show under her skirt.

"Follow me," Davis said, as he jumped out of the car and opened the back door. Flashbulbs began popping again. Police still kept the reporters and cameras at a safe distance. Davis elbowed his way through the group crowding around the open grave and deftly maneuvered himself next to Mr. Jackson, then swiftly stepped away to make room for Don. Karen, her shoulders stiff, barely moved from the edge of the crowd. I faded back, both as a defensive measure and because I felt somehow out of place, uncomfortable. Why was I here? The cameramen moved quickly to the other side of the grave, holding their cameras high to get "the picture." The coffin was lowered into the ground. Voices cried out as the first thump of earth pounded against the hollow surface.

It was the end of Marlena, the gazellelike black girl. The fire was out.

As if in anger, the rain came down in earnest as the workmen began shoveling the earth swiftly into the hole.

Mr. Jackson knelt at the graveside, smoothing down the earth and arranging flowers along its top. Don stooped down beside him, as if to help. The flashbulbs popped.

When we were back in the car, Don borrowed my penknife to clean his shoes.

XXXIX

The front page of the *Washington Chronicle* lay flat on the president's desk with its four column picture of Senator James and the father of the dead girl kneeling beside her grave. Grasped in the old black man's gnarled hands was a tiny bouquet of white flowers. Senator James seemed to be patting the earth of the grave, his face composed, saddened it seemed by the injustice of premature death. The photographer had frozen the moment exquisitely, the misted overlay, the anguish of the black man, even the bouquet seemed marvelously radiant, a fitting offering to dead youth. Death had come too soon, the picture said. Man grieved. The loss was irrevocable. It evoked the universality of art.

"The son-of-a-bitch," Baum said.

"You've got to hand it to him, Baum. He's a clutch player."

"Who's going to believe this crap?"

"Many people unfortunately."

The president tapped an ash from his cigar, pushed a lever for the ashes to drop into the false bottom of the tray, the laid the cigar carefully against its lips. He looked over his scrawled notes on the yellow pad of lined foolscap.

"We've got lots of work to do," the president said. "Playing the demagogue is an art that the good senator has honed pretty well, but he underestimates the power of the presidency."

"I'm glad you feel that way, Mr. President. I have some ideas of my own."

"Good."

The president stood up and faced the window of the oval office. He enjoyed the view of the well-kept lawn, greener now for the rain that came down in sheets.

"I want that man destroyed. He is a danger to everything we stand for. He's taken a desperate gamble. But no matter what, he's still a formidable opponent, the strongest of all the possibilities. What he represents has great currency in America, that dream of Utopia through simplistic compassion, simplistic solutions. He'd give the country to the bleeding hearts. He would see things different from this vantage point."

"As always," Baum pointed out, "people like that are grist for the Communists' mill. They'll burrow inside his organization. They'll manipulate his people. Why can't people understand?"

"We know that, Baum. But it's an old line. Americans just can't believe that Soviet Communism hasn't changed its motives. We've grown fat with materialism and make-work. This man would have us with more bureaucracy, more government interference. Hell, the government can barely operate now; it's so leaden with inefficiency and indifference. Why can't they see the dual threat to our society? Weaken us by sloth inside. Deaden us by softness outside. It's so damned frustrating."

Baum nodded. He said nothing.

"Unfortunately, we can't tell it like it is. We're too committed to détente. It would blow our credibility sky high. The old style red-baiter is a dangerous image to project. They think you're using the scapegoat techniques. Let's all hate something that we can all agree to hate. Baum, why do we have such a bad way of saying things publicly?"

"The media distorts whatever we say, anyway."

"The media is just a pack of howling wolves. Why don't we feed them the right meat?"

"Anything we say is distorted. Look at that picture. It's a deliberate appeal for understanding and forgiveness. If it were you, they'd paint you at your worst."

"I don't expect any better treatment. It's as if a disease was running rampant in people attracted into that business. Freedom of the press! How can the press be free if it's controlled by bleeding hearts?"

The president shrugged. He was straying again, he thought. How his gall rose when he began to go down that road. It was not constructive to lose his cool on the subject. He couldn't operate at white heat. He needed calm, calculation, well thought-out tactics, strategies formed by intelligence, not emotion.

"We need a new device, something people will understand, that the press cannot ignore. We need to assassinate publicly the good Senator James, to push him over the brink."

The president turned from the window, sat down again at his desk, and looked over his notes.

"I want this committee formed, totally political, outside the White House orbit. I want loyal men, reportable directly to you." He looked into Baum's steel-grey eyes. "When I say loyal, I mean loyal. Soldiers to the cause. No weakbellies. We'll feed them with everything we can turn up. He's a philandering bastard. I'll get the raw FBI files on him. Then I want to know everyone he's ever fooled around with. I want names. I want these names leaked to the press, until they can't ignore it. Even if they found the sources, they would still have to tell the story. I want a full field investigation of the man's life. I want to know all about his wife, his mother, father, brothers. I want to know everyone who has ever given him a dime for his campaign. I want to know what the source of his income is. I want his life turned inside out."

His anger rose in him as he spoke. He stopped himself again, picked up the cigar and puffed to quiet himself.

"And if the information isn't enough to warn the American people about his character, if they're so debased and degenerate as not to see through him, I want more and more and more, until they see the truth about him. That man is a danger and a threat to this country."

He looked at the picture of Senator James and the black man. "This is arrogance, pure arrogance." The president stood up again and held up the picture for Baum to see. "It's sophistry. Propaganda.

Worse than Goebbels I wouldn't be surprised if he actually murdered the girl."

He watched Baum's reaction, although he knew in advance what
it would be. Baum was the perennial flunky, the obedient func-
tionary to whom every presidential opinion became gospel instantly.
He never disagreed, but made notes endlessly in a loose-leaf notebook which bore the presidential seal.

"Figuratively speaking, of course. What's so incredible is that he
has the gall to deny it publicly, on television. And worse, the
American people could buy it. Put the power of television in the
hands of a natural and, by God, they could buy it. Lord help us all."

"I'll move ahead immediately on this." Baum got up and began to
walk toward the door.

"And Baum," the president called after him. "I want this handled
in the usual way. I want the option of credible denial. No details
please. But, by God, Baum, I want both barrels aimed at that man's
guts. Do whatever is necessary, even what might be characterized as
extracurricular or quasi-legal."

"Yes, Mr. President," Baum said with relish.

When he had gone, the president leaned back in his chair. If only
he could make them see the truth. That was his main failing.
Somehow he was missing that extra measure, that indefinable aura
required for mass persuasion. It was a mystique. He had to plod his
way through, bull it through. If he had that extra measure, he would
not be going through this hell of frustration. He started to tear up
his notes of yellow foolscap. History would prove him right. Of that
he was dead sure.

XL

Ernie lay on his bed, hands clasped behind his head, staring at the ceiling. The ceiling wobbled, he had concluded, and the paint-covered crack along the center gave evidence that somewhere deep in the apartment building's foundation all was not quite right.

He had by now grown used to the sour stench of his body and the stale air, layered with the stinks of human consumption, cigarette smoke, rotting pizzas, bones of stripped chicken, fruit cores, and banana peels. For three days he had locked himself away in his lair, an injured lion, licking his wounds, waiting for healing, a process that had eluded him.

Why did it not come? Rage ebbed. Indifference set in. Then the damned rage returned in gale force. He had actually quit his job, had opted for blind purity, for haughty principle. He had tasted, very briefly, the ecstasy of heroics, the heady brew of martyrdom. Then he had gone home, locked his door, refused to answer his phone, told Ellen to please, please leave him alone for a few days. Within the first few hours the plateau of joy collapsed under its tentative pilings as if they were made of balsa wood.

He did manage a few monosyllabic phone calls.

"You did what you had to do."

"It was stupid."

"It was worse than that."

"I'm sure you'd get the job back. All you'd have to do is ask. Chalmers knows you're good."

"I can't bring myself to do it. I think I'm crazy."

"Maybe a little self-righteous."

"A little?"

"Lots."

Why didn't his feeling of exhilaration sustain itself? Where was the fucking catharsis? He had done that thing that was a far far better thing to do than he had ever done. But at least Sidney Carton didn't have to dwell on the abject stupidity of his action. Zap went the guillotine! And here Ernie was still conscious, bleeding like a sieve all over his rumpled bed, on to the floor of his pig sty of an apartment.

Inflexibility. Martyrdom. He cursed at himself. Silent martyrdom no less. Only three people in the world knew about it, and one of them was him. Worse. He had two hundred bucks in the bank, owed five payments on his car, and he liked—loved—his job.

But when self-pity retreated and his mind cleared momentarily, he felt more analytical about what he had done and less self-immolating. Wrong is wrong! It wasn't a question of judgment. You just don't compromise the fact of truth. That man got up on the boob tube and lied like hell. That was wrong. But worse, Chalmers didn't want the truth. The smugness of Chalmers irritated him the most. The bile rose again—anger, rage.

What people were capable of doing in the name of political ideology was incredible. Chalmers sucked the teat of the liberal bitch while the president stroked the conservative hound. How did such moral illiterates ever get so powerful! But that was the way it was, they all had said. Indignation was for suckers. The objective was to become powerful, to get into the position to state your message, the real message. Although, by then, after the rot of compromise had eaten away your gut, you wouldn't have a message to state. Like Senator James, like the president, like all the rest in between. Let them all rot in hell, wherever that was.

How many of us would finally be left? Was the movement decimated, the sweet, brave movement of love and truth, defeated? Where were his comrades? Hell, he couldn't fight off the bastards all alone, not forever. The fucking foxhole was flooded. He was running out of ammo, and his courage—what courage—was evacuating him like rats from the hold of a doomed ship.

He rose from his bed and put his bare feet into a pair of loafers, threw a sweater round his neck, and went out. Stiff and tired for lack of use, his legs rebeled against walking swiftly. He fought it, felt the pain in his shins, and pressed on. People observed him and then turned away. He knew he must have looked like a derelict, but he had to get out into the air to move with speed, to feel the blood pulse.

Perhaps, he thought, he could tell Chalmers, "Give me only assignments on which the truth is essential, where only the absolute truth counts." "What is the absolute truth?" Chalmers would say. Nothing is absolute. Nothing but the truth. But to deliberately abuse a fact by filtering it out—that is wrong. He couldn't redeem Senator James. He was finished, a turd like the rest of them.

Maybe he should never have left good old Williamsport, P.A. Ambition, restlessness, opportunity had goaded him away. All these small-town boys slugging it out in the big cities—what good was it being a small-town boy if they didn't break your heart in the city, as your mom and dad had warned?

But who was ever really safe in Williamsport, P.A. where the mind caved in at thirty. Besides, technology had obliterated all the Williamsports, and Main Street now came crawling through the television set, and the White Charger was pots of glue and dogfood, or would be soon—very soon.

Perhaps, in the end, he would have to go back to Williamsport P.A. wherever that was now, repack the battered suitcase, and roll back home. He could again smell his mother's hard cookies, the ones with the raisins, and his father's cigar-soaked breath; and with it, the memories returned of the old corny dreams. Old illusions. Dead dreams.

He passed storefronts. Cars rolled swiftly by. Voices filtered past. Martyrdom somehow didn't seem contemporary. He wasn't a Thomas More, and, Christ, he wasn't Christ. He began to look into the store windows, watching his own disheveled image float by. He passed bars, gift shops, antique stores. At an optical store, he paused and watched an old craftsman grind a lens. The man's craggy fingers seemed sure. Perhaps he would become a skilled craftsman, deft fingers merged with roughhewn material, carving the truth from a piece of wood or metal or glass. There was greatness in that act. It wasn't trivia. It couldn't be bent or battered by compromise. He looked at his hands. They were clumsy, indelicate.

He turned from the storefront and looked about him. People were scurrying about on their daily rounds, quite oblivious to his great act of moral indignation. The traffic along M Street seemed endless. A supermarket across the way was crowded with housewives engaged in the mundane chores of human sustenance. Children straggled to school, across traffic laden arteries controlled by intense women with red chestbands.

The sun was trying to work its way through the smog. Occasionally, a glint of its reflection would bounce off a metal sign. He breathed deeply, listened to the sounds of the street as if hearing them for the time.

He yearned to be part of that throbbing mass again, not alone in himself, locked away in his apartment, morbid with self-pity. It was life that he wanted to sink his teeth into—life. He had built up too many expectations—great expectations. Perhaps Chalmers was right after all. Perhaps wisdom came only in tiny steps, a messenger wending his uncertain way through the crowded human experience.

If he could only see it all as a mere difference of opinion instead of an irrevocable betrayal of principle. Was it pride? Or was it plain stubbornness, something injected into his blood by a long line of Pennsylvania Dutchmen on his mother's side. Later, perhaps, he'd call Chalmers and ask for his job back. Yes, later, he'd call Chalmers. Tonight he'd see Ellen and get back to the land of the living.

Turning a corner, he saw an old copy of the *Chronicle* lying on a pile of trash. Familiar faces appeared vaguely visible on the front page. He picked up the paper and carried it into a nearby coffee shop, crowding into a small booth in the rear.

Spreading the paper, he saw the picture. And yet, the details of it, which he might first have studied, seemed obscured by the by-line: "Photo by Charles Hershey." "They set 'em up, I shoot 'em," he remembered Charlie saying.

He looked about him. Nothing had changed. An old man was drinking coffee at the counter. A woman's voice drifted in from the kitchen. It was as if he shared a secret with very few men. Perhaps, instead of indignation, blunted now, he should substitute admiration. It was a dazzlingly masterful technical performance by the senator and his people. By God, they had done it, or seemed to have done it; they had shoved it right up the kazoo of fat-assed America.

When the coffee came, he blew on its surface and sipped. A drop spilled on the picture, hitting the black man directly on his bowed head, fading away some of his image.

The old enemy was a crafty cat, he thought. No, he couldn't go back to the *Chronicle*. That play was over now. He knew his head had cleared, the emotion subdued, the judgments clear. A standing target couldn't just stand there, after all, and take the shot. Sooner or later they'd gun him down.

He had to think clearly, go over his options carefully, just as they did. Surely, there were others like him. He was a fool to think he was alone. And they could use a good man, someone who knew how the enemy did it. He'd find them. And somehow he would get that story published. For the one thing that DBJ and his crowd might never suspect was that somewhere out there was a human time bomb ticking away—ticking.

He walked out of the coffee shop and flipped the paper into a trash can.